THE GOURLAY GIRLS

MARGARET THOMSON

DAVIS

GOURLAY
GIRLS

B&W PUBLISHING

First published 2000
by B&W Publishing Ltd
Edinburgh

ISBN 1 903265 08 8

British Library Cataloguing in Publication Data:
A catalogue record for this book is available from
the British Library

Cover illustration:
Detail from *Portrait with Still Life* by G. T. Bear
Photograph courtesy of The Bridgeman Art Library.
Copyright disclaimer: whilst every effort has been made
to find the copyright holder of this work, this has not been possible.
The publisher would be most grateful to hear from anyone
who can provide further information about this matter.

Poetry by Michael Malone, except for
the poem *Glasgow*, which is by Albert Goodyear

Printed by Omnia Books, Bishopbriggs

1932

I

Wincey stood very still and watched her grandfather. He was choking, gasping for breath. She had seen him taking seizures before. He had a heart condition and on the few occasions when she had been present, her grandmother had ordered her to run upstairs and fetch the old man's tablets from the bathroom cabinet. Upstairs and downstairs she'd flown, so that Grandmother could take a tablet from the bottle and press it into Grandfather's mouth. It only took a few seconds after that for the seizure to calm and for Grandfather to seem perfectly all right. A bit tired looking perhaps. Otherwise he was to all appearances her big, good natured, kindly, smiling, loving Grandfather Cartwright. George, to his wife Penelope.

Wincey wasn't sure now which one she hated more—so called loving and devoted Grandfather or unloving, uncaring Grandmother.

Grandmother was different with her brother Richard. Richard, five years older than Wincey, was the clever one and the favourite of the family. How Grandmother's beady-eyed, long-nosed face would soften at the sight of 'her handsome boy', as she called him.

Wincey didn't mind. That was something she could understand. Richard was easy to love and admire—he was tall and slim, dark-eyed and dark-haired like her daddy, and just as handsome. Quite unlike Wincey with her fringed red hair and freckles, or their mother who had fair, golden hair.

Sometimes her mother and father would laugh and say, 'I don't know where Wincey came from.'

She came from them, the same as Richard. But her mother and father seemed to think that she was different. Most of the time they completely ignored her, lavishing all their attention on the literary and political friends who were so often in the house.

Her mother and her first husband, James Mathieson, had never had any children. Mathieson was one of her mother's set. He had divorced her for adultery not long after the Great War. Her mother had no shame. She and her father had been lovers for years. Wincey had overheard her grandmother and grandfather talking about it. Grandmother never tired of saying that it wasn't decent the way the two men had become friends, and 'that dreadful communist revolutionary', as she called Mathieson, visited Nicholas's house.

Richard was at boarding school in Edinburgh, but he returned home to Glasgow most weekends and saw a lot of their grandparents. They both loved Richard, especially Grandmother. When she came to visit them, Wincey was usually sent to keep her grandfather company. His heart condition often prevented him from getting out and about. She saw this as yet another example of her parents trying to get rid of her one way or another.

She was supposed to be her grandfather's favourite. Grandfather was supposed to love her best.

For most of her twelve years, she had believed this. Now she knew better. Yet the truth was so terrible, so painful, so confusing, she couldn't cope with it. Her mind, as well as her heart, ached with it. It paralysed her.

Earlier, when she'd cringed away from him, he'd pushed

money into her pocket. 'A wee present,' he'd said, 'for being Grandfather's good girl. You buy yourself something nice, eh?'

Now all she could feel as she stood staring at the old man was bitterness and hatred. He was trying to mouth the word 'tablets'. His eyes bulged with pleading. He clawed the air. She didn't move. The expression in his eyes changed to disbelief, then to terror. Eventually his gasping stopped. His body slumped. His mouth sagged.

The room weighed heavy with stillness, then gradually—in the far distance, as if coming from another world—she heard the faint rumble and clang of tram cars. The sound frightened her. It brought an air of reality back into the room. Her grandfather was still slumped in his chair, his head twisted to one side, his mouth hanging open. His eyes were open too. It was his eyes that brought the full realisation of what had happened crashing in on her. She began to tremble and moan with the acuteness of her distress.

The emotional confusion that had been plaguing her became stronger. To it was now added terror, and the need to escape became overwhelming.

She raced from the room and out of the house onto Great Western Road. She was oblivious of the rain gusting along the wide street, with its large stone villas set well back on either side and partly hidden by trees. She was panic-stricken, especially when she realised that she'd reached the part of the road that reared up to form Kirklee Terrace, where she lived with her mother and father. One of them could be looking out over the grassy bank, down onto Great Western Road.

At the end of the terrace was the private entrance to the park known as the Botanic Gardens. Further on, level with the street, was the main entrance. Wincey ran through it and along the nearest path, knowing that now she'd be well hidden by trees. Even if anyone in the family looked out of one of the windows that faced onto the park, it would be impossible to see her.

Yet she felt no satisfaction at this thought. She desperately longed to be able to run to her parents and be comforted by them, to be told that everything would be all right. She ached to be made to feel loved and secure. But they'd never made her feel that. She didn't dare think how they would be towards her now. Yet she wept with her need of them.

Tears mixed with the rain, blurring her vision and she began to shiver as she became aware of her white blouse, navy cardigan and pleated skirt clinging wetly against her. The path had disappeared under angry puddles that were being whipped by rain and wind. Everywhere was fast becoming a quagmire. Her stockings were spattered with mud, her shoes sodden and squelchy with water.

She tried to get onto the grass to escape from the puddles but slipped and fell. Now everything was covered with mud. Her fringe stuck wetly to her forehead; her white blouse, her cardigan, her skirt, her shoes—everything was ruined.

Trying to scramble to her feet, her skirt caught on a bush and, desperately tugging at it to free it, she caused a ragged tear. Almost mad with panic now, she ran, stumbled, fell, ran again.

Eventually she reached another gate, ran through it, and found herself on an empty, windswept street. She kept running this way and that until she was exhausted. Then she remembered the money her grandfather had pushed into her pocket. She boarded a tram car and sat shivering on the nearest seat. The conductor looked at her suspiciously. 'Where are ye goin'?'

Wincey just held out some coppers without saying anything.

The man shrugged and handed her a ticket. Her mind was in such a turmoil, she just wanted to be safely home in bed, with the events of the last hour never having happened.

But they had happened, and she shivered all the more at the thought of her parents' coldness. Now they'd have very good reason to hate her. She couldn't bear the thought of their cold, shocked faces, so she blanked them out of her mind.

It was early evening but it was already getting dark and the rain was beating relentlessly against the tram windows. The tram was lurching to a halt now as the conductor approached her and said, 'Ye'll huv tae get aff noo, hen. Either that or buy another ticket.'

Dazed and without a word, she left the tram and started wandering about the dark, mean looking streets between the high tenements. She had no idea where she was. After what seemed like hours, she could walk no further and sank down on to the pavement. With her back propped against a tenement wall, she wept broken-heartedly.

'What's up, hen?'

Wincey wiped at her eyes and saw a young girl crouching down in front of her.

'I don't know where to go,' Wincey managed.

'How? Huv ye no' got a mammy an' a daddy an' a home tae go tae?'

Wincey shook her head. The girl, Wincey later discovered, was fourteen-year-old Florence Gourlay, two years older than herself. Florence had a highly dramatic turn of mind and thrived on crises, real or imaginary.

'So ye're an orphan?'

Wincey nodded.

'So ye've run away so they won't put you into an orphanage—or into the workhouse?'

Forgetting her tears, Wincey stared curiously at the girl. She managed to nod again.

'Och, never mind,' Florence said. 'Ma mammy'll take ye in. She's always takin' folk in.'

'Is she?' Wincey said in surprise.

'Och aye, our place is like a doss house sometimes. Girls come down from the Highlands an' stay for a few days at our place until they get fixed up wi' a nurse's job at wan o' the hospitals. Ma mammy used tae come from the Highlands. Come on.' Florence got to her feet. 'I'm soaked an' freezin' tae death. An' starvin' intae the bargain.'

Wincey struggled to her feet. The streets glistened darkly with rain. Greenish pools of light wavered under gas lamps. The high black tenements dwarfed the two bedraggled figures as they began trudging along.

'Whit's yer name, by the way? I'm Florence.'

'Wincey.'

'Wincey! Where did a funny name like that come from?'

'I was christened Winsome.'

'That's even worse,' Florence laughed.

'Then when I went to school we learned that rhyme about Incey Wincey Spider and everybody started calling me Wincey—even at home.'

'Ah hardly ever went tae school so ah dinnae know any rhymes. Is that like a poem?'

'Sort of, I suppose.'

'Didn't ye mind?'

'What?'

'Bein' called after a spider?'

'I never thought of it like that. It just sounded better than Winsome. More friendly, somehow.'

'Aye, right enough.'

Wincey managed to find out from Florence as they went along that she lived in Springburn, in one of the tenements in Springburn Road. Wincey had heard about Springburn at school. Most people in the area had worked in the building and maintenance of the railways, in the workshops and repair yards of the North British Railway Company at Cowlairs, of the Caledonian Railway Company at St Rollox, and the North British Locomotive Company, the largest of its kind in Europe.

She remembered her teacher saying that no-one knew for certain how Springburn had originally got its name, but that among the nearby hills there were many springs and burns and wells. With the coming of the railways and new housing, however, there was certainly nothing rural about the place now. The teacher had shown the class pictures of the streets black with workers pouring out of all the railway works, but now there was a depression and many men were unemployed, hanging about aimlessly on street corners.

'Have you any brothers or sisters?'

'No brothers, but ah've an older sister, Charlotte, an' two younger ones. They're twins—Euphemia and Bridget. We tried tae call Euphemia Phemie but ma mammy wouldnae let us. She likes tae be proper.'

'Are they all living at home?'

'Aye, ma granny as well. Here we are.'

They stopped at a dark close-mouth, one of the many tunnel-like entrances to the tenements. Wincey groped her way nervously along.

'Isn't there a light?'

'Naw, the leerie's supposed tae come but he hisnae done anythin' wi' this close for ages. Maybe it's run out o' gas. I don't know. Just hang on tae me goin' up the stairs, ye'll be all right.'

Three flights of stairs up, Florence thumped loudly on one of the top flat doors. It was opened by a tall, delicate looking girl with a pale face and fair hair pinned back with kirby-grips. As they all walked through the small box of a lobby, and then into a gas-lit kitchen, Florence nodded towards the tall girl.

'That's Charlotte.' Then, once in the kitchen, she announced, 'This is Wincey. Her mammy an' daddy died o' the flu an' she wis goin' tae be locked away in an orphanage an' she didnae want tae go. So ah brought her home wi' me. She can stay here, can't she, Mammy?'

'Would ye listen tae the cheek o' that?' This came from an elderly woman of ample proportions, who filled to overflowing a rocking chair by the fire. She had floppy cheeks and no teeth. 'As if we huvnae enough tae contend wi' here!' Red rimmed eyes glared at Wincey. 'Away ye go back where ye belong—ah dinnae care if it's the orphanage or the workhouse, ye cannae stay here.'

Tears of disappointment and fatigue overflowed and spilled

down Wincey's cheeks. A thin, bent woman with wispy salt and pepper hair knotted back into a bun was standing over at the sink. She said in a soft Highland voice,

'Now, now, Granny. We can't turn a poor bairn out on a night like this.'

She smiled at Wincey. 'It's all right, dear. Come over here and wash your face and hands. I'll make a cup of tea and you'll soon feel better.'

'Florence Gourlay,' the old woman raged, 'will get us aw intae serious trouble yet wi' that imagination o' hers, an' aw the downright lies she tells. You mark ma words!'

She turned to the man wearing a cap—or bunnet—with the skip pulled well down over his eyes who was sitting on one of the chairs jammed close together around the cluttered table.

'Are ye a man or a mouse, Erchie Gourlay? Are ye just gonnae sit there an' allow this? We'll aw end up in the workhouse at this rate. How many mair mouths can we feed? We cannae feed oursels.' She cocked a thumb towards her daughter-in-law. 'Thanks tae her extravagance.'

Erchie appealed to his wife. 'We'll manage, sure we will, hen.'

Teresa smiled and Wincey wasn't sure then what age she might be. Her smile made her look younger than the scant faded hair suggested. She was a patient, good natured woman but there was a thrawn bit—even a slyness—about her at times. She secretly enjoyed getting any small victory over her mother-in-law.

'Yes, of course we'll manage,' Teresa said calmly. 'With God's help.'

Florence led Wincey over to the black sink. She winked at her and whispered, 'Ah told ye.'

'You give your feet a wipe,' Teresa instructed Florence. 'You're getting mud all over the floor.'

'What God'll help you?' Granny asked.

'We all worship the same god, Granny,' Teresa said gently

as she settled the kettle on top of the glowing embers of the fire.

'You're a Pape,' Granny accused. 'You worship that picture.' She pointed to the painting of Jesus that hung on the far wall of the recessed bed. 'Wearin' a gownie! Ye worship beads an' idols an' graven images. Ah'll never know what possessed ma Erchie tae marry a Pape. An' us a respectable Orange family an aw.'

'Ma,' Erchie protested, 'ye're no' tae upset Teresa.'

'Upset her?' Granny scoffed. 'Upset *her*! Nothing ruffles that one's feathers. It's well seen who that lyin' wee trouble-maker takes efter.'

She glanced over at Florence who was going into contortions in her efforts to wipe the mud off her bare feet. Charlotte spoke then.

'Mammy, I'd better away through and finish that dress.'

'Charlotte is a lovely sewer and dress maker,' Teresa told Wincey. 'Between us we make a decent living.'

'Decent? Decent?' Granny bawled out. 'Whit's decent aboot livin' here?'

Wincey couldn't help thinking the same thing. The gas mantle over the mantelpiece barely lit the kitchen. Even with the bright flames of the small, barred fire, most of the room was shadowy. Wincey couldn't imagine where everybody slept—there was only one recessed bed and hardly an inch of floor space.

As if reading her mind, Florence said, 'Come on through and ah'll show ye where we'll sleep.'

Teresa called after them, 'Take your wet clothes off and I'll get them dried.'

As they were crossing the lobby, there was knock at the front door and Florence opened it to reveal two small girls, both with mops of curly brown hair.

'This is Wincey. She's an orphan an' ah found her lying half dead in the street an' Mammy said she could stay here. Wincey, they're ma twin sisters—Euphemia an' Bridget.'

'Hello,' the two girls murmured. They looked tired and cold and their clothes clung wetly to their bodies. Each was carrying a shopping bag from which issued the tantalising aroma of fish and chips. Suddenly Wincey realised how hungry she was. She couldn't remember when she'd last eaten.

'You couldn't have timed it better,' she heard Teresa tell the girls. 'I've just this minute masked the tea. Och, poor wee things, you're soaked. Never mind, you'll soon dry out and once we've had a nice cup of tea and a fish supper, we'll all feel fine and happy.'

Wincey couldn't believe she'd ever feel happy again. At the same time, she was grateful to have found shelter. The front room, as Florence called it, was not much bigger than the kitchen. It too had a curtained recessed bed with a high mattress. Opposite there was a fireplace, in front of which sat an ancient looking sewing machine and a stool. The fireplace had a surround of dark maroon tiles but the grate was empty and the room gripped with an icy chill.

A settee covered in cheap leather substitute and two matching easy chairs were crowded into the room. The back of the settee had a row of tiny wooden pillars topped with a padded rail. The floor was covered with linoleum which was referred to as wax cloth. On the walls, a dark brown varnished dado was topped with heavily patterned wallpaper.

'Where does everybody sleep?' Wincey asked.

'Mammy an' Daddy are through in the kitchen bed. Granny sleeps on a hurly bed in front o' the fire. She couldnae climb up to the bed.'

'What's a hurly?'

'Ye don't even know what a hurly bed is!' Florence shook her head in disbelief. 'It's a wee bed that hurls out from under a big bed. You an' me'll have a hurly bed from under this room bed. Charlotte sleeps in the big bed—she's sixteen. The twins—they're just twelve—and they sleep wi' her.'

'Goodness!'

'What's wrong wi' that?'

'Nothing,' Wincey assured Florence hastily. 'Nothing at all.' But she'd never heard the like of it in all her thirteen years. At home she'd always had a room of her own and a much bigger room than this.

'Right,' Florence said, struggling out of her thin dress, 'get yer clothes aff an' we'll go through an' get somethin' tae eat.'

Wincey was both shocked and frightened.

'I couldn't do that.'

'Why no'. They're soaked.'

'But . . . but . . . Your father's through there.'

'What's wrong wi' that?'

Florence looked perplexed and annoyed, as if Wincey was implying some sort of criticism of her father.

'It's just . . . I'm a bit shy, I suppose.'

Florence laughed. 'Don't be daft. We keep our knickers an' simmets on. So there's no need. It's not as if we're grown up, like Charlotte.'

Wincey was afraid not to go along with Florence, in case she caused offence and was ordered to leave. But she was more than afraid. She was feeling so vulnerable, she was almost in a state of collapse, as she eventually—dressed only in her knickers and vest—followed Florence through to the stuffy, gas-lit kitchen.

2

Teresa manoeuvred the steel poker through the ribs of the knee high fire and made the flames spark brighter. The fire was part of a black, cast iron range that had a high, overhanging mantle shelf. Along the mantle shelf, Wincey could see by the light of the softly hissing gas mantle a tin tea caddy, a box of matches, candles, a spare mantle for the gas, a pile of pennies for the gas meter, a pair of china wally dugs, a pair of brass candlesticks, a green packet of Woodbine cigarettes and a brass ashtray. Hanging on one side of the mantle shelf was a triangular box of stiff card holding spills.

From the other side hung a ladle and partly along the front, a potato masher, a toasting fork, a cheese grater, and a frying pan. Also along the front was fastened an expanding rod. Draped over it were a tea towel and several pairs of socks. A stone hearth was bordered by a brass fender with a padded box on either side.

Euphemia and Bridget were each sitting on one of the boxes. They had stripped off their dresses and steam was rising from their vests as they crouched as near as possible to the fire.

Teresa went to a hook that was on the wall beside the curtained bed and undid the rope that was twined around it. A four barred pulley came trundling and squeaking down from the ceiling and hung over the table.

'Give me all your wet things,' she said. 'They'll soon dry on the pulley.'

Wincey's hands trembled as she handed over her skirt, cardigan, blouse and stockings. She felt naked and painfully vulnerable without her clothes. The strange place and so many strange people confused her. She wondered hopefully if it was just a dream, one of the too-frequent nightmares she'd been having recently. She tensed her body, willing herself to wake up, willing everything and everybody to disappear. But they didn't.

Teresa said, 'Sit down at the table, Wincey, and drink your tea. It'll heat you up. Wincey? That's an unusual name. How did you get that, dear?'

Before Wincey could reply, Florence announced breathlessly, 'The minute she was born, a spider dropped from the ceiling on tae her, so it did. That's why they called her Wincey—because there's a rhyme, *Incey Wincey Spider*. They called her after the spider, so they did.'

'Ooh!' All the females in the room made a face.

'That's horrible,' Bridget said.

Erchie laid down the *Daily Worker* newspaper he'd been reading and gave Bridget a warning look. 'Watch your tongue. You'll upset the wee lassie.'

He was sitting next to Wincey and he put an arm around her shoulders. 'Never you mind them, hen. I think Wincey's a lovely name, and you're a lovely wee lassie.'

The sleeves of his striped shirt were rolled up and Wincey could feel the heat of his skin and the hairs on his arm. She shrank back trembling with agitation, but he didn't seem to notice. Nobody did. They were now all enjoying their tea, especially old Granny. She was making noisy slurping sounds and stuffing chips and bits of fish in between her gums. Her rocking chair squeaked backwards and forwards.

'Wire in, hen,' Erchie said. 'There's no standin' on ceremony here, it's every man for himsel'.'

The keenness of Wincey's hunger stoked by the hot smell filling the small room overcame every other feeling. She picked up a chip and began to eat. The fish supper was delicious—hot, salty and vinegary. She'd never tasted such delicious fish and chips. Nor had she ever eaten fish and chips with her fingers—especially out of a newspaper. Teresa was right, the hot tea and the food did make her feel better. Only she wished Erchie wasn't sitting so close to her. She kept trying to shrink further away. She kept giving him sidelong, apprehensive glances. He seemed harmless enough.

But then, so had her grandfather.

Teresa said to Bridget, 'Away through and tell Charlotte to come and get her supper.'

Wincey became aware of the rattle and whirr of the sewing machine. It didn't stop and when Bridget came back into the kitchen, she said, 'She's no' hungry and she has tae get that dress finished for Mrs Tompkinson.'

Teresa shook her head. 'No wonder she's so thin. I'm really worried about her.'

Granny's gums stopped their munching. 'It wid fit you better tae be through there workin' instead o' sittin' here talkin'. That girl's aye gettin' the heaviest end o' the load.'

'Now, Granny,' Teresa said calmly, 'you know fine I do my share. But I have to see to the cooking and cleaning and other things as well.'

'Cookin'?' Granny scoffed. 'When did ye cook this?'

'I'm going to make a nice pot of broth for tomorrow.' She turned her smiling attention on Wincey. 'Eat up, dear. Mr Nardini always gives us extra pieces of fish so there's plenty. He's a good soul, and nobody can make a fish supper like the Italians.'

'Same wi' the ice cream,' Erchie said, smacking his lips. 'An ice cream wafer,' he added wistfully. 'Oh, ah could

16

murder wan o' them right now.'

'I hadn't enough left for that,' Teresa said apologetically. 'But never mind, Erchie, you'll be able to get a job soon and we'll be all right.'

Erchie sighed. 'Ah wish ah could believe that, hen.'

Teresa turned to Wincey and said proudly, 'Erchie was in the navy. Everything was fine until they cut his money. A right disgrace it was, wasn't it, Erchie?'

'Aye, ten per cent. An' it wisnae as if we were well paid in the first place. It wisnae sae bad for the officers. It wis just a drop in the bucket tae them. But tae us matelots, it wis terrible. A real disaster, especially for men like mysel' wi' a wife an' family tae support. We were at Inver G when we heard about it.'

'That's Invergordon,' Florence interrupted for Wincey's benefit. Florence had obviously heard the story many times before.

'Aye,' her father sighed, 'ah must admit there wis a right panic at first. Before anyone wis briefed right, the newspapers got hold o' the story, ye see, an' got it aw wrong. They were sayin' it wis twenty-five per cent so ye can imagine how we aw felt.'

Florence cut in again. 'Ye mutinied, didn't ye, Dad? There wis a big mutiny an' aw the men stopped the ship frae sailin'. An' aw the captains were furious an' threatened aw the men—'

'Hang on,' Erchie laughed. 'Ye're an awful wee lassie for gettin' carried away. We had meetin's in the canteen an' on the fo'c'sle an' there wis a lot o' speech makin' and cheerin' and singin', an' some o' the ships couldnae sail, right enough.' He became serious again. 'Ah wis lucky, ah suppose. Ah wisnae wan o' the men who were jailed. Ah wis just wan o' the crowd o' matelots who were discharged from service.'

'An' now,' Florence said, 'he cannae get a job anywhere. Poor Daddy has tae sit here aw day long just twirlin' his thumbs, so he has.'

'Will you be quiet, Florence,' Teresa scolded. 'Your daddy does *not* sit here all the time. He keeps trying his best to get a job. It's not his fault there's no jobs going.'

'Ah never said it was.'

'Just be quiet, I said.'

'Aye,' Granny agreed. 'She blethers on far too much, that yin. If ah've said it once, ah've said it a hundred times—that girl'll get us aw intae trouble yet.'

Teresa was gathering up a few chips and a bit of fish onto a plate. She placed a fork beside it. 'Nobody touch this. I'll go through and take over the machine and make Charlotte come for a bite. She's very finnicky,' Teresa explained the plate and fork to Wincey. 'I'm usually the same myself but a fish supper out of a newspaper has a special taste, don't you think?'

Wincey nodded her agreement.

'And you pair,' Teresa addressed Euphemia and Bridget, 'get rid of all the paper and give the table a wipe over. I'll put this plate in the oven for a minute to heat it up again.'

The oven was part of the range and situated on the left side of the fire. Teresa had to squeeze sideways from her side of the table to go over to the oven. Everybody had to squeeze sideways to go anywhere in the kitchen—it was so small and packed—although it only contained a table, four wooden chairs, four stools, a rocking chair and a basket chair. The bed recessed into the wall opposite the sink was draped with fawn curtains and valance, and was a permanent fitment. Now it was in deep shadow. The gas light was not strong enough to brighten any corner of the room. The coal bunker was opposite the fireplace and had a long shelf above it. The kitchen was not even as big as the pantry at Wincey's Grandmother Cartwright's house. That kitchen was like a ballroom in comparison with this one.

In a minute or two, Charlotte entered and sat down at the table.

Erchie said, 'Is it nearly done, hen?'

'Mammy's just finishing it off. I'll be able to deliver it first thing in the morning. It'll just need a wee press.'

'Great! That's great, hen. Come on, eat up. Ye deserve it.'

The younger girls cleared away the debris the others had left, and gave the table a wipe before taking the plate out of the oven. Charlotte smiled her thanks at them and began daintily forking bits of food into her mouth. She was poorly but cleanly dressed and with her straight brown hair held back behind each ear with a kirby-grip.

'I hope she likes it,' she said, 'and gives me another order.'

'It's terrible,' Granny shook her head, 'that we've tae be dependent on rubbish like that.'

Charlotte flushed. 'It is not rubbish. I do a good job. It's a beautiful dress.'

'Och, ah dinnae mean the dress, ye silly bissom. Ah mean that woman ye've got tae slave for, an' aw the rest o' the toffee nosed bitches over in that West End.'

'Mrs Tompkinson is not rubbish. She's a nice woman in her own way. She just doesn't know—doesn't understand— anything about how other people have to live. People in places like the West End and Bearsden and Giffnock and Newton Mearns live in a different world from us.'

Wincey wanted to say a heartfelt 'How right you are!' but didn't want to risk giving anything away about herself.

Erchie said, 'Her in the West End—Tompkinson, did ye say her name was, Charlotte?'

'Yes.'

'That wis the name o' our rear admiral. He wis senior officer o' the Atlantic fleet. Ah wonder if she's any relation.'

'Oh, I shouldn't think so, Daddy.'

'Ask her when ye deliver the dress tomorrow.'

Charlotte laughed. 'I'll just be checking on the fitting and collecting my money. I'm not likely to be chatting to her. People like that don't chat to servants, Daddy.'

'Bad bitches,' Granny growled. 'Aw tarred wi' the same brush. Think they're better than us but they're no'.'

Erchie laughed and said to Wincey, 'Ma's a bit of a commie. She used tae march behind Maclean. An' she'd be out there supportin' Jimmy Maxton if she wis able.'

Wincey wondered what everyone's reaction would be if she told them that her mother and father had known Maclean and now knew the equally charismatic but more eccentric looking Maxton. She had been brought up on stories about Maclean, and even had a vague recollection of being carried on her father's shoulders at his funeral nine years ago in 1923 and feeling frightened at the size of the vast crowd. Maclean had been a hero—a pacifist who had been sent to prison on several occasions for upholding his beliefs. He had also formed what was called the Tramps Trust Unlimited and campaigned for a miner's wage and a six-hour day, and full wages for the unemployed. He also established the Scottish Workers' Republican party. Oh, she knew all about politics and politicians, all right.

Her mother was always out with them, or working on their behalf, or entertaining them in the house. Her father would join them if they came in the evening. There was always much serious talk and discussion then. During the day, he'd stay shut away in his writing room.

Grandmother Cartwright disapproved of all of this, particularly their involvement with James Mathieson. 'What's going on, that's what I would like to know?' she never tired of asking her husband, her son and anybody else in her circle. 'A *ménage à trois?*'

Grandfather usually shook his head at this. 'Shouldn't think so. It's just they've got all that socialist nonsense in common.'

'And who's fault is that?'

Few things made Grandmother more furious than the mention of socialism. 'Our Nicholas had no interest whatsoever in anything like that. To think we sent him to the best boarding school in the land! Then Sandhurst! To think he got his commission in the army—he was a good loyal subject of the king. It's been that girl who's corrupted him.'

'I know,' Grandfather would agree. 'But unfortunately there's nothing we can do about that now. The damage has been done.'

'That's what happens when somebody moves out of their class.' Grandmother liked to think she resembled a thin version of the old Queen Victoria, and judging by some of the late queen's photographs, Mrs Cartwright did have the similar beady eyes and small tight mouth. 'Virginia is—and always will be—nothing more than a common scullery maid. I don't know what my son ever saw in her. Or rather,' she paused and sniffed her distaste, 'I do know but it's something too disgraceful to talk about.'

Everybody knew, including Wincey. While Virginia had worked as a scullery maid for Mrs Cartwright, she'd had a love affair with the only son of the house, and while he'd been away in the War, Virginia had his child. That was Richard.

After Nicholas had been reported killed in action, Mrs Cartwright had taken the child from Virginia. Some time later, Virginia had married Mathieson. Then Nicholas had turned up in a hospital in England. Nicholas had been badly injured and suffered loss of memory, and the trauma of shell shock. He had lain in the military hospital for a considerable time before his identity was discovered. It had been this hospital experience that had given him sympathy for and understanding of Mathieson—who had later suffered a stroke and had also spent a traumatic time in hospital. As a result the two men had become firm friends.

But Mrs Cartwright could never understand their relationship. The whole set-up of her son's house in Kirklee Terrace—indeed his whole life—was beyond her. He had become a writer and she had no time for any of his literary and artistic friends. Every one of them horrified her with their loose, bohemian ways. As she often said, it was that awful girl who encouraged him with this writing business in the first place. She still referred to Virginia as a girl, although Virginia was now thirty-three. She still thought of Nicholas as a boy although he was now thirty-seven.

'That's why,' she told her husband, 'we must encourage Richard to spend as much time as possible with us when he's on holiday from boarding school. We don't want him corrupted by that awful girl as well.'

As usual, her husband agreed wholeheartedly. He shared her horror of all things socialist. 'Communist revolutionaries and trouble makers, the lot of them,' he said bitterly. As well as owning munitions factories before he retired, he had also owned tenement property in Glasgow and still remembered the trouble the rent strikes had caused him. Wincey had heard the other side of the same story from her mother, from Mathieson and even from her father. For a long time she'd been confused by the conflicting versions she'd heard in her mother's house and her grandparents' house, but now seeing for herself the conditions people had to live in, she could well understand why people went on strike and refused to pay increased rents. Especially when, during the war, most of the men were away fighting for king and country. It was a disgrace, her mother had said, and now Wincey agreed with her.

She became aware of Charlotte speaking to her.

'Can you sew, Wincey?'

'I've done a little embroidery but I've never used a sewing machine.'

'Embroidery?' The others laughed uproariously, and Wincey suddenly realised that, to them, embroidery was a luxury, a pastime for those who didn't have to spend every waking moment trying to earn a living.

'Just at school,' Wincey hastily explained. 'The sewing teacher was only showing us what it was.'

She felt shaken. The realisation suddenly came to her that she could never go home. No-one must find out what she'd done. No-one must know who she was. She was isolated in this awful place for ever. But then, she'd always been isolated. And at least here, people seemed to care about her.

3

Nicholas was at a crucial stage in the creation of his new novel. He had never found novel-writing easy. People often said that poetry must be easier to write because it was so much shorter, but as far as he was concerned, all writing was hard work. Not that he was complaining. He loved his work and felt very fortunate that he was now able to make a living from his novels. There might be praise for poetry, but, he had long since discovered, little financial benefit.

Some verses written in a few snatched moments of privacy while he'd been at school and then in the army had been all he could manage at first. For a long time, they had to be kept secret. He knew only too well how disapproving his mother and father would be if they found out. Only Virginia knew and understood. And she was encouraging—he could never thank her enough for that.

He had thanked her many times, through his poetry. In his first novel, too, he'd managed to express his love for her. Now, it pained him to see her so unhappy. He was equally distressed at the disappearance of their daughter, but he was also secretly ashamed of the recurring feeling he had that his father's sudden death and Wincey's inexplicable disappearance were having an adverse effect on his novel. Even at normal times he resented anything that disturbed his writing.

Virginia had long since learned not to enter his writing room while he was working, and the children had quickly realised that the good-natured, smiling father they knew outside the writing room was very different from the impatient, angry character inside that room, if they interrupted him.

Very few things made him lose his temper, but having his work interrupted was certainly one of them. He had been suppressing these feelings since Wincey's disappearance. At first, he had gone out to look for her. He had co-operated with the police search, his mind aching with trying to think of where she might have gone and what could have happened to her. He and Virginia had talked endlessly about every possibility. Friends kept dropping in or telephoning to ask for news or to offer any help they could. In the end, everyone feared that when she had found her grandfather dead, she had run from the house in a blind panic and fallen into the river.

But the River Kelvin had been dragged and nothing was found. Even his mother, who had never shown all that much interest in or concern for Wincey before, was now looking pale and withdrawn. Naturally, she had been shocked and distressed at the death of her husband, although even then she had succeeded in hiding her emotions. That was her way. She became stiff and dignified, her face closed, her eyes hardened. But she had asked about Wincey.

As the days and weeks dragged past without any news of Wincey, they all tried to carry on as normal. But even when Richard came home at weekends, the underlying tension and strain was always there. Nothing was quite the same. Nicholas went out drinking with his literary friends—which was something of temporary help—and at least they understood about his novel. People like Mathieson and their more politically active friends, good and sympathetic though they were, had not the same understanding. His life was in chaos. He felt

24

everything was slipping away from him, never to return.

Eventually, sitting listlessly with Virginia over a cup of coffee in the kitchen, he suddenly burst out,

'We can't go on like this, Virginia. We have to get our lives back to normal. I'm going to start writing again.'

'Normal?' She gazed at him with sad eyes and a bitter twist to her mouth. 'What can be normal now?'

'We can't go on like this,' he repeated.

'How can you even think of writing at a time like this?'

'I'm not doing any good sitting here like this, am I? Nor are you. We've done all we can. We'll just have to leave it to the police now.'

'They haven't done any good either.'

'I'm sure they've done their best and will continue to do their best, Virginia. It's not helping the situation allowing ourselves to be overcome by depression. Look at you. You don't look well. I'm worried about you.'

'Worried about me,' she scoffed. 'Don't give me that, Nicholas. I know you. All you're worried about is your precious writing.'

'Are you accusing me of not caring about my own daughter?' he suddenly shouted at her, as he half rose, sending his chair crashing back. He knew he was over-reacting because of guilt. He was angry at himself more than her. All the same, he did care about Wincey.

Virginia had no right to imply that he didn't. She was nursing her head in her hands now.

'Oh, shut up, Nicholas. Run away to your damned writing room, for pity's sake, and give me some peace.'

'I've done everything I possibly could. No-one could have done more,' he insisted. 'I've walked the streets for days. I've—'

'Yes, all right, all right. I wasn't accusing you of anything.'

'And after all, I've a living to earn, and Richard's school fees and God knows what else to keep paying.'

'I said all right, Nicholas. Just leave me alone.'

25

He left the kitchen and once in his room, he still felt angry. Yet there was relief too. He did care about his daughter. He cared about her acutely, painfully, but here—in his sanctuary—he could escape the pain. He could enter another, different world. Here he could change things, create problems and then solve them. He could make people sad, and then happy. Danger could turn to safety. Here he was all powerful. Here he *could* do more.

★   ★   ★

Virginia's emotions were in turmoil. She felt absolute anguish every time she thought of Wincey. It was everyone's unspoken opinion that she must be dead. She had drowned and been washed away, either in the River Kelvin or the River Clyde. There could be no other reason why she had not been found alive and well. Her disappearance had been reported in the *Glasgow Herald*. There had been pictures of her. Her auburn hair, her face, with its dusting of freckles, were unusual in a way, but she had a sultry beauty despite the fact that she was obviously just a child in school uniform.

A reward had been offered for any information. The size of that reward, the police assured Virginia, would encourage someone to come forward. But no-one had. A thousand times in her imagination Virginia had suffered the agonies of drowning with Wincey. It was unbearable to think of the child suffering alone. Yet, at the same time, she clung to the hope that somehow, somewhere, Wincey might still be alive. It was true what Nicholas had said—they had done everything they could.

Yet the many unanswered questions about the dreadful day Wincey disappeared continued to haunt Virginia. Mrs Cartwright had been worried about the state of old Mr Cartwright's health before she had left for her bridge afternoon. As a result she had returned much earlier than usual, only to find that her husband was dead and Wincey had vanished into thin air. The child had no money. She wasn't wearing her coat or hat or gloves. They had all been lying in the Cartwright hall where she had left them when she arrived. It had been a wild afternoon with wind gusting furiously along Great Western Road. Rain had been streaking down, hardening into hailstones to drum against windows and doors. What could have made Wincey rush out unprotected on a day like that?

Virginia wept. Then she dried her eyes, overcome with bitterness. It was all right for Nicholas. He could escape into his fictional world. That was where he really belonged— where he was truly happy. He could shut Wincey out. He could shut everybody and everything out. That's what he always did. It had never bothered her before, she had simply accepted it, but now she almost hated him for it. She wondered if he cared at all about Wincey.

She tried to tell herself that she was being unfair. Of course he cared about his daughter. His love for the child had been expressed in his poetry. She remembered a poem he had written about Wincey:

Minutes rush
A tiny yawn holds parents
Captive in a cocoon of wonder.
What dreams visit her
As perfect hands stretch
To grab at the hope charged air.

Minutes rush
While lashes, long and dark,
Lie pillowed by cheeks
Of impossible softness.
Milk sated lips pout
With contented sighs.

Minutes rush
As varied and fleeting emotions

27

Vie for attention.
But mother and father dare not blink
As they attend the next murmur,
The next tiny movement,
The next breath,
And still, the minutes rush.

She remembered him gazing in wonder at the baby, tenderly nursing Wincey in his arms. Of course he loved the child. Of course he'd done his best for her. But still the irritation, the resentment against him, lingered, refusing to be completely banished.

Unable to sit alone with her thoughts for a minute longer, she rose and went for her coat and hat. She decided to go and see Mathieson. At least he would be able to take her mind off all her troubles, even just for a short while. He was not long back from London where he had been supporting the Hunger Marchers. The marches had been flash points for violent anti-government protests across Britain in the past two weeks. The last time she had seen him was when he came for lunch and he had given her and Nicholas a vivid description of the fifteen-thousand-strong rally in Trafalgar Square and the scene when two thousand marchers from the provinces joined thousands of supporters in Hyde Park. Nearly five thousand police fought with them for two hours. Fifty people were injured and fourteen arrested. During an East End visit, Prince George had been met with shouts of 'Down with the means test, we want bread'. Mathieson had hardly changed since she first knew him as a zealous young socialist during the war. Despite the disabilities he'd suffered since his stroke, he was still able to give lectures on politics and economics at the Scottish Labour College. One side of his face still bore the unmistakable signs of his stroke, and he had to walk with the help of a stick, but despite all this it seemed as though nothing could slow him down or deflect him from his devotion to the 'Cause'.

Mathieson now lived in a one-bedroomed flat above the shops in Byres Road, within easy walking distance of Kirklee Terrace. Virginia was glad of her long coat with its high fur collar and her tight fitting cloche hat as she braved the bitter November wind outside. It had been a cold day like this when Wincey disappeared, and her thoughts returned once more to her lost daughter as she hurried along Great Western Road, then turned down into Byres Road.

She felt as if she was going mad. It was the not knowing, not understanding what had happened. The growing possibility that she would never know. At the same time she couldn't imagine herself ever giving up hope. One day, she would uncover the truth.

4

'How about this, Daddy?' Charlotte said. 'When I was delivering Mrs Tompkinson's latest outfit, I saw a broken down sewing machine left out at the back of the house for the bin men to collect. How about if you collect it instead, bring it back here and see if you can mend it? If you could fix it up, I could teach Wincey and Florence to use it. They could work shifts on that machine. Then with Mammy and me on the one we've already got, we'd be able to take on more work.'

Erchie's face brightened. 'Here, that's a great idea, hen. It'll give me somethin' tae dae an' ah'll no' be much o' an engineer if ah cannae manage tae fix a wee sewin' machine.'

'It'd be a real help, Daddy. We'd be able to make more money.'

'Right, hen. You give me the exact address an ah'll be off. Ah'd better look nippy or the bin men might get there before me.'

Charlotte scribbled the address on to a piece of paper and Erchie hurried to snatch his jacket from the peg in the lobby. Within seconds the outside door banged shut and he was away. He could be heard whistling as he clattered down the stairs.

Teresa's tired eyes glowed with enthusiasm and gratitude towards Charlotte. 'You're a clever girl, Charlotte. That'll give your dad a job—just what he needed.'

'Huh, some job,' Granny grunted. 'What good's a job wi' nae wages?'

'Once the four of us really get going, we could earn enough to give Dad something,' Charlotte said. Wincey, now settled in and feeling like one of the family—indeed more so than she'd ever done in her own family, spoke up with enthusiasm.

'Yes, and maybe we could even find more machines and have more people work on them. That's how big businesses are built up.'

Granny scoffed. 'What would the likes o' you know about big businesses, or any kin' o' business, ye cheeky wee tramp!'

'Now Granny,' Teresa said, 'there's no need to talk like that. Wincey's a good girl and she's been a great help to us.'

It had always been Bridget and Euphemia's job to go on errands to the shops. They had become quite expert at tracking down bones for soup, or stale cookies or bread that a baker in town was going to throw in the bin at the end of the day. Local bakers were more likely to ask for a penny or two for their stale bread and scones. While her mother was taking her turn at the sewing machine, Florence helped with the cooking— at least Florence would peel the potatoes and scrape the vegetables for the soup. She boasted she once made scones, but mostly she was out wandering about, asking for trouble as Granny said. Wincey opted for the scrubbing and cleaning of the house. Teresa said she didn't need to do that because the three girls, Florence, Euphemia and Bridget, usually took turns doing the cleaning. Instead, Charlotte said Wincey could accompany her on her rounds, collecting or delivering clothes for different customers. 'That way,' Charlotte said kindly, 'you'd be able to get away from here for a wee while and see all the lovely houses the gentry live in.'

But Wincey insisted she'd rather stay in and clean and scrub. It wasn't just her fear of being seen and recognised in one of the more prosperous areas that made her want to stay indoors. She had discovered she preferred to do things on her own. Not only that, there was an obsessive streak about her at times. Concentrating completely, silently, going to extremes, scrubbing the floors, the sink, the outside of the coal bunker, the fire, polishing the black grate, washing the windows—it somehow made her feel safe in herself. It also gave her a deep sense of achievement. This total obsessiveness even overcame her revulsion at cleaning the outside toilet.

'Never,' Teresa told her, 'since this building was built, has that toilet been kept so spotless.'

It was a tiny cubicle situated downstairs on the half landing and shared by two other families, next door neighbours of the Gourlays on the top floor. It had a cracked wooden seat and a cistern mounted over six feet up the wall, and it was flushed by pulling a hanging chain. It had been a dark, putrid smelling place before Wincey attacked it. She had even scrubbed the walls and the cistern, climbing on to the toilet seat to reach it.

'Ye must be mad,' Florence said. 'It's no' as if we're the only wans makin' a mess o' it. It's that McGregor bunch. There's sixteen o' them. Filthy wee middens o' weans!'

Teresa tutted. 'Och, poor Mrs McGregor has her hands full trying to cope with so many, and her always pregnant with the next. I am sorry for her, right enough.'

'I don't mind keeping the toilet clean,' Wincey assured everybody. 'Honestly, I enjoy working away by myself.'

Florence laughed. 'Enjoy, did ye say? Enjoy cleaning filthy toilets. You definitely are mad!'

'You can cut up Erchie's old *Daily Workers* for toilet paper, if you like,' Teresa suggested helpfully. The *Daily Worker* was Erchie's only luxury in life, except the odd Woodbine cigarette, but that was only an occasional treat.

'Oh, thanks Teresa,' Wincey said. 'I could put holes in

each bit and thread string through them and hang them all onto a nail on the wall.'

'Och, we aye take a bit o' our Daddy's old paper down wi' us anyway,' Florence reminded her.

'I know, but this is more efficient. I mean it's tidier, and it helps everyone.'

Eventually Teresa said, 'That toilet's like a wee palace.'

And everyone—including the McGregors and the other family on the landing, the Donaldsons—wholeheartedly agreed. Both families began boxing their children's ears or slapping their legs if it was discovered they had made a mess in the toilet, or the lavvy as it was more commonly known. Teresa and family were more polite and proper than most of their neighbours. Granny was a trial, however. She couldn't get down to the toilet since her arthritis was so bad and she'd gained so much weight.

'Ma hips are murder,' she kept informing everyone, 'an' it's even gone intae ma gums. That's why ah cannae wear ma teeth.'

'Och well,' Teresa said with a look of wide eyed innocence, 'it hasn't affected your jaws, Granny. You're still able to talk, dear. Your jaws never stop moving.'

'What dae ye mean by that?' Granny demanded angrily.

'Now, now, Granny, you know fine we're all concerned about you and do our best for you.'

They certainly did do their best for Granny, as Wincey soon discovered. When Granny needed 'to go', as she called it, it was a real challenge of strength and endurance for everyone who happened to be in the house. The challenge arose again now. Erchie was out collecting the sewing machine. Euphemia and Bridget were out looking for any vegetables that had been thrown out by the fruit shops in town. Their bins at the back of the shops could prove a treasure trove of food. Other grocery stores in the centre of the city could delight the sisters with tasty morsels, often in packets or tins, which had just been burst or bashed and didn't have the perfect appearance that fussy people with too much money always insisted on.

Florence was out trying to scrounge some bits of coal lying about in one of the coal yards.

'Ah need tae go,' Granny announced, her small rheumy eyes betraying some anxiety.

Teresa said, 'Can't you wait a wee while until someone else comes in, Granny. There's only Wincey just now.'

'What's up wi' her then? Is she paralysed, or what?'

Teresa rolled her eyes. 'You know fine she's only a wee slip of a thing, and there's not much more of me. I don't think we'd be able to lift you. The girls won't be long. Just try to hang on a wee while longer.'

'Ah cannae.' Granny's voice rose to a wail. She was obviously in genuine distress.

'All right, all right, we'll do our best,' Teresa said hastily. 'I'll fetch the chamber pot,' she said, giving it its proper name. It was a chanty to everyone else. Once the chamber pot was ready at Granny's feet, Teresa told Wincey, 'Now you get a grip of her at one side and I'll hang on at the other and we'll both try and heave her up.'

In a matter of seconds both Teresa and Wincey were scarlet faced and panting with their exertions. Granny felt like a solid and immovable mountain. But eventually they did manage to prise her out of the rocking chair and stagger forward with her.

'Wait a minute,' Teresa gasped, 'till I pull her knickers down. Hang on.'

Like grim death, Wincey hung on.

'Right, lower her down now.'

The lowering down proved to be worse than the raising up. Wincey felt her legs and her back would never be the same again. Once safely deposited onto the chamber pot, Granny's face acquired an expression of deep concentration and Teresa cried out, 'Och, not number two, Granny!'

Granny grunted, 'Ye'll be auld yersel' wan day.' This was

an expression Granny often used in self defence.

'Never mind,' Teresa said to Wincey. 'I'll empty it, dear.'

Afterwards Wincey swung the outside door to and fro to allow comparatively fresh air to waft in. She also opened the kitchen window while Teresa masked a pot of tea 'to help us get our strength back'.

'Are you two tryin' tae freeze me tae death noo?' Granny wailed.

'Now, now, Granny,' Teresa said, 'a nice cup of tea will soon heat you up.'

'There's never any biscuits these days,' Granny complained. 'I used tae enjoy a nice digestive tae dip intae ma tea.'

'Never mind. Once we get another machine, we'll be able to make more money, as Charlotte says. Then you can have your digestives.'

'Ah'll believe that when ah see it.'

'Are you all right, dear?' Teresa gazed anxiously at Wincey.

'Yes, fine, thank you.'

'Here, drink up your tea.'

'Thank you.'

'You're such a polite wee girl. Where did you learn such nice manners?'

Wincey shrugged. 'My mother, I think. She was . . .' An idea occurred to her. 'She was from the Highlands, like you.'

'Ah, that explains a lot dear. As well as your nice voice. You don't sound a bit Glaswegian. Your parents died in an accident, did you say? Or was that Florence? I get mixed up with all her stories.'

'I'd rather not talk about it. It upsets me even to think about. Please don't ask me.'

'Oh, I'm so sorry, dear,' Teresa interrupted hastily. 'it's not like me to be nosy.'

'Ha,' Granny snorted. 'That's a laugh!'

'Now, now. I've never asked Wincey anything about her background before, have I, Wincey?'

'No, everyone's been very good. I'm so grateful.' And she

was. She didn't feel that she'd ever been accepted just as herself before. To her grandfather she had been nothing more than a sex object. To her grandmother she had been a younger edition of her mother, and it was only too obvious that her grandmother hated her mother. To her mother and father, she barely existed at all. They were so caught up with all their clever, articulate friends. She was a joke. They often laughed at her shyness and the way she could get tongue-tied. Sometimes she even stuttered. She never stuttered here, no longer even felt shy. She was as happy as could be, as long as she was able to blot out the past and keep her guilty secret locked safely away in a dark recess of her mind.

5

'What does Nicholas think of Galsworthy getting the Nobel prize for literature?' Mathieson asked once he'd led Virginia into the kitchen. 'I've just made a pot of tea—do you want a cup?'

'Yes, all right.'

She sat down on one of the wooden chairs at the table and watched her ex-husband limp towards the press at the side of the grate and fetch a cup and saucer. The kitchen was almost identical to the one they'd had when they lived together in the Calton. It even had the same furniture. Yet Virginia experienced no feelings of nostalgia. In those days Mathieson had been as totally immersed in politics as Nicholas was now totally taken up with writing. She suspected that this obsessive devotion was one of the things that both men knew right from the start they had in common.

Nicholas had been good to Mathieson while he had been lying in his hospital bed, unable to move or talk. Nicholas had kept him in touch with everything by reading the newspapers to him every day. She suspected that, with such a silent listener, Nicholas had also poured out his heart to Mathieson.

He'd certainly told him all about his passion for writing, even reading out chapters of his new novel to him.

At first, when she'd discovered that Nicholas had gone to see Mathieson, she was both horrified and afraid. After all, she had been having an affair with Nicholas and had had his child. That was before she had met Mathieson. She was married to him by the time it was discovered that Nicholas had not been killed in the trenches. And when she'd married Mathieson, he knew nothing about either the affair or the baby.

After Nicholas had returned, they had restarted their affair and eventually she confessed everything to her husband. She told him she was leaving him. As a committed socialist, Mathieson had always hated the rich and powerful—men like Nicholas's father. As well as the munitions factory in which Virginia's brother had been killed, George Cartwright had owned property in many of Glasgow's most notorious slums. At that point, however, Mathieson had not met Nicholas. She tried to tell him how different Nicholas was from his father, but he had refused to listen and became more and more enraged. That was when he had taken his stroke. For a long time she had blamed herself. She had been so distressed that she had stopped going to see him in hospital. She couldn't bear to look at his grotesquely distorted face. She had believed that he was not aware that she was even there, that he was not aware of anything.

Nicholas had been appalled when he heard this. 'I know what it's like to lie alone and confused in a hospital bed.' And that was when he took over the visits. It must have been during this time that Mathieson had come to accept that Nicholas was indeed different from his father. Nicholas had learned to embrace socialism himself since his experiences in the war. He wasn't as radical as Mathieson, but a socialist nevertheless.

'I express my beliefs in action,' Mathieson once told him. 'I spread the word by teaching and I take an active part in protests and the like. You express your beliefs in your writing. Who's to say which of us is more effective, Nicholas?'

The divorce had been traumatic for all of them, even though they'd all agreed that for Mathieson to divorce Virginia on the grounds of adultery was the best and quickest solution. Long before Mathieson had got out of the hospital, she had already set up house with Nicholas.

If anyone had told Virginia before Mathieson had taken ill that one day he and Nicholas Cartwright would become firm friends, she would never have believed them. But friends they had become. She often thought that they got on better together than she'd ever got on with either of them. They seemed at times to have far more in common.

'We've been thinking, and talking about, nothing else but Wincey,' she told Mathieson now.

'Oh yes, of course,' Mathieson said. 'It's awful for you both, and I suppose it hasn't got any easier as time has passed.'

'It's got worse, if anything. It's beginning to affect our relationship.'

'How do you mean?' He poured out two cups of tea.

She shrugged. 'Oh, I don't know. All the tension and worry, and not being able to do anything, I suppose.' She took a few sips of tea. 'I as much as told him this morning that he was totally selfish and didn't care about Wincey. He'd just announced, you see, that he was going back to work in his room.'

'He does care, Virginia.'

Miserably, she nodded.

'It's just not being able to do anything, not knowing.'

'We've all done everything we can, especially Nicholas. What more do you expect him to do?'

'I know. I know.' After a few minutes she added, 'I'm dreading Christmas.'

'There's a few weeks to go yet. You could still hear good news.'

'Do you really believe she could still be alive, James?'

'People go missing all the time and many of them do turn up again, often in another big city, like London.'

'London?' Virginia echoed incredulously. 'How on earth could the child get to London?'

Mathieson shrugged. 'It has been known. I've read about cases like that, haven't you?'

'I suppose so, but I can't imagine Wincey being so resourceful. She's always been such a quiet, slow kind of child. She never did very well at school, you know. Not compared with Richard. Richard has always been so clever, and self-confident, and outgoing.'

'And everybody's favourite,' Mathieson said.

Virginia paled. 'You don't think . . . I mean, have we been unfair or unkind to her? Did we neglect her? Oh James! Whatever she might have believed anyone else thought of her, she definitely knew her grandfather thought the world of her. We used to smile when he called her his clever girl. Poor Wincey. She was probably so grief stricken, she couldn't cope, didn't know what to do except run away from the awful truth of her grandfather's death.'

'Maybe she imagined she'd have nobody to care about her after he'd gone.'

'But we did care about her, James. Maybe we've been thoughtless. Maybe we didn't spend enough time with her, pay her enough attention. But we did care. We still do.'

'Of course you do,' he soothed. 'Children are always getting strange ideas into their heads. I haven't worked for a lifetime as a teacher not to know that, and especially young people of her age. Once they get into their teens, life can be terribly difficult for them—and for their parents.'

'I'm sorry to keep bothering you like this, James. You've been very supportive.'

'You're not bothering me. I only wish I could be of more help.'

'Were you not at the College today?'

'It's Saturday.'

She rolled her eyes. 'I really have lost track of things, haven't I?'

'It's time you showed some common sense like Nicholas. Get on with your life. You're not going to do yourself or anybody else any good by cracking up.'

'It just shows you, though. Saturday, Sunday, come hell or high water, it doesn't matter, it doesn't make any difference to Nicholas as far as his writing is concerned.'

'It's the nature of his work, Virginia. You always knew that.'

She sighed. 'I suppose so.' Then after a minute, 'Would you like to come to lunch tomorrow. Maybe you'll be able to drag him away from his desk.'

It was Mathieson's turn to sigh. 'You just can't accept it, can you?'

She thought he was going to add, 'Just as you could never accept the time and commitment I gave to politics.' She almost dared him to say it, so that she could argue with him, take her frustration out on him. After all, she'd helped him as much as she could and in every way she could. She even spoke at political meetings. But in the end she'd seen that all of Mathieson's passion was for politics. His political work and the time he spent on it took precedence over everything else.

It seemed to her now that, although Mathieson's work and Nicholas's were very different, they had much the same attitude to it. But Mathieson added nothing to his statement and so she repeated, 'Will you come?'

'Yes, all right. But don't expect me to go into Nicholas's room and drag him out.'

'Maybe if I ask George or Jimmy as well?'

George Buchanan was Labour MP for the Gorbals. James Maxton was MP for Bridgeton.

'Maxton's too busy fighting Ramsay Macdonald and opposing rearmament just now to be socialising with us. Buchanan's been having a go at Macdonald as well. I'm hard put to it to decide which of them is the more brilliant speaker. I think George is the more fiery one—him and his red hair, but they're both equally charismatic as far as I'm concerned.'

'So they're in London just now?'

'As far as I know.'

'Oh well, make it about one o'clock, James. That'll give him a morning on his own. He surely can't complain about that.'

'One o'clock it is. And try to discipline your mind to concentrate on something else. Invite some of Nicholas's friends for supper. He won't mind that and you enjoy listening to them.'

'I suppose I could. You know them only too well, don't you. None of them would leave their desks early enough to come for lunch. Writers!'

'Well, you know what Nicholas always says. He'd never have continued with his writing in the first place if it hadn't been for you.'

'I sometimes wonder now if I did the right thing.'

'I've never been more certain about anything, Virginia. You did the right thing. One day, it might be Nicholas receiving that Nobel prize. In my opinion, Nicholas is a far better writer than Galsworthy, and his work shows him to be far more committed to social reform.'

'You think so?'

'I always say what I think.' At least this was true.

'All right, I believe you. But living with a writer is not easy.' She wanted to say, 'any more than it was easy living with a politician.' But she didn't. And she left Mathieson's house feeling even more frustrated than when she'd arrived.

6

'You're really a very smart girl,' Teresa said. 'You've picked up sewing so quickly.'

'I'd like to learn the cutting too,' Wincey said eagerly.

Teresa looked doubtful. 'Oh, that's a bit more tricky, dear. Maybe you'd better leave that to Charlotte and me for a wee while yet.'

'Yes,' Charlotte agreed. 'But you're doing very well, Wincey. I will let you do some cutting eventually, but it's so important— it's not a thing you can rush. I could start taking you out with me and show you the measuring and fitting. That's very important too.'

Wincey shook her head. 'No, I'd rather stay here and work.'

'You are a funny child,' Teresa said. 'Any of the other girls would jump at the chance to see into some of the houses that Charlotte goes to. You can't be that shy. You're not shy with us.'

'It's different here. I feel at home. I'm not frightened any more.'

'What on earth is there to be frightened of?'

Wincey shrugged. 'I don't like posh places or posh people.'

Granny, who had been dozing by the fire, spoke up with a splutter, 'Bloody parasites, the lot o' them. Ah'd put them up against a wall an' shoot them.'

'Now, now, Granny,' Teresa said. 'You know fine well you would never do any such thing.'

'They've done it tae oor kind though.' Granny raised her voice. 'Shot decent pacifist lads an' poor fellas who were aw tae bits wi' shell shock. Called them cowards an' shot them in cold blood.'

'Yes, all right, Granny. Just try and calm down now. You know what getting too excited does to you.'

Getting excited caused Granny to lose control of her bladder. Sometimes, a whole row of Granny's knickers festooned the pulley above the kitchen table.

'They as good as killed poor Johnny, the way they tormented him in prison. Did ye know that?'

'Yes, Granny, we know how poor Johnny Maclean was treated in prison. You've told us before.'

'Aye, but no' often enough, it seems. They'll be doin' the same tae Jimmy Maxton if we let them get away wi' it. He's a pacifist as well, don't forget.'

Wincey imagined how amazed and fascinated Granny and all the Gourlays would be if she told them that she had met Maxton—first of all when she'd gone with her mother and father to hear him speak, and later when he had been invited to Kirklee Terrace. Like Mathieson, he had been a school teacher and she'd heard him say that he had been converted to socialism by speakers such as Keir Hardy, Philip Snowdon and Ramsay Macdonald. But none of these men, Wincey felt sure, could match James Maxton as a dramatic and witty speaker. During the war, he was dismissed as a teacher, charged with sedition, found guilty and imprisoned for a year. Her father said that his suffering in prison was still etched on his lantern-jawed face. His long hair was, her father suspected, one of the ways Maxton had of cocking a snook at the

44

establishment and its conventions. In appearance at least, he was very unlike his fellow socialist MP, John Wheatley—a short, serious man with a chubby, bespectacled face. Wheatley had been both her father and mother's favourite. They admired his courage and intelligence and supported his campaign for better housing in Glasgow. Wheatley had proposed a scheme for the building of municipal cottages instead of tenements in Glasgow, and he'd succeeded in getting his Housing Act passed successfully. His plan was to create a partnership between political parties, local authorities and building employees and build as many new council houses at modest rents as possible.

Wincey had been brought up on stories about socialist politicians like Maclean, Maxton and Wheatley, but these stories had seldom, if ever, been told directly to her. She had heard them discussed between her parents and their friends. Her parents had seldom even noticed that she had been there. How Granny Gourlay would have loved to hear some of those stories about her socialist heroes—but Wincey couldn't risk breathing a word of any of this.

Instead she said, 'I've read all about them. The socialists, I mean. And seen pictures of them.'

'Where did you get the books and pictures?' Teresa wanted to know.

'The library,' Wincey said hastily, wishing that she had just kept her mouth shut as she usually did about anything outside of the house and the immediate concerns in it.

'I'm surprised you had the time, dear. But I'm glad you did. I know how happy I am if I can find a few minutes to get to the library and pick up a nice romance. But as you can imagine, it's not so easy getting the time to read it. Now with Christmas and the New Year coming near, all our clients will want party dresses made.'

'Aye, they'll aw be lookin' forward tae toastin' anither happy Hogmanay,' Granny growled, 'while aw we huv is the clankin' away o' these sewin' machines.'

45

'That reminds me,' Charlotte said. 'It's time I was getting back to the room and getting on with it.'

'Och, have another wee cup of tea. You've been at it since the break of dawn, Charlotte,' her mother said worriedly.

'It's just we're doing so well now,' Charlotte said. 'It's word of mouth, you see. One satisfied customer tells another. We're even getting a pound or two in the bank. Come on, Wincey, it's time you relieved Florence. She's been through there on her own for long enough.'

'If you're hinting at me,' Teresa said, 'I had to see to Granny as well as make a bit to eat for everybody.'

'I know, I know. I'm sorry. It's just that we're really beginning to get somewhere, so it's important to keep going.'

'I know, dear, but what's the use of having money in the bank when we're still having to scavenge for food.'

'Capital, Mammy. We need capital for a successful business.'

Erchie arrived in the kitchen then, rubbing his hands and going over to try and heat them at the fire. 'Whit's this, hen?' He peered up at Charlotte from underneath the skip of his bonnet. 'Are ye turning intae a capitalist or somethin'?'

'I'm only trying to make a decent living for us all, Daddy. Have you seen any more machines yet?'

'What on earth do you need any more machines for,' Teresa said. 'Where would we put them. The room's packed as it is, and all that cloth lying about—we've hardly an inch to put our feet.'

'I know!' Wincey suddenly exclaimed. 'How about asking around to see if anyone else has a machine and asking them if they would do some work for us, but in their own houses.'

Teresa was silent for a moment, and then Charlotte said, 'You might have something there, Wincey.'

'Aye, she's a clever wee lassie, right enough,' Erchie said in admiration. 'How aboot Mrs MacIntyre? She used tae huv a machine, didn't she. Ah wonder if she's still got it.'

'She used to make lovely wee things for her children when they were small,' Teresa said. 'But that was when her man was alive and making some money. I don't know how the poor soul survives nowadays, since wee Betty and Andy died of the cholera. And then losing her man in that pit accident. I often wonder why God gives some folk such a heavy burden. I thought she looked thinner the last time I saw her. Her shawl was awfy frayed and worn.'

'I'll speak to her,' Charlotte said. 'I'll go right now.'

'Och, it's pouring doon and pitch dark outside, Charlotte. It's terrible the way they don't mend these lamps. Wait until tomorrow, dear.'

'I'll come with you,' Wincey said eagerly. She hardly ever set foot out of the house but was beginning to feel hemmed in. In a way, it was as if she was in prison, albeit a self-imposed imprisonment.

'You are a funny child,' Teresa repeated. 'You can't face visiting posh houses but you're perfectly happy to go out on a dark, wintry night to visit Mrs MacIntyre in her wee single end.'

'All right,' said Charlotte. 'Come on, Wincey. Can she borrow your shawl, Mammy?'

'Yes of course, dear.' Teresa fetched the faded tartan shawl, draped it over Wincey's head and tucked it around her shoulders.

7

For Richard's sake, they felt they had to do something about Christmas and the New Year. Nicholas was not all that enthusiastic about Christmas. But then he never had been.

'It's a holiday in England, not here,' he always insisted. Which was true, but she knew that Nicholas just grudged taking time off from his writing on Christmas Day. He hated holidays at the best of times.

'Everyone else works on Christmas Day,' he said in self defence when Virginia accused him of this. 'Why shouldn't I?'

'Not everybody,' Virginia insisted. 'And anyway, you're different. You don't need to work.'

Nicholas raised a sarcastic brow. 'Really?'

Virginia felt irritated. He knew perfectly well what she meant. His books had already made enough money to keep them in comfort for years. There was no excuse for him not taking a whole week off over Christmas and New Year, never mind one day. Eventually he agreed. Virginia could see, however, that he was restless and resentful. Nowadays, out of his writing room, he was like a lost soul. It made her so angry—it was all very well for him to escape into his fictional world, but what about her? Didn't she deserve something more from him, some support in the real world that she was having such a struggle to survive in? He might as well have deserted her, walked completely out of her life. She knew that even outside of his room, he was not really with her. His mind was still far away.

'Why don't you switch off when you come out of that room? Is that too much to ask?'

'You don't understand,' he protested. 'It's not as easy as that. Not when I'm in the middle of a book. The characters are still speaking and living their lives in my head. It's not like being a shopkeeper and just shutting up shop and walking away from it. Creating a book isn't like that.'

The conversation ended abruptly as they had to go out, but the bad feeling between them remained in the room, like an enemy lying in wait until they returned. They had booked seats for the Alhambra theatre for Mrs Cartwright, Richard and themselves. Mrs Cartwright was still in mourning for her husband and wore a heavy, ankle-length black dress and a silver fox stole. Her black hat was festooned with a veil shaped to fit under her chin. Virginia wore one of the new style three-quarter length astrakhan coats, with leg of mutton sleeves and a perky little hat balanced on one side of her head. But she didn't feel perky, although she did manage to smile at Will Fyfe's antics on the stage. Nicholas laughed uproariously, as if he hadn't a care in the world.

They had Mrs Cartwright to Christmas lunch with turkey and all the trimmings, followed by the traditional exchange of expensive gifts. Virginia couldn't help remembering her childhood Christmases. There were no turkeys then, and they were lucky if their mother could find scraps with which to make a pie. She remembered the excitement of hanging up her stocking on Christmas Eve and praying for a doll. On Christmas Day she'd find her stocking three quarters filled with ashes, with just an orange or an apple on top, and, if she was lucky, there would be a bar of Fry's Cream chocolate. Her brothers usually got the same and, if they were lucky, a torch or even a mouth organ. The Co-op always had a Santa and if her mother and father could scrape up a few extra pennies, they'd take her to the Co-operative Hall where Santa sat at the bottom of a big chute. After you paid your sixpence, Santa pulled a lever and your present came down the chute.

Richard had been brought up in the lap of luxury by the Cartwrights for his first five years or so, and had never known poverty—or any deprivation whatsoever. Nor had Wincey. Virginia kept telling herself that she had done her very best in every way for Wincey. She kept going over everything that had happened with Wincey since the year of her birth. She had loved the child from the first moment she had seen her little red wrinkled face, and the downy crop of ginger hair. Nicholas had laughed at the first sight of her.

'Where on earth did she get that ginger mop?'

The bright ginger mop had darkened as Wincey got older until it was a rich auburn. She was a lovely girl—despite her freckles. Nicholas and Virginia had given her everything— there had never been any stockings filled with ashes for her. Each Christmas, she had been given whatever she asked for, although she never asked for very much. She was a quiet, introverted child, but nobody could be blamed for that. She just had a different nature, a different personality, from Richard. They hadn't sent her to a boarding school like Richard, but that was for her own good, and anyway, she didn't want to go. Nicholas didn't want to send Richard either, as he had unhappy memories of his own time at boarding school. Eventually he had been persuaded by Mr and Mrs Cartwright, who had insisted Richard should have the best education in the country. And after all, Edinburgh wasn't far away and he could come home for weekends and holidays.

Nicholas had agreed on condition that, if Richard was not happy there, he had only to say and they'd immediately take him out of the school. As it turned out, Richard was always perfectly happy, but then Richard had never been a problem.

Wincey, however, had always been shy and awkward. They had many clever and talented friends. They had lots of lovely parties but the child had always hung back when anyone tried to include her in the company. Both Richard and Wincey had been given piano lessons, and even when he was quite small Richard would often entertain everyone with a tune. He was naturally talented and everyone went into raptures of praise. Then when Wincey was also asked to perform, it was a terrible carry-on to persuade her. Once or twice, she did play and made a quite unnecessary and stumbling mess of the piece which she could play perfectly well when she wanted to. She only seemed to want to play when she was alone.

Eventually they gave up asking her to do anything. She was such a difficult child. Immediately the thought made Virginia feel guilty. No, she was not difficult. She was just a very shy wee girl. No two children were the same in any family. Why should they be? No doubt Wincey was relieved when everyone stopped asking her to do things she didn't want to and just left her alone.

Mrs Cartwright thought Wincey was like Virginia, but Virginia believed that was quite wrong. Wincey had not her mother's light golden hair, for a start, and as far as her nature was concerned she was more like Nicholas if she was like anyone. Not in looks, but in some aspects of her nature. Nicholas could be quite a loner, and was not afraid to disagree with everyone else. Virginia could go out and speak at political meetings to support the socialist cause, especially to support Mathieson in his arguments for Home Rule for Scotland. Nicholas would not entertain any ideas about Home Rule, despite the fact that it had been seriously debated in the House of Commons.

'It'll come eventually,' Mathieson insisted.

'That may be so,' Nicholas said, 'but I believe we should be trying to get on better with each other, not splitting up.

I'm surprised at you, James, for advocating such an aggressive policy.'

'It's not an aggressive policy,' Mathieson insisted, and so the argument went on—but they never fell out over politics, or anything else. They just agreed to differ. Nicholas would never agree to speak about politics in public, although he was a socialist—much to his parents' fury and disgust. They had always been true-blue Conservatives, and they blamed Nicholas's political conversion on Virginia, just as they blamed her for everything else. They had certainly always held her responsible for encouraging Nicholas to take up writing, and they were not at all proud of his success.

As well as being a loner, Nicholas used people. He did what he called 'research'. He went to Salvation Army hostels and mission halls and spoke not only to the inmates, but to the people who were in charge. He gathered and used everyone's experiences, including his own. Virginia did not know what he was writing at the moment—since Wincey's disappearance he had stopped talking to her about his work—but she was sure he would be using Wincey's disappearance as the basis of a plot, and exploring how such an occurrence could affect everyone. He had probably even used his father's death in a dramatic scene. He was quite ruthless when it came to his work.

Virginia could see that now. It had never occurred to her before—she had always believed he was a very sensitive man. But now, looking back, she could see that he'd always been using people and experiences, especially emotional experiences, for his own purposes. Even—come to think of it—in his poetry. Once, her favourite had been 'Shy Love'. She had read it so often in the past, she had the words off by heart. Now she realised that, even so many years ago, he'd been using their private sexual experience.

Passion eased
Wearing the same skin

52

Your breath flows
Like slowing winds in my ear
Afloat on a pontoon of tenderness
Fleetingly, we forget
The flinty landscape
That encircles us.

Ardent for expression
I want to honour your kisses
Sing of your soothing skin
Celebrate your languid smile.

Instead I stutter raw whispers
Into the pliant flesh of your neck
Pray you unravel
The braille from my lips
And read those three little words.

It had just been another opportunity for him to put words together. She had begun to feel cynical about everything, even about the favourite songs that everyone else loved. 'Love is the Sweetest Thing' and 'Love's Last Word is Spoken' and 'Night and Day' were continuously on the wireless. More and more now, she could not bear to hear them and switched off. When Nicholas did take the occasional hour or two away from his work, it was to take his mother out to lunch. The old woman didn't want to come to visit them at Kirklee Terrace for lunch or anything else, if she could avoid it, unless Richard was there. Mrs Cartwright had always disliked and disapproved of Virginia, and that animosity had grown over the years.

'She's lonely without Father,' Nicholas explained. 'She misses him more than she will admit.'

'She has Richard often enough,' Virginia said. 'And you.'

'Do you really begrudge an old woman the occasional company of her son and grandson, Virginia?'

She hated Nicholas for making her feel guilty and ashamed. 'No, of course not,' she protested. 'It's just that you never seem able to take any time off to be with me.'

'What nonsense! We have every evening together.'

'Most evenings I have to share you with friends, and even when there's no-one else here, you're not really with me. Your mind's on your writing.'

'When I'm with you now, you seem to do nothing but nag. It's enough to drive me back to my room, mentally and physically.'

Virginia didn't think she nagged. He was only using that as an excuse. She could complain a lot more about his mother but didn't. The visit to the theatre and the Christmas lunch had been more of an ordeal than a pleasure, thanks to Mrs Cartwright and the way she had of looking down her long nose at Virginia, especially when she used her lorgnette. Hopefully New Year would be better. At least Mrs Cartwright would not be at Kirklee Terrace on Hogmanay. James Mathieson and their other friends would be coming to bring in 1933 with them.

The company would perhaps help her to keep her mind off Wincey, at least for an hour or two. She doubted if Nicholas gave the child much serious thought now. Poor Wincey would now be little more to him than a character in his book. She had asked Nicholas what the name of his main female character was in his current book and he'd reluctantly muttered, 'Cathy.'

'Young?' she'd queried.

'Yes, but I don't like having to put up with pointless questions about my work while I'm in the middle of it, Virginia. So just leave it, will you.'

Oh yes, Cathy was Wincey all right. And he was feeling furtive and guilty about it. Virginia was sure of it. She didn't say any more. She just walked away from him thinking,

'How could you? How *could* you?'

8

The Gourlays had been very busy with all the extra work that was now coming in. Mrs MacIntyre proved a fast, willing and efficient machinist. Wincey usually collected work from her which was not only beautifully sewn but carefully pressed and folded. On one occasion, Wincey asked her if she knew of anyone else who owned a machine.

'It doesn't matter how old or broken down it is. Erchie's great at fixing anything.'

Mrs MacIntyre looked worried.

'If you get someone else, would it mean I'd get less work?'

'No, no,' Wincey assured her. 'The more people we have working for us, the more customers we can take on.'

'Well, there's Mrs Friel up the stairs. She has one. And maybe Mrs Andrews in the next close. I know she used to have one, but that was years ago.'

'Great!' Wincey said. 'I'll go and check on them right now. And don't you worry, Mrs MacIntyre. This way things can only get better.'

Both machines were in a pretty bad state, but Erchie lost no time in repairing them and getting them into good working order. He was a happy man now, revelling in his new job—especially as he was being paid a wage, albeit a small one. Charlotte had suggested to Wincey that she could take charge of organising the wages for each member of the family who helped in what was known now as 'the business'. It was recognised that Wincey was old for her years, and more serious than other girls of her age. She was more intelligent too.

'How did you learn so much?' Charlotte asked. 'You even seem to know all about politics.'

'Not really,' Wincey laughed, secretly regretting offering an opinion when Erchie had been pontificating on the subject. So often, when she opened her mouth, she had given something away about herself. 'I used to hear my father talking about what was going on in Parliament and he used to let me read his newspaper as well. I'm just good at remembering things, that's all.'

The truth was she had heard her mother and her mother's friends talk more about politics than her father ever did. Also, she'd had a very good education, including a private tutor one evening a week after school hours, and twice a week during school holidays.

Between them, she and Charlotte worked out a system of payment for everybody, including themselves. They kept proper books listing all income and expenses. Wincey had saved most of her money and was now able to start a Post Office savings book. Charlotte had opened a bank account for the business. Having a bank account had been unheard of in the family before.

'You've brought us luck, dear,' Teresa told Wincey. 'Everything's gone that well ever since you arrived. It's a good job,' Teresa cast a sly, triumphant look in Granny's direction, 'I didn't listen to Granny. If she'd had her way, you would have been back out in the street.'

Granny gave a loud snore that didn't fool anyone. She was obviously just pretending to be asleep.

One day the local Co-op couldn't supply them with the particular shades of thread they needed and Charlotte asked Wincey to go into Copeland and Lye's in Sauchiehall Street to buy a stock of the necessary colours. Copeland and Lye was one of her grandmother's favourite stores. She often shopped there and had morning coffee or afternoon tea in their restaurant. Wincey refused to go for the threads, and Charlotte became annoyed. She was a mild natured girl, rather like Teresa, but on this occasion—partly, no doubt, because of the stress of the heavy workload she had taken on—she lost her temper with Wincey.

'This is getting ridiculous, Wincey. You're like a hermit. Why won't you set foot anywhere out of Springburn? It's not as if you even belong to the place. Where exactly was it you lived before?'

This frightened Wincey. Nobody had quizzed her in detail about her origins. They'd taken it for granted, helped by the hints she'd given them, that she did indeed belong somewhere in the Springburn area. After all, it was in Springburn that Florence had found her. Charlotte though was smarter than the rest, despite her quiet and modest manner. It had obviously not escaped her that Wincey spoke with a different accent— the others had thought that she must have taken after the Highland mother she had told them about, but Charlotte, judging by other questions she'd asked, had also been wondering about her standard of education.

To avoid answering any more questions Wincey said, 'Oh, all right. I'll go into town.'

As she set out, she felt so tense and nervous that pains stiffened up the back of her neck and gripped her head like a vice. The town was busy with pre-Christmas shoppers, despite the wind and rain. Women were protected from the weather with long fur coats and little head-hugging hats. Brollies were being blown inside out by the wind. Wincey was wearing a raincoat she'd picked up at Paddy's Market on her first journey outside of Springburn—she'd had no fear of meeting anyone from her other world among the 'shawlies' at the Market. Business men, lawyers, accountants, insurance brokers and bankers all wearing bowler hats were thronging into Langs Restaurants in Queen Street and St Vincent Street. Langs had been a favourite place of her grandfather's, where self-service was *de rigueur*, the price of every item was clearly marked, and each customer simply announced his total to the cashier when leaving. Her grandfather said that this self-regulating system was rarely, if ever, abused. If anyone was spotted trying to abuse it, the regulars would be quick to point them out to the management. This would result in the offender being called into the manageress's office, only to be freed after a generous contribution was made to a favourite charity.

Wincey reached Sauchiehall Street, keeping her head down and her eyes furtively glued to the pavement. The worst ordeal was entering the old established and highly thought of Copeland and Lye's. She made straight for the haberdashery department and the thread counter. Rows and rows of trays packed with reels of every shade of every colour were stacked against a wall behind the counter. Wincey showed the assistant the bundle of small fragments of cloth she carried. The assistant went to the trays and, with amazing speed and accuracy, picked from each an exactly matching shade for each cloth sample. Then she packed the whole order into a bag and Wincey handed over the correct money.

Trying not to look around, she hastened out again by the side door, but she didn't feel in the least relaxed until she had boarded the red tram car bound for Springburn and it was swaying and clanging its way back along Springburn Road. Only in the jungle of towering black tenements could she feel safe.

'There you are,' Charlotte greeted her. 'I knew you could do it if you wanted to.' She examined Wincey's purchases. 'We should really get all our threads from them. They have such a good selection.'

Granny piped up then, Wid ye listen tae her! She's really gettin' above hersel' noo. What about the Co-op divvy? Many's the time ye've been glad o' that, the lot o' you. The Co-op's been good an' loyal tae the workin' man. The least we can dae is be loyal back.'

'Och Granny,' Teresa said, 'we get everything else in the Co-op. You know fine we do. We've been loyal members all our days.'

'Aye, well, ye'd better watch her. It's that Wincey's fault, if ye ask me. She's too hoity-toity for ma likin'. It's no' natural.'

'Nobody's asking you Granny.'

The twins came trailing through from the room.

'Can we knock off now, Mammy? We're tired.'

'Me too.' Florence followed them and slumped down onto a chair. 'You're gettin' to be right slave drivers, so you are.'

'Now, now, Florence. You're glad enough of your wee wage at the end of the week. You can't get out quick enough to spend it.'

There was no hope of either Florence or the twins saving, it seemed, but they did work hard and still managed to do most of the scavenging for cheap food. Wincey thought they looked too thin and were probably anaemic, or worse. There were a great many people in the area going down with tuberculosis. Or consumption, as it was called. One of the women down the stairs had lost a son to the disease only a few weeks ago.

'Yes,' Teresa agreed, 'you do look tired, right enough. Sit down and I'll make us all a nice cup of tea. I've no milk though.'

The girls groaned. 'Och Mammy, we cannae go for any noo. We huvnae any energy left.'

'I'll go,' Wincey offered. 'I'm the one with the waterproof coat and it's pouring with rain.'

'Thanks, dear.'

Teresa carefully examined what she had in her purse

59

before handing over some coppers to Wincey. 'See if the Co-op has any rolls left as well. That would be a nice treat for us. Either that or a wee pot of jam, I've still got half a loaf here.'

Wincey nodded and struggled back into her coat. She liked to get out on her own to roam around the Springburn streets. The crowded room and kitchen could get so claustrophobic at times. Sometimes it felt as if it was suffocating her. However, on this occasion, she knew that she mustn't waste time roaming about. They would all be waiting eagerly for the rolls or the pot of jam to enjoy with their tea.

When she was on her way back, she met Erchie trundling the battered old pram he used to transport sewing machines. He had his latest find balanced on top of the pram.

'Gosh, another one,' Wincey gasped. 'That's great, Erchie. But where will we put it.'

'Och, there's surely a wee bit space left in the room. Ah picked it up in a rubbish dump. It must've come from a big house somewhere. It's in quite good nick. Believe me, it'll be perfect after ah've had a go at it, hen.'

'You're soaked.' Wincey stared worriedly at him as they passed under one of the street lamps. Rain was dripping off the skip of his flat bonnet and darkening his thin jacket.

'Och, never mind, hen. Ah'll soon dry off.'

Once in their close, Erchie heaved and bumped the pram up the stairs while Wincey balanced it and tried to help lift it at the other end. They were both panting and out of breath by the time they reached the top landing. Wincey pulled the bell and the door was opened by Teresa.

'My, my, another one, Erchie. I expect Charlotte will be pleased.' She sighed. 'But soon the place'll be that full of sewing machines, there'll be no room for any of us.'

'Och well, never mind. We'll manage somehow.'

Erchie lifted the machine off the pram and staggered into the house with it.

'My God,' Granny howled. 'No' another yin. The noise o'

them's sendin' me aff ma heid. Ah'll be endin' up in Lennox Castle next.'

Lennox Castle was the local mental asylum.

'Now, now, Granny,' Teresa winked at the others, 'Lennox Castle isn't such a bad place.'

9

Wincey enjoyed her late night walks. She was no longer afraid of the dark. In a way, it had become like a friend. It was good to escape from the cramped conditions of the Gourlays' house and the constant whirr and clatter of sewing machines. Not that Springburn Road was quiet. There was the clanging of tram cars, and the hustle and bustle of people streaming out of the Prince's Picture House, the Wellfield, and the Kinema. The latter was nicknamed 'the Coffin' because of its shape and its proximity to Sighthill Cemetery. This did not put anyone off visiting the Kinema, and Wincey had recently gone with Florence for a special treat after they'd finished an important order sooner than they had expected.

On that occasion, they received praise as well as payment from their satisfied customer. It had been a Saturday afternoon and Florence had thoroughly enjoyed herself at the Kinema. Wincey had found the Flash Gordon serial more ridiculous than exciting. In one scene Flash had been blown up but, she was quick to notice, he came down with his hat still on. There were equally ridiculous cliff-hangers with heroines tied to railway tracks who somehow never got run over. Tom Mix was another hugely popular hero who failed to excite Wincey.

Florence complained, 'Och, ye take everythin' far too serious, so ye do.'

But life had become a serious business. Wincey did not want to lose the new home she had found, and felt anxiety whenever Charlotte asked her to run errands far from Springburn. Once, Charlotte had insisted she accompany her to deliver wedding outfits to customers over the other side of town. Each of the customers had two outfits made—bride and mother of the bride.

'I'm not going to have any more of your nonsense,' Charlotte said. 'I can't carry all this. You'll just have to come with me, whether you like it or not!'

Wincey had been terrified but after racking her brain, she couldn't think of anyone who knew her, or her family, in the area where these particular customers lived. All the same, she felt sick at taking such a risk. Fortunately all had gone well, and she had remained in the kitchen while Charlotte and one of the maids carried the garments upstairs to the lady of the house.

Coming back through the town to Springburn on the tram car, a drunk had got on. Like many Glasgow drunks in this situation, he had a burning desire to communicate and it was only a matter of time before the dreaded 'Hey youse' broke the silence. Then came the problem of deciding if he was the type who, if ignored, would keep demanding attention with self-fuelling indignation. Or would he take the opportunity to lapse into lengthy and maudlin reminiscences about his time serving in the HLI.

Now, as Wincey and Florence made their way back, it was closing time and drunks were spilling out onto the pavement, many of their voices raised in song. Sometimes a prancing, staggering attempt at a dance accompanied their words.

Just a wee doch an dorris,
Just a wee yin that's aw,
Just a wee doch an dorris,
Afore ye gang awa'.

One man coming out of Quinn's pub at the bottom of the Balgrayhill accosted Wincey, clutching at her arm and staggering against her.

'Hello, hen. My, ye're a bonny wee lassie, eh?'

She flung his arm off and began to run, the man's indignant words ringing in her ears, 'Och, ah wis only tryin' tae be friendly.'

Probably he was, she thought, once she had reached a safe distance and had slowed down. But she still had an underlying fear and distrust of men. She managed to hide it, or to control it, most of the time. Sometimes she even convinced herself that she had lost it, that she had cured herself. Then, unexpectedly, it would return in a rush of panic. In her distress, she suddenly found that she had run off the main road and was in a dark cul-de-sac, at the end of which was a derelict looking warehouse. Propped in front of it was a sign which read *To Let. Apply Belling & MacKay*, followed by an address and telephone number.

Wincey felt excited. It suddenly occurred to her that the next step in the business had to be getting premises in which all the sewing machines could be kept and worked. The women with machines of their own could continue working in their own houses if they wanted to. But the machines in the Gourlays' house and any other machines Erchie or anyone else could find could be put in a place like this, and other women in dire need of a job could be engaged. There would be no shortage of willing workers, Wincey felt sure.

She began to run again, this time happily, eagerly. She could hardly wait to tell Charlotte. Along the gas-lit road she flew, in the close and up the stairs two at a time. The older girl was collapsed into the hole-in-the-wall room bed and half asleep when Wincey reached the top floor house.

'Charlotte, Charlotte,' Wincey cried out. 'I've just had a wonderful idea.'

The twins stirred beside Charlotte.

'For pity's sake, shut up, Wincey,' one of them groaned.

'Aye,' Florence agreed from her hurly bed on the floor, 'we've aw had a hell o' a hard day an' need our sleep.'

But Charlotte was too good a business woman to miss any opportunity, no matter how exhausted she felt. She propped herself up on one elbow. 'Never mind them. What is it, Wincey?'

Wincey told her about the warehouse to let and what she thought could be done with it.

'Yes, yes, you're right. But it would depend on the rent, wouldn't it? And then we'd need more machines and more work to keep us going.'

'It looks pretty run down. I shouldn't think the rent would be too much, and maybe we wouldn't need to stick to just private customers. Maybe we could ask about supplying shops, or wholesalers, or something. I mean, who makes all the shirts for men's shops and departments? They've got to be made somewhere. They must come from somewhere.'

'It's worth a try,' Charlotte said. 'We could inquire about the rent first and if that was something we could afford, then we could try and find out about other kinds of work. Oh, Wincey, I'm so excited now. I'll never be able to sleep a wink.'

Teresa had appeared at the room door, her shawl wrapped over her nightie, her thin hair loosened from its bun and straggling down to her shoulders. 'What's going on. Granny's complaining like mad through there. She's cursing me for giving you a door key, Wincey. This is a bit late to be coming in. You know we're all up early for work in the morning.'

'I'm sorry,' Wincey said. 'I'll be as quiet as a mouse after this if I come in late. But something exciting has just happened and I had to tell Charlotte.'

'What's that, dear?'

Charlotte answered her mother before Wincey had the

chance. Teresa was impressed but worried. 'Do you think you can do it, dear? It's all right Wincey coming out with these grand ideas but it's not so easy to put them into practice. A lot could go wrong, couldn't it.'

Wincey said, 'We'd never get anywhere if we didn't take any risks. What's the good of just staying as we are. I suppose we could stay as we are for the rest of our lives. Is that what we want? Is that what you want for the family?'

'Well, dear, we've got a lot better life now than we had. I mind the days when we couldn't even afford a loaf of bread.'

'You see, we can afford lots more now. That's because we moved on. We took a risk with the extra machines, and we took another by starting to employ more people.'

'Yes, Mammy,' Charlotte agreed. 'Wincey's right. We've at least got to try to do this. We might not even manage to get the warehouse in the first place but we've got to try.'

Teresa sighed. 'I expect you're right, dear, but right now we all need our rest.'

'Tomorrow's Saturday,' Wincey suddenly remembered. 'Maybe the office will be shut. The one on the To Let notice.'

'No, no,' Teresa said. 'They'll be working, same as us. Everybody's got to make a living.'

Charlotte lay back on her pillow. 'I'll go round there first thing in the morning, Wincey. I can hardly wait.'

Teresa sighed again as she turned away. 'Try and get some sleep.'

Wincey couldn't go out with Charlotte next morning because it was her turn at the machine. She didn't stop working but her mind was waiting in an agony of suspense for Charlotte to return. Right away, she knew that it was all right. She had only to look at Charlotte's bright eyes and flushed face.

'It's a giveaway price,' Charlotte sang out. 'It's been lying empty for so long, apparently. It's an awful big place. They sent someone from the office to show me over it. Far more space than we'll need. But we can just shut some bits off.

They offered to sell it to me but that would be stretching things a bit far just now. I said I'd consider that in due course, though. Meantime I've to go back tomorrow to confirm everything.'

'Great, great!' Wincey caught Charlotte's outstretched hands and they hugged one another in triumph and delight.

'She'll huv ye goin' too far, that yin,' Granny said, meaning Wincey. 'She'll mean trouble tae us aw yet, you mark ma words. She's gettin' beyond hersel' wi' aw them grand ideas.'

'Och, never mind Granny,' Charlotte told Wincey. 'If this succeeds and we get it going, I'll make you my partner, Wincey. Would you like that?'

'Thank you, Charlotte. That would be wonderful, and I just know we can make it succeed. I'll work my fingers to the bone to make it succeed.'

Charlotte hastily washed her face and hands and brushed her hair. Wincey polished Charlotte's shoes. She also loaned her her waterproof coat. Granny was persuaded to part with a pair of gloves she'd worn in better days when she was able to get out to attend the church and the Orange walks.

'You mind them good gloves noo,' Granny warned Charlotte. 'If ye lose them good gloves, ye neednae show yer face back here again.'

'Don't worry, Granny. I'll take good care of them, I promise.'

'Aye well,' Granny muttered. 'Ye'd better.'

'Do ye want yer daddy tae go wi' ye, hen,' Erchie asked. He was rubbing his hands together and almost dancing with excitement. More than any other member of the family, Erchie was full to overflowing with enthusiasm for every aspect of the business.

'No thanks, Daddy. I'll be fine. As well as working on the machines, me and Wincey are going to be in charge of organising and planning everything. You have to be in charge of the machines.'

'Aye, right ye are, hen.' Erchie gave her an exaggerated

salute. 'Ye're the boss. You an' wee Wincey. Ye're a couple o' wee stoaters.'

Soon Charlotte had returned from town and everything was signed, sealed and delivered.

'I've just thought of something else,' she told Wincey. 'I wouldn't be able to do all the cutting if we're going to expand. Even both you and I couldn't manage it, could we?'

'It depends on what orders we get, and the size of them, I suppose,' Wincey replied. 'Anyway, no doubt we'll be able to find unemployed cutters if we try.'

They had already found that married women who had been experienced workers in the clothing trade before their marriage and whose children were now more or less off their hands were the best bet. But they soon discovered a pool of younger women too. Mrs McGregor's eldest was a trained cutter. 'Wan o' the very best,' Mrs McGregor assured Charlotte and Wincey. 'Cuts like a flash. Naebody tae beat her.'

They were all set—at least they'd scrubbed out the part of the warehouse they planned to use. The place now awaited more machines before they could go any further and recruit any more women workers. Erchie set to like a greyhound after a hare. He shot about everywhere—back courts, back gardens, the Corporation rubbish tip, the Barras market and Paddy's market. He knocked at doors, asking for old machines. 'Ah'll take it oot yer road, hen,' he'd say.

Eventually he had found and repaired seven machines and he'd picked up a couple of tables suitable for the cutting. And so, counting the ones from the house, they had eleven machines ready to start in what was now called the factory. While he'd been doing his bit, Charlotte and Wincey had been out searching for orders. To their delight, they had found a big one for shirts and it looked as if it would be a regular order.

'They said if we made a good job of the first order, we're in,' Charlotte announced joyously. 'And of course we will.'

They did, and they were.

But not without difficulties, setbacks and worries. One worry in particular Wincey had not foreseen and—much as she tried—could do nothing about.

1936

10

'Noo ah'm no complainin', hen,' Erchie told Charlotte. 'Ah'm just sayin' that if ye could let me fix masel' up wi' a tradesman, or some sort o' strong young fella, it wid be an awfae help tae me. Ah'm no' as nippy as ah used tae be an' these past couple of years, ah've been a jack o' aw trades. It's no' just been the machines. It's been mendin' the lights, an' the plumbin', an' God knows what else. But ah'm no' complainin', hen. Ye understand me.'

'Of course, Daddy,' Charlotte said. 'I'm so sorry. I've been treating you like a slave, expecting you to do so much. You're right, we definitely need another man to take over some of the workload. Will I advertise, or do you know somebody?'

'Aye, ah know a few good lads who served their apprenticeships an' now cannae find work. Just leave it tae me, hen. Ah'll send a fella tae ye, an' ye can tell him what ye'll pay him. Ye're the boss.'

'Fine. Do it right away, Daddy. I feel terrible about this. I've been so caught up with the women's work. You look dead beat—I'm so sorry.'

'Och, be quiet. Ah'm aw right. Just a bit tired.'

73

'Come to think of it, Daddy. Now that we've got over twenty machines and opened up another couple of areas, we could do with two extra men. There's the new office to paint and fit out—it's a right dump at the moment.'

'Well, we'll see how it goes, hen. Ah'll talk tae wan or two fellas first.'

The first result of Erchie's intervention was the appearance at the factory of Malcy McArthur. Wincey suspected right away that he could mean trouble. But she was suspicious of all men. That was just how she was. Unlike most local unemployed men, Malcy was not thin and pale and emaciated. He boasted a hard muscular body, a head of fair curly hair and light blue eyes. He had done some boxing, kept himself fit by regularly working out at the boxing club, and often went running or hill climbing out at Campsie Glen. He was a Glaswegian born and bred, but had the cheek of the Irish and sounded at times as if he'd kissed the Blarney Stone. He had tried his best to charm Wincey, without success. She ignored his compliments and returned them with cold stares.

Once, in the course of trying to tease her, he put his arm around her. She had furiously shaken him off and ordered him to go about his business and not waste time. If he continued to waste time, he'd end up without a job. She'd see to it. And she could, now she was a legal partner in the business.

The trouble was that it wasn't long before Malcy had turned his full attention on Charlotte, and he was far more successful in charming her. More than a few times Wincey had seen Charlotte go all giggly and blush when Malcy was speaking to her in the factory. Wincey tried to warn Charlotte against him.

'Charlotte, he's a right rascal and out for all he can get.'

'Nonsense,' Charlotte laughed. Wincey had never seen her look so happy. 'He's a marvellous worker. We couldn't do without him now. He can turn his hand to anything, and he's always so cheerful and willing.'

'Oh, he's willing, all right,' Wincey said sarcastically.

Charlotte shook her head. 'What on earth has made you such a man-hater, Wincey? Other girls of your age are courting. You've never even looked kindly at a boy. I appreciate all the time and dedication you give to the business, but now it's so established, Wincey, there's no need to devote every hour of the day and night to it.'

'I enjoy the work.'

'But it doesn't seem natural, all work and no play—you know the saying. You need some fun in your life.'

'It's natural for me, Charlotte. There's no need to worry about me. It's you I'm worried about.'

'Why, for pity's sake? I'm perfectly fit and happy. I've never felt so happy in my life.'

Wincey groaned to herself. Charlotte had obviously fallen in love with Malcy.

'For one thing, he's too old for you.'

'Who?'

'Charlotte, don't act daft. You know perfectly well who.'

Charlotte giggled. 'For goodness' sake, Wincey. He's only been joking and having a bit of a laugh with me. He's good fun. And anyway, what's a few years between friends.'

'Ten years to be exact. And he's not your friend, he's your employee.'

'Oh, don't be such a snob. And a man should be older and more mature than a woman. My daddy's a few years older than my mammy, and it's never bothered them.'

Wincey felt a real stab of fear. Surely Charlotte had not _ marriage on her mind? But if she was really honest _ Wincey knew that it was the business more than _ rried about. If Charlotte loved the man— _ in her opinion—that love would _ ppy enough. Wincey was concerned _ kely to be the business that was in _ ar was on the make, she felt sure of it. _ han once in a nearby close making bets with the local bookmaker did nothing to help her peace of mind. A gambler was an untrustworthy person to have near money, and Wincey began to keep a closer eye on Malcy's activities. She discovered he was not just an occasional, but a frequent visitor to whatever close the bookie was using for business. She'd pass along the street and see the crowd of men making their bets, and the runner hovering about outside, watching for the police and ready to shout the warning cry of 'Edge up'. Hearing it, everyone would scatter. Malcy was a gambler all right.

One day she caught sight of Erchie handing over money to Malcy. Later she questioned Erchie about this.

'Och, it's all right, hen. Ah was just givin' Malcy a wee loan until pay day. He had a wee bit o' bad luck on the horses.'

'Gambling, you mean?'

'Och, now, there's nae harm in a fella havin' a wee flutter now an' again. He deserves a wee bit pleasure. He's a hard workin' fella, ye can't deny that.'

She couldn't say any more on the subject, either to Erchie or Charlotte, or even to Malcy. The retort would be that what Malcy did in his own time, or how he spent his hard earned wages, was Malcy's business. She tried to tell herself that this was true and there was nothing more to it, but in her heart of hearts, she knew perfectly well that there was much more to it. Or at least there would be in the future, if something wasn't done to stop him. She believed he was taking advantage of Charlotte's love and trust, and she couldn't help being reminded of how a man had once taken advantage of her. It was a very different situation, but nevertheless Malcy McArthur *was* taking advantage of Charlotte. Wincey had seen him flirt with other women. Not in the factory—oh no, he was too clever for that. She had seen him, however, at street corners laughing and carrying on with girls.

Even Charlotte had caught him on one occasion. It had been at a hen party at Green's Playhouse. A neighbour's daughter, Mary Purdie, was getting married. Mrs Purdie had been a good friend and neighbour to Teresa for years and all the Gourlay girls and Wincey had been invited to a fish and chip tea in a local chippie and then a noisy ride in a tram into town to the famous Green's Playhouse.

Green's Playhouse had the reputation of being the largest picture house in Europe, and high up at the top of the building was a dance hall that always had the best bands.

Wincey hadn't wanted to go but both Charlotte and Teresa more or less bullied her into it—or as near to bullying as their natures allowed. Charlotte especially was a gentle soul.

Teresa said, 'Now, now, Wincey, Mrs Purdie has been good to me and it'll really upset me if you insult her daughter by refusing this invitation.'

'Yes, you've no reason not to go,' Charlotte said. 'You're just being difficult for no reason at all, Wincey.'

And so she'd gone.

Once safely inside the building, Wincey began to relax. Out on the streets in the centre of the city, there was always the chance of someone recognising her. Her mother, or grandmother, or some of their friends, might well be out shopping. But no-one had recognised her, and certainly there would be no danger of anyone of her mother and grandmother's generations cavorting about up in the dance hall in the skies.

The ladies' room was like a bird sanctuary. It was crammed with loudly chattering girls. There was a crush at the mirror, as a whole crowd of them strained to check their hair powder puffs over shiny noses. Dresses rustled and rainbow of bright colours.

Charlotte was wearing a short-sleeved plum dress with a demure little collar and a flare favoured a long-sleeved dress in dark g spotted bow tie under a flat collar.

The crowd of Gourlay girls and burst from the ladies' room on a wave ot been joining in the banter and laughter. Un all the couples locked in each other's arms on t.

77

She hadn't realised how most of the dances meant full frontal contact. Waltzes, foxtrots, quicksteps, tangos—it was all the same, it seemed. Along one wall stood a row of girls and across the moving throng of dancers, a line of young men stood nonchalantly smoking cigarettes.

Occasionally one of them would nip the lighted end of his cigarette and tuck it into his pocket. Then he'd swagger across to the line of girls and put out an inviting hand. In a second, he'd be clutching her against him and they'd be circling the floor.

The last thing Wincey wanted was to be clutched in any man's arms for any reason. However, she didn't want to appear a spoilsport and so she joined the line of girls along with Charlotte and the others.

As luck would have it—bad luck as far as she was concerned—she was the first to be lifted. He was a tall thin man wearing horn-rimmed spectacles. His body was hot against hers.

'What's your name,' he asked, his feet making fast, complicated movements that Wincey was having to concentrate on in an effort to keep up with him.

'Wincey.'

'That's a funny name. What's it mean?'

'Short for Winsome. I was christened Winsome. Don't ask me why.'

'I love your red hair.' Next he'd be telling her he loved her freckles. 'My name's Ian, by the way.'

She made no comment.

'Is anybody seein' you home?'

'I've only just got here.'

'Later on, I mean.'

'I'm with friends. I'll be going home with them.'

'Oh.' He sounded disappointed. 'Couldn't you—'

'No,' she interrupted.

'Oh well, if that's how you feel,' he said huffily.

Before the music had finished, he'd begun leading her

back to where they'd started. Fortunately, the music had stopped by the time they'd reached the others and so Wincey was saved from making any explanations.

It was then that she noticed Malcy leading a girl back just a few yards from where they were standing. He had his arm around the girl's waist and was laughing down at her. He kept his arm around her as they stood for a few minutes and then, as soon as the band struck up again, he began a smoochy dance with her.

'Look at that,' Wincey said. 'What did I tell you, Charlotte.'

Charlotte looked upset but she tried to put a brave face on by saying lightly, 'For goodness' sake, Wincey. He's not married to me or anything. We haven't even been walking out together.'

'But he has asked you, hasn't he?'

'The fact remains, we still haven't been out together. Between you and me, I was a bit worried about what would happen. I mean, about discipline in the factory, if the girls found out. You might think I don't care as much as you do about the success of the business, Wincey, but I do.'

'Of course you do. I know that. I just worry about you sometimes, Charlotte.'

Charlotte gave an unhappy smile. 'There's no need. Oh dear, I think he's seen us.'

Malcy, dancing cheek to cheek with his partner, was passing quite near to them now. As soon as he saw them, he immediately held his partner at arm's length. Then after the dance, he made his way over to Charlotte.

'Charlotte! Now the whole evening's turned to magic because I've the chance to dance with you.' He held out his arms invitingly, his eyes soft and loving. Wincey had to admit to herself that he did have a most attractive smile, and who could resist that look? She could, but she feared that Charlotte could not.

11

During the Glasgow Fair holiday in July, the Gourlays and Wincey decided to go 'doon the watter'. They planned to stay for a whole week in Dunoon. It was the first holiday the family had had in years and everybody was looking forward to it. They had booked a two-room and kitchen. They were used to a two-room and kitchen house now since some of the profits from the business had gone into the removal and renting of a bottom flat in the same close in Springburn Road. Money had also been spent on a wheelchair for Granny which meant that she could now get out and about, and even come on holiday with them. Although it was hard work pushing the chair, especially up the gangplank of the ship.

The factory had closed for the fair fortnight but after the week's holiday, all the family—and the family now included Wincey—were going back to the factory to catch up with some odd jobs that needed to be done. Somehow there wasn't usually much time for any extra jobs, especially if they'd a big order in. Joe, the odd job man, couldn't be at the factory during the holiday week because he was going to Rothesay with his family for the whole fair fortnight.

Teresa had her hands full all the time attending to the domestic chores, the shopping, and looking after Granny. She had had plenty of practice pushing the wheelchair to the shops for the 'messages', which she piled onto Granny's lap—not without some complaints from the older woman.

Malcy had volunteered to help out in the factory during the second week of the holiday. Another volunteer was the latest cutter they'd got, a man called Bert Brownlee. He was in charge of the new electric cutting machine. A woman would spread out the pattern on top of layers of cloth. Then Bert used the huge upright thin blade attached to an electric belt from above. Twisting and turning the blade, he could slice through over twenty layers of material without any difficulty.

Then another woman collected all the cut material into a basket and hauled it through to the machinists. The machinists sat in rows now at their machines in the biggest area of the factory, a vast high-roofed hall of dark brown wood. It had rows of pegs along part of one wall on which the machinists could hang their coats. A lavatory out in the back yard served their other needs. Disappearing out to the back yard too often, or for too long, was disapproved of, however, and a sharp eye was kept on any movement away from the machines. Even the twins and Florence came under the same scrutiny as all the others.

At first they'd complained bitterly about this. 'We're the boss's sisters, for goodness' sake,' the girls protested to Charlotte.

'All the more reason,' Charlotte said, 'for you to show a good example to the others.'

Charlotte had a quiet authority that was respected by all of her employees. Wincey was respected too, but regarded as more of an unknown quantity. Most of the time she was shut away in the office doing the books. Also she was the one who every now and again disappeared from the premises to go and negotiate or seek out new orders. Charlotte could on occasion have a pleasant chat or even a laugh with the girls, when they had a brief break to eat their sandwiches. Wincey was more reserved. They called her Miss Wincey to distinguish her from Miss Charlotte, because as far as everyone at work and most other people knew, they were both Gourlays.

The twins and Florence had been instructed—indeed, were made to swear—that they would never divulge the way in which Wincey became part of the family. This was really unnecessary because they had long since accepted Wincey, and more or less forgotten that she wasn't originally part of the family.

Because Malcy and Bert had been 'good enough'—to use Charlotte's words—to volunteer to work a week of the holidays, they were allowed to accompany the family on their sail 'doon the watter'. Their fares were paid, also their wages, but not their holiday accommodation in Dunoon. The two men were going to share a single end in one of the side streets near the pier. Not far either from the two-room and kitchen that was to house the family.

First there was the exciting and wildly enjoyable sail in the packed paddle steamer. Even before the paddles were thumping and the boat had started waddling away from Bridge Wharf across from the Broomielaw, a band had started playing cheery tunes and people were singing. Women were chattering and laughing. Children were racing about getting lost.

The band consisted of four men in navy blue suits and caps. One man, with great concentration, strummed the banjo. Another had a white hanky spread over his shoulder on which rested his fiddle. Another energetically squeezed a concertina and a fourth, with concentration equal to that of the banjo player, thumped on an ancient piano.

The gangplanks were lifted, ropes flung aboard, the steamer gave a warning hoot and then, with much creaking and groaning and splashing, the ship's paddles were set in motion. Slowly at first, the water foaming and frothing, then gradually, as it pulled away from Bridge Wharf—just by the George V Bridge—

the paddles quickened and found their joyous rhythm. The steam drifted away, past giant cranes jagging the sky and over the silent shipyards which, like everything else, were closed for the fair.

Normally the shipbuilders—swarms of men high up like ants on the sides of hulls, noisily banging and clanging, or leaning over, or up in the clouds working cranes—would stop and wave hands or caps and bawl friendly greetings at any passing ships. Today, however, there was nothing to compete with the noisy paddle steamer except the hoots of other ships and the raucous screeching of gulls. The white breasted birds swooped and dived alongside, and followed the holiday cruises from Glasgow, knowing that there would be plenty of eagerly proferred handfuls of food.

All the old Scots songs were being bawled out now—'Roamin' in the Gloamin'', 'Road to the Isles', 'Stop your Ticklin', Jock', 'Ah'm the Saftest in the Faimily' and 'I belong to Glasgow'.

Wincey enjoyed the sail and breathed deeply of the tangy fresh air. The journey was only spoiled for her by the sight of Malcy following Charlotte around. Eventually he managed to detach her from the rest of the family and walk with her on his own. Wincey kept getting glimpses of the pair of them on deck, with him gazing fondly down at Charlotte, and Charlotte looking up at him with an even stronger emotion.

Everyone wanted to visit the engine room and Wincey was no exception. Every steamer had a vantage point from which passengers could watch the enormous drive shafts, pistons and valve gear, and experience the thunderous, deafening noise. Through the latticed paddle boxes could also be seen revolving wheels with torrents of water gushing from the blades.

It was while Wincey was watching this scene that she noticed Malcy and Charlotte again. Now he had his arm around her waist. Feeling suddenly depressed, Wincey turned away and climbed back up to the deck. She loved Charlotte like a sister and she had become more and more concerned about her involvement with Malcy. What depressed Wincey was the knowledge that there was nothing she could do. Charlotte was twenty now and free to do as she pleased. She could of course marry if she wanted. And in marriage it was going to end—that much was perfectly obvious. They had now started walking out.

All during the holiday, Malcy stuck by Charlotte's side. Bert, an older man than Malcy, spent most of his time in one or other of the local pubs. The twins and Florence disappeared every morning and only reappeared at mealtimes. During the day, Erchie took his turn with Teresa at pushing Granny's wheelchair along the front. Often they met their neighbours from Glasgow and it seemed like the whole close—indeed the whole street—had come on holiday because it was the fair.

Wincey was quite happy to be left to her own devices, walking for miles to reach lonely and deserted places. She enjoyed climbing the Castle Hill, then sitting on the grass hugging her knees, gazing down at the pier, and listening to the kilted piper playing one of the steamers away to the haunting lament of *Will ye no come back again.*

'Oh, we're no awa' tae bide awa'', the ship's passengers lustily sang. 'We're no awa' tae leave ye. We're no awa' tae bide awa', We'll aye come back an' see ye.'

It was agreed at the end of the holiday week that it had done everybody good. Even Granny's sallow complexion had acquired some colour, so had Erchie's, and even Teresa's thin face had a bit of a glow about it. But no-one was more glowing than Charlotte. Wincey had worn a wide brimmed straw hat most of the time to protect her skin because she burned so easily.

'Red haired folk are aye like that. Right nuisances,' Granny said. 'Ye cannae take them anywhere.'

Then of course there was the struggle to heave Granny's wheelchair up the gangplank again and squeeze a place for her among the throng.

'Oot o' ma road,' she kept bawling and jabbing mercilessly at all and sundry with her umbrella.

★   ★   ★

Back in the house in Springburn Road at last, Teresa said, 'I'll put the kettle on.' In this house, they had the luxury of not just one gas ring on which to boil the kettle, but two gas rings on the range. Nowadays, Teresa didn't even have to balance her soup pot on the fire.

The kitchen was much bigger too than the one they'd had in the house upstairs. There was the usual hole-in-the-wall bed but now in each of the two rooms at the front, there were two recessed beds. As a result, Charlotte and Wincey had a bed each in one room, Florence and the twins occupied the beds in the other, Florence having one of the beds to herself. Granny still had to have the hurly bed in the kitchen. Teresa and Erchie attempted to relegate her to one of the rooms but she was having none of it.

'Ah've slept in ma hurly bed in front o' the kitchen fire for years,' she insisted, 'an' ah'm no gonnae change noo.'

She'd also accused Teresa and Erchie of wanting to get rid of her.

Teresa said, 'Now, now, Granny. You know that's not true. It's just that Erchie and I would like a wee bit privacy.'

'Whit fur?' Granny wanted to know.

Neither Erchie nor Teresa had the nerve to tell her.

On the whole, the quality of Granny's life was much better since they'd moved downstairs and had the extra accommodation and the wheelchair. Now she could be wheeled into one of the front rooms and parked at the window so that she could watch the world go by on Springburn Road. This at least gave Teresa some peace to do the cooking, baking or cleaning without sarcastic comments or a string of instructions, or stories of how Granny used to do everything so much better in her day. From the front room, Granny kept roaring things out like, 'There's that Mrs Fisher wi' her fancy man, brazen as ye like. A right disgrace.' Or 'There's her frae up the stairs wi' anither mucky wee wean. How many's that she's got noo? Must be surely a hundred or mair. It's absolutely terrible!'

Teresa was in a state of constant anxiety in case anyone outside could hear Granny's comments. Probably they did but were just suffering in silence because Granny was an old woman. Teresa, Erchie and the whole family agreed that Granny was a terrible trial of an old woman, although sometimes they couldn't help laughing.

It was no joke, however, trying to get her to take a bath. They could now hurl the wheelchair to the steamie. As well as a big area for washing clothes, the steamie had cubicles, and in each cubicle there was a bath. As a result, Teresa insisted that they no longer used the zinc bath in the kitchen. It had always been a terrible struggle to get Granny in and out of the bath. For one thing, it was too tight a fit. Every time she plumped down in it, a surge of water flooded out, soaking everyone around her.

'You're going to the steamie, Granny, whether you like it or not. You've got far too fat for that wee zinc bath,' Teresa told her, but she also told the girls, 'You'll all have to come and help me. I can't manage to bath Granny on my own at the steamie, any more than I ever could here in the kitchen.'

'You know fine Wincey and I couldn't be of much help, Mammy,' Charlotte said. 'Just take Florence and the twins. They're heftier and stronger than us.'

While this was an exaggeration, they were certainly growing into big healthy girls, helped no doubt by their improved diet.

After some discussion, it was agreed that Florence and the twins would accompany Teresa to the steamie and do battle with Granny.

'The real reason I couldn't go,' Charlotte confided in

Wincey after the family disappeared up Springburn Road, 'is because I'm meeting Malcy. Oh Wincey, try to be happy for me. Malcy and I are so much in love.'

Wincey tried to smile reassuringly but her heart was not in it.

12

It was on the front page of the *Daily Record* — 'A Scots Queen. King George VI and Queen Elizabeth to be proclaimed. Coronation next May.'

Erchie read the headlines out to Granny and continued with, 'Future plans of Edward VIII. As the unparalleled drama of the abdication King Edward VIII unfolded itself yesterday, a wave of relief swept over the country, spreading right throughout the Empire. The succession of the Duke and Duchess of York to the throne is being hailed as not only the best, but the only solution to the crisis.'

'Aye, a great relief tae us aw, ah don't think!' Granny said. 'It disnae matter wan jot tae us whit that crowd dae. If that whole crowd o' royals went up in a puff o' smoke, it wouldnae matter wan jot tae a soul in Springburn.'

'The King's going to broadcast tonight.'

'Which wan? As if ah cared!'

'Edward.'

'Him an' his fancy woman. They don't know they're born, that lot. They'd know aw aboot it if they had tae try an' survive on a few bob in a single end in Springburn. That's how me an' ma man started our married life.'

Erchie laughed. 'It'd be the death o' them, Ma.'

'An' brought up five weans there as well. Four o' them carted off on the fever van, wan by wan, an' ah never saw any o' them alive again.'

Teresa joined in the conversation. 'Aye, they were hard times in those days, Granny.'

'Whit dae ye know? Ye were enjoyin' yersel' up among the hills an' glens. Whit dae ye know about life in Glasgow?'

'Now, now, Granny. You know fine I've lived here most of my life. But I remember when I was a child, what a hard life my mother and father had, trying to make a living on a wee croft. I'm sure they were glad to come to Glasgow. I know I was.'

'Aye,' Erchie said. 'It's no' such a bad place.'

'It's aw right fur you noo,' Granny scowled at him. 'Ye're a bloody capitalist!'

Both Teresa and Erchie laughed and Erchie said, 'Ye're bletherin' now, Ma. Ah'm still as much of a socialist as ah ever was.'

'Ye cannae say your Charlotte's no' a capitalist,' Granny insisted. 'An' she's tight-fisted as well. She must be makin' a fortune in that place, an' we're aw still livin' up a close in Springburn Road. No' that ah'd want tae be livin' any place else,' she hastily added.

'There's a lot more room, Granny, without the machines cluttering up the place. You were always complaining about the noise of the machines.'

'Aye, it's a funny old world,' Erchie said, and went back to reading his *Daily Record*. It wasn't long before he was interrupted by the jangle of the doorbell.

'That'll be Charlotte now,' Teresa told Erchie as he went to open the door. 'She said she and Malcy would be going to the first house of the pictures and she'd be bringing him home for a cup of tea. I've made some nice salmon sandwiches.'

'Any digestives,' Granny asked hopefully.

'Yes, Granny, there's plain and chocolate.'

Erchie was now returning along the lobby with Charlotte and Malcy.

'You two look happy,' Teresa greeted them. 'Was it a good picture?'

'Mammy,' Charlotte cried out excitedly, 'Malcy and I are engaged. We're going to be married in the spring.'

'Oh, congratulations to the both of you.'

'Here,' Erchie said, rubbing his hands, 'this deserves a wee celebration. Never mind the tea, Teresa. I've got a bottle of whisky in the press.'

He went over to the cupboard and produced a bottle of Johnny Walker.

'Nothing but the best for Charlotte an' Malcy. Come on, Teresa. Get some glasses oot, hen.'

They were toasting the happy couple and Erchie was refilling the glasses when Wincey arrived back from one of her solitary walks.

'What's going on?' she asked, but with a sinking heart, she knew.

'Charlotte and Malcy are engaged, dear. They're going to have a spring wedding. Isn't that lovely? It'll give us all something to look forward to.'

'Congratulations,' Wincey muttered, but she could have cheerfully killed the grinning Malcy. 'Smug bastard,' she thought.

'Well?' Malcy came swaggering towards her. 'Am I not going to get a kiss from my future sister-in-law?'

Wincey turned her cheek just in time as his lips were about to meet hers. She hated the proximity of his face and the mocking, triumphant look in his eyes. It occurred to her that he'd never forgotten or forgiven the way she'd spurned his original advances. It took an almost superhuman effort on her part to raise the glass Erchie gave her and wish the engaged pair every happiness. She sincerely wished Charlotte every happiness. The trouble was she now very much doubted if

90

Charlotte would get anything but worry and grief from Malcy.

Florence and the twins arrived and they all had another few whiskies. Then they had a sing-song. Even Granny joined in. Eyes closed with emotion, she gave a gumsy rendering of

> *'If I can help somebody as I go along,*
> *If I can help somebody with a word or song,*
> *If I can help somebody as I go along,*
> *Then my living has been worthwhile.'*

Everybody gave her an enthusiastic clap and cheer. Erchie sang, or rather droned, 'The Bonny Wells o' Weary' and Malcy sang to Charlotte, 'Just the Way You Look Tonight'. The romance of this rendering was somewhat spoiled by Granny dropping off to sleep and loudly snoring.

'Oh here,' Teresa said, 'we'd better get Granny to bed while the rest of us are sober enough. It's such an awful struggle.'

'I'd better go,' Malcy said.

Charlotte gazed up at him, her soft brown eyes adoring. 'I'll see you to the door.'

It was quite a long time before she reappeared. Erchie had climbed into bed with all his clothes on and Wincey was closing the bed curtains. The twins and Florence were helping Teresa to get Granny's clothes off. Wincey pulled out the hurly bed.

Wincey turned to Charlotte, 'It's time we moved again. We still could do with more space, and we could afford a bigger place now. Even one of these nice red sandstone tenements up the Balgrayhill. That would be nearer the park. Then we could take Granny there without having to struggle all the way up the hill every time.'

Granny liked to watch the crowds in the park and listen to the brass band. She especially enjoyed the Salvation Army band, and she could often hear them and watch them from her window when they played in Springburn and marched along Springburn Road. Like the Pied Piper, the Sally Army band attracted all the children in the neighbourhood to follow it.

Teresa shook her head. 'When Charlotte gets married, you'll have the room to yourself, dear.'

'I wasn't thinking of myself. I was thinking of Granny. And it can't be a perfect situation for you and Erchie having Granny sleep in the same room as you like this.'

'That's true, dear, but you know how she likes to be near the fire. She likes to be cosy.'

'But she could go on sleeping in the kitchen, but by herself. There could be another room for you and Erchie. We could get a three-room and kitchen.'

Charlotte spoke up then. 'If that's what you wanted, and Wincey agreed, it would be all right with me. Wincey got a great order the other day. But don't tell Granny, for goodness' sake. It's for shirts for the Army. Wincey has been marvellous. I don't know how she does it. We're having to take on more girls, men as well.'

'It's not so much me,' Wincey said. 'It's the quality of the work. Our reliability in getting orders done on time, and our prices. But mainly I think it's the high standard of work.'

'That's good, dear, but I can see what you mean about Granny, with her being a pacifist, and having all these pacifist folks as her idols.'

'She'll be telling us that her Johnny Maclean would birl in his grave at you helping the armed forces.'

'We're not going to war, Mammy. We're just sewing clothes.'

'Does your Daddy know yet?'

Charlotte shook her head and Wincey said, 'I don't suppose he's going to like it either. But we can't help it, Teresa. It's going to be the making of us. If we do well with this first small order, we could end up supplying the whole of the Army, and maybe the Air Force as well. We're in line to make a fortune.'

Charlotte laughed then. 'You're about as bad as Florence with your imagination, Wincey.'

'It's not imagination. It's hard facts. Why shouldn't they give us bigger orders if we show we can do a good job with this one. And we can. You know we can.'

'All right, dear, but it's time we all went to bed. Och now, look what's happened. The girls have fallen asleep and we haven't got Granny sorted yet.'

Florence and the twins were slumped over the table, head down on the crook of arms, eyes shut, mouths hanging open.

'We'll try and help,' Wincey said. 'Come on, Charlotte.'

Before long, they were scarlet-faced with their exertions at trying to get Granny to bed. Then they had to half drag, half carry Florence and the twins through to their beds.

'Don't bother lighting the gas,' Charlotte said, once she and Wincey were in their own room. 'If we don't pull the blinds, there'll be enough light from the moon and the streetlamps.'

'That's another thing,' Wincey said. 'It's time we had a place with electric light. Or at least had electricity put in here.'

'Well,' Charlotte sighed, 'it's up to you, Wincey. Malcy and I are going to start looking around for a place of our own. You mentioned up the Balgrayhill and the park. I was thinking of buying one of these nice villas in Broomfield Road, opposite the park.'

'Buying? A villa?' Wincey echoed incredulously. The villas in Broomfield Road opposite the park housed lawyers and doctors and ministers.

'Yes. Fancy me buying a house—and a villa of all things! Actually, Wincey, we've already been looking at one. It was Malcy's idea.'

'I'll bet,' Wincey thought.

'He just loves Springburn Park,' Charlotte went on. 'It's always been his dream to live in one of those houses looking onto the park. It would be a dream come true for him, he said.'

'I'll bet,' Wincey thought again.

13

An unshaven, shabbily dressed man was crouched on the bottom step of the stairs outside the Gourlays' door. He was greedily supping a bowl of soup and tearing at a hunk of bread with his teeth. As Wincey was putting her key in the door, he jerked his head towards it and said, 'She's an awfae kind wuman, that, for a teuchter.' Wincey couldn't help smiling at the Glasgow word for a Highlander. Teresa often gave soup or bread to beggars who asked for it. So did many folk up other closes.

For years now there had been quite an army of beggars, the plight of many, Wincey suspected, caused by the Depression. They were unemployed men who, through no fault of their own, were reduced to either begging or starving.

'That man out there is fairly enjoying your soup, Teresa.'

'Oh, there you are, dear. You look tired. Sit down and relax and I'll dish your soup. Have you had a busy day?'

Wincey flopped into a chair. 'Yes, but it's better to be busy than idle, like some of these poor men.'

'That's true, dear, and I know you've done your best in giving jobs to as many as possible.'

'There's only so many we can take on, unfortunately.'

'You do your best, dear. Would you like a wee nip of whisky to help you get your strength back?'

'No thanks, Teresa. I'd rather wait for your soup.'

'I'll go and get my plate back from that poor soul out there before I start setting the table.'

'Is Granny at the front room window?'

'Yes, I'm going to bring her through in a minute.'

'I'll fetch her.'

'No, you sit where you are, dear, and rest yourself.'

'Have the girls been home yet?' Florence and the twins had recently escaped from the factory. Florence was working in the millinery department of Copeland & Lye's and had become quite toffee-nosed, or so her father said.

'I have to speak proper in the millinery department of Copeland's, Daddy,' Florence had explained. 'It's all posh customers that go there.'

The twins had found jobs in the Co-op. Euphemia was in ladies' underwear, and Bridget in hosiery. They too had polished up their accents.

'Yes, the girls have been in and away again. Since they've all started courting, they're hardly ever in. I'm looking forward to Charlotte's wedding, though. Aren't you? Just three months to go now.'

Wincey nodded but looked away.

'You never seem all that enthusiastic about it, Wincey. Aren't you pleased that she's happy.'

'Of course I want Charlotte to be happy. It's just . . .'

'What, dear?'

'I'm not all that keen on Malcy. I just hope she's not making a mistake, that's all.'

'Och, Malcy's a good lad. What on earth can you have against Malcy? Erchie says he's a hard worker, and he's been that nice and polite to me, and to Granny. He brought us a box of chocolates last week, and look at the nice presents he gave us all at Christmas. Erchie got that box of Woodbines and that was a lovely scarf he gave me. And—'

'I know, I know,' Wincey cut in. 'Just forget I said anything. Have you made up your mind what you want to wear at the wedding yet? You just need to tell us what you want, you know, and we'll make it up for you.'

'No, dear. Thanks all the same, but I know how busy all of you are at the factory, and Florence was telling me of the lovely dresses there are in Copeland's. Lots to choose from, she said, and I could try hats on while I'm there. Match colours and everything. So that's what I plan to do. Malcy was saying that Charlotte should get her wedding dress there. Nothing but the best, Malcy says. Charlotte's started an account there. Fancy!'

'And I expect Malcy will be getting everything he needs there too.'

'I don't know, dear. Why?'

'Well, nothing but the best, as he says.'

'You sound—'

A roar from the front room cut Teresa short.

'Are you gonnae let me sit through here till ah die o' starvation or whit?'

Teresa tutted. 'I was forgetting about poor Granny. She has been sitting through there for quite a while.'

She hurried from the kitchen and in a few minutes returned pushing Granny's wheelchair.

'Ah wis frozen stiff as well.' Granny stared at Wincey. 'Whit's up wi' your face?'

'Hello, Granny. Nothing.'

'I'll dish the soup. That'll soon heat you up, Granny.'

Teresa hustled over to the range. These days she had her hair professionally conditioned, cut and finger waved. She wore a pretty floral pinny over her navy skirt and frilly lavender blouse. Wincey thought how different and how much better she looked now than when she'd first set eyes on her. That seemed a lifetime ago now.

'Wincey and I were talking about the wedding, Granny.

May's usually a good month for weather. It makes such a difference to photographs if the sun shines.'

Wincey said, 'You'll have to get a new dress as well, Granny. We're all going to be dressed up to the nines.'

'Ah've already got a good dress. The one ah used tae wear tae church.'

'Granny, it's reeking of mothballs,' Teresa said, 'and it's an old thing.'

'Ah'm an auld thing.'

Wincey and Teresa laughed. 'Yes, and a right awkward torment of an old thing. Here, eat up your soup. There's nice lamb chops as well.'

'Any puddin'?' Granny had a sweet tooth.

'Of course. Guess what it is. Can you not smell it?'

Granny's nose twitched at the spicy air. 'No' a clooty dumplin'?'

'The very same.'

Sheer joy flashed into Granny's eyes but hastily she lowered her head and began slurping at her soup, muttering in between slurps, 'Aye, well, it's taken ye long enough. Ah've been askin' for years aboot a clooty dumplin'.'

Teresa winked at Wincey. 'Now, now, Granny. You're getting worse than Florence for exaggerating.'

Soon Erchie had arrived to join them at the table. At least he—like his mother—had never changed, Wincey thought. He still wore his skipped bunnet all the time and a comfortable old jacket and trousers.

'Huv ye seen the papers yet, Ma?'

'Ye know fine ah cannae read noo wi' ma eyes. How? Whit's been goin' on?'

'Lots of men are goin' over tae Spain tae fight in the Civil War. Mind the other day I read tae you about whit's happened there.'

'Naebody'll thank them for it,' Granny said.

'It's a good cause, right enough,' Erchie conceded. 'It's against Fascism. It says in the *Record* crowds o' intellectuals are goin', even fellas from Cambridge. An' fancy! The British government has warned Britons who enlist on either side that they're liable to two years in prison.'

'Och, it's gettin' beyond me,' Granny complained. 'Wan minute they're jailin' men for no' goin' tae fight—good men like our Johnny Maclean. Noo they're jailin' men who *are* goin' tae fight. Whit dae they think they're playin' at?'

'Never mind, dear,' Teresa said. 'Here's a nice pork chop.'

'Ah know whit their game is,' Erchie said. 'It says in the *Record* here they're goin' tae spend one thousand five hundred million—fancy!' His voice rose to a screech. 'One thousand five hundred million—to build up arms stocks. They're plannin' another bloody war, that's whit they're playin' at.'

'Now, now, Erchie, watch your language.'

'Well, it's enough tae make anybody swear. They told us the last war was tae be the war tae end all wars.'

'Ah never believed a word o' it at the time,' Granny growled.

'No, Ma, an' neither did ah. Ye cannae believe a word they say.'

'Remember how Johnny prophesied another war wis on the cards?'

'Aye, we could always believe whit Johnny said. He wis an honest man. An' his prophesy'll come true. You mark ma words. It says in the *Record*—'

'Och, Erchie,' Teresa protested. 'Will you put that paper away and let us have some peace to enjoy our food.'

'All right, all right, hen. It's just that Ma likes tae be kept up tae date wi' whit's in the paper.'

'Well, dear, you can read every page of the *Record* to Granny later. Through in the front room.'

'She's aye shovin' me through there oot the road. Ah've been sittin' through there frozen stiff aw day.'

Teresa sighed. 'I'll light a fire for you, Granny. Then you and Erchie'll be nice and cosy while he reads you the paper.'

'Aye, well . . .' Granny said grudgingly, but with one eye

on the clooty dumpling now drying out at the fire. A fine sight it was—fat, dark brown, fruity and spicy and with a beautiful shiny skin.

'I've cream as well, Granny.'

'Cream? Cream?' Granny echoed incredulously. 'By Jove, it's well seen we're well off nooadays.'

'I was just thinking,' Teresa said, 'what with Charlotte getting married, and no doubt Florence and the twins won't be long behind her, and there's you as well, Wincey . . .'

'Oh no,' Wincey said, 'I'll never get married.'

'Nonsense, dear. Of course you will. One day. But you're still young, so don't worry.'

'I'm not worried. It's not that.'

'I was just thinking, you see,' Teresa interrupted, 'there would be no point in us going through all the upheaval of moving again. This'll do fine for us, won't it, Erchie? It's such a nice close and we've such good neighbours.'

'Aye, ye're quite right, hen. This is where we belong, no' among the toffs up the Balgrayhill.'

Wincey shrugged. 'Well, if you're happy here, it's all right by me.' And yet she felt a pang of sadness. She didn't know where it came from.

1937

14

'Don't be ridiculous, Nicholas,' Mathieson said. 'You're forty-two.'

'So? What does age matter?'

'I would have thought you'd have had more than enough of fighting. I thought you'd become a pacifist.'

'This is different, James. It's against the growth of Fascism. I think it should be nipped in the bud before it spreads any further. Derek and Nigel and Peter have already gone.'

Mathieson sadly shook his head. 'Good men, and we'll never see them again. Good, intelligent men who could have been an asset to Scotland.'

'What a pessimist you are, James. Of course we'll see them again.'

'Have you forgotten all you told me about what it was like in the trenches? And how many good friends you lost there? The flower of British manhood was sacrificed in that war.'

'This is different.'

'Not as far as suffering and killing are concerned. We must find other ways, Nicholas. Socialists all over the world must use every means at their disposal to stop every country building up arms. A lot of good Stanley Baldwin was. It was him who started it all again here. Remember George Lansbury's last speech? He quoted Jesus. "Those who take the sword will perish by the sword." But it's the arms dealers and the men who make fortunes out of munitions factories who are at the root cause of war. They encourage war because it feeds their greed.'

Virginia had come into the sitting room then and said, 'Well, that was a bit tactless of you, James.'

'Oh sorry, Nicholas. I'd forgotten about your father.'

Nicholas smiled. 'It's all right.' He turned to Virginia. 'James has been trying to talk me out of my idea of going over to Spain.'

'I should think so too,' Virginia said with feeling.

'Think of Virginia,' Mathieson said. 'She still hasn't completely recovered from losing Wincey.'

'I doubt if I ever will. But there's no point using me in trying to persuade him, James. You're far more likely to succeed if you use his precious writing.'

'She hates my work,' Nicholas told Mathieson sadly.

'No I don't,' Virginia protested. 'It's just the way you always put it first—before me, before everything.'

Nicholas shook his dark head and said nothing.

It was Mathieson who spoke up. 'Don't be so selfish, Virginia.'

'Selfish! Me?' She flushed with anger. 'You've got a nerve!' She glared at his twisted face, his shaggy mop of prematurely grey hair and bent shoulders, and suddenly her anger seeped away. She thought—what was the use.

Mathieson spoke again. 'Nicholas has been a good husband and provider for you, Virginia. Not only that, he has given pleasure to thousands with his books. But as well as all that, he has conveyed the socialist message more effectively and reached more ordinary people than you or I or any of our friends have done in all the years of our work in politics. You should be proud of him.'

'I am, I am.' Tears filled her eyes. 'It's just . . . I can't bear the thought of him going away again.'

'All right, darling.' Nicholas hastened to put his arms around her shoulders. 'I won't go. I promise.'

'I still think of Wincey,' Virginia said.

'So do I, darling, and I worry.' He gazed over at Mathieson. 'Do you think she felt neglected, James?'

'Why should she? She had a good home here. She had everything any child could have wished for.'

'Every material thing, yes,' Nicholas said. 'That's not what I meant. Remember our get-togethers with all our friends when she was here, James. You think of it. Where was she? Who spoke to her? Did I speak to her? My God, James, I can hardly remember seeing her. I've got now so that the more I try to remember what she was like, the less I can remember. Sometimes I think I've never known her at all.'

'Now you're being ridiculous again, Nicholas. She was a shy girl, that's all. She kept herself in the background. She didn't want to mix with everybody. And why should she, when you think of it? It was always adult company. She was just a child.'

Virginia spoke up then, her tone as worried as Nicholas's. 'We should have invited more children to the house for her. We should have encouraged her to bring her friends home.'

'But as far as I could see,' Mathieson said, 'she didn't have any friends. It wasn't your fault. There are people like that— loners. It's just their natures.'

Virginia chewed at her lip. 'She was far too much in her grandfather's company. I used to say to her, Be a good girl and keep your grandfather company. When I think of it now, I shouldn't have said that. I shouldn't have done that.'

Nicholas gave her a little shake. 'You must stop tormenting yourself like this, Virginia. You're only harming yourself.'

'Yes,' Mathieson agreed. 'It's time you faced facts, Virginia. And you too, Nicholas. Because if you ask me, you're just as bad. Wincey is long dead and it was nobody's fault. She loved her grandfather. She liked him and wanted to be with him. Her death was a tragedy but nobody's fault. You've got to accept that—both of you. It's the only way. Your child wouldn't have wanted you to be so unhappy and tormented like this. She loved you too, you know.'

'Do you really think so, James?' Virginia gazed anxiously over at him.

'Of course she loved the pair of you. How can you doubt it? It was perfectly obvious to everyone else.'

'Was it, James?' Nicholas asked with an anxiety that matched that of his wife.

Mathieson rolled his eyes. 'For God's sake, you're both being ridiculous now. I've never been more certain of anything in my life. Of course Wincey loved you. And she was proud of you both. I used to see it in her eyes every time she looked up at either of you.'

'Thank you, James,' Virginia said quietly.

'Yes,' Nicholas echoed. 'Thank you.'

'Nothing to thank me for. I'm just stating facts. Now, you've had your grieving time, so put it behind you. Get on with your lives. And try to be happy, for God's sake.'

'All right. All right.' Nicholas smiled. 'We take your point. Now let's have a drink. Let's drink to the future.'

'That's more like it.' Mathieson gave one of his grotesque twisted grins. 'How's Richard these days?'

'Better you didn't know,' Nicholas said.

'Don't tell me he's taken after your father and gone into munitions?'

'No, but my father would have been pleased, I suppose. He's joined the Air Force. He's training as a pilot and loving it.'

'So he's going to be cannon fodder this time around.'

Virginia cried out in horror, 'James, don't say that. I can't bear it.'

'I'm sorry, Virginia. But it does look as if there's another war brewing.'

'You're such a pessimist, James. You always have been.'

'Well, I only hope I'm wrong.'

Suddenly Nicholas said, 'There's still that money, you know.'

'What money?' Mathieson asked.

'In my father's will. He left Wincey a large sum in trust until her twenty-first birthday. It gave my mother quite a shock when she found out about it. I'll never forget her face at the reading of the will.'

Virginia said, 'She never really liked Wincey. She thought she was too much like me—which was utter nonsense, of course. Poor Wincey wasn't a bit like me, either in looks or in any other way.'

'What are you going to do about the money?'

'She would have been seventeen now. We can't bear to touch the money yet. After her twenty-first, we'll see. But at the moment, both Virginia and I feel we'd rather give the whole lot to charity. It's not as if we need it.'

Virginia said, 'You'll stay for dinner, I hope, James.'

'Thanks. If you're sure it's all right.'

'When has it not been all right, James?' Nicholas laughed. 'You're one of the family, and always welcome. You know that.'

'I'll go through and see to it.' Virginia went through to the kitchen. She had a daily cook and a cleaner—Mrs Rogers and Jessie Conway. Mrs Rogers was just taking off her apron when Virginia arrived in the well-equipped, spacious kitchen.

'I've left the potatoes peeled and ready salted in the pot,' Mrs Rogers said. She was an efficient cook and enjoyed the job, but she was glad to be heading home regularly every afternoon. She was a widow with two children at school. 'And the pie's all ready there just to pop in the oven. There's fruit salad in the fridge and a jug of custard. Or you could heat up an apple pie. I made two yesterday.'

'That's fine. Thanks, Mrs Rogers. Now off you go. Jessie got away on time, did she?'

The cleaner just came in for four hours.

'Yes, she did the stairs and the bathroom and cleaned up here.'

'Fine. See you tomorrow then.'

After Mrs Rogers had gone, Virginia switched on the kitchen wireless. It was a request programme and George Formby was twanging away at his ukulele and cheerily singing 'Leaning on a Lamppost'. Then came a woman vocalist who began the sad refrain, 'Can I Forget You'. Virginia rushed over and switched the wireless off.

15

Wincey knew it was only a matter of time. She knew it would come, and it did.

Charlotte said, 'It's only right that we should make Malcy a partner, Wincey. He can't just go on working in the factory as an ordinary employee.' Her eyes shone. 'I thought I could make a partnership my wedding gift to him.'

Wincey took a deep breath. She must try to keep calm and not criticise Malcy. She knew it would only make matters worse. Charlotte would never listen to a word against him.

'I'm sorry, Charlotte. I can't agree to that.'

'Why not? What have you got against Malcy?'

'It's just that I believe the secret of our success is *our* partnership—just the two of us. I don't want to spoil it by changing anything. We could give Malcy another job. He'd make a good salesman. He could travel about as—'

'I don't want Malcy to travel about, as a salesman or anything else. I want him here beside me. No, it has to be a partnership, Wincey. I can't disappoint him.'

'So you told him.'

'Well, just hinted a bit when he was so worried about how

awkward it was going to be at work once we were married.'

'I see.'

Charlotte brightened again. 'So it's all right with you?'

'No. I'm sorry, Charlotte. It isn't, and it never will be.'

'So Malcy was right.' Charlotte sounded bitter now. 'He said you would try to spoil everything for us. He said he didn't know what he's ever done to you to make you dislike him so. And neither do I, Wincey.'

'Can we just leave it now, Charlotte?'

'No, we can't. I'll go to a lawyer. I'll get Malcy a partnership one way or another.'

'Well, you'll no longer have me as a partner. Or anything else. I'll wash my hands of the business altogether.'

'You can't do that.'

'Just watch me.'

'You know I can't do without you. Especially now. You're the only one who knows—'

'That's right, Charlotte. And what does Malcy know?'

Charlotte's cheeks were crimson. Wincey had never seen her look so angry. 'I'd give up the factory and sell everything and be content to be Malcy's wife, rather than hurt or insult him.'

'I don't want to hurt or insult him, Charlotte. And you can give up the factory if you like. I've no doubt that I can find other work if I have to. I have plenty of contacts now.'

Charlotte left in high dudgeon. She was off to meet Malcy— their last meeting before the wedding, in fact. Wincey was confident that Malcy would not welcome the idea of Charlotte killing the goose that laid so many golden eggs. Charlotte returned late that night and Wincey pretended to be asleep. She knew, however, by the way Charlotte was banging about the room that she was angry—and it was with her.

Next morning at breakfast, Charlotte addressed Wincey with bitterness. 'Well, it's only too obvious that my Malcy is a lot more reasonable and generous-hearted than you.'

Before Wincey had time to say anything, Teresa asked,

'What's wrong? What do you mean, dear?'

'I wanted to give Malcy a partnership in the firm as a wedding present. As I told *her*, it would be awkward for us both if he continued as an ordinary employee after we were married. But oh no, she wouldn't have it. She threatened to ditch the business altogether rather than have my Malcy as a partner.'

'It has never worried you,' Wincey struggled to control her temper, 'to have your father working as an ordinary employee.'

'That's different.'

'Yes. Erchie is a much more experienced and more senior member of the staff, as well as being the head of the family.'

Erchie said, 'Ah appreciate what you're saying, hen, but ah've always been quite happy to leave the runnin' o' things to you an' Charlotte.'

'I know, Erchie. But what do you bet Malcy wouldn't be. That's what I'm afraid of. I don't blame Charlotte for not understanding and being angry with me. She loves Malcy and good luck to her. I sincerely wish her and Malcy every happiness as man and wife.'

'Och aye, hen, ah'm sure ye do. Come on, Charlotte. Ah don't like tae see you an' Wincey fallin' out. Ye've been like sisters tae each other for years. Closer than the twins.'

'That's right, dear. We don't want either of you to be upset so near to the wedding. What did Malcy say? Is he angry as well?'

'No, he is not.' Charlotte assumed a quiet dignity. 'That's what I was trying to say. He simply told me that he would be the last one to come between me and Wincey, or have us give up the factory, even though he'd have loved to have me just stay at home and look after him all the time. I tried to insist that he was the only one who mattered to me, and I'd gladly give everything up for him. But he wouldn't hear of me giving up the factory.'

'I'll bet,' Wincey thought, but she said nothing.

'How about making Malcy the manager, hen? That would

be something, would it no'?' Erchie turned to Wincey. 'How about that, hen?'

Wincey shrugged. 'Yes, that's all right with me.'

'Charlotte, hen?'

'I suppose it's the next best thing. I'll mention it to Malcy and see what he says.'

'Good, good.' Erchie rubbed his hands. 'An' whit are ye aw goin' tae dae wi' yersels the day?'

Florence and the twins had already left for work but Wincey and Charlotte were not going in to the factory. It was the day before the wedding and there was still quite a lot to do.

Teresa said, 'We're having our hair done for a start. And there are dresses to collect. Away you go out the road, Erchie. And remember, keep in the pub with your pals tonight. We're having Charlotte's hen party.'

'What? In here?'

'Yes. Charlotte doesn't want to be traipsing away into town and coming in late at night. She wants to get her beauty sleep tonight. We're just going to have a few of the neighbours in for an hour or two and a bite of supper. But no men allowed. Do you hear?'

'Poor old Erchie,' Wincey thought. 'He's not even been invited to Malcy's stag party.' No doubt Malcy would be living it up in town, treating all his gambling pals, lording it, showing off. She prayed that he would be kind to Charlotte. Charlotte had always been such a loving and generous-hearted person. She deserved someone who would love and cherish her.

Gradually, during the rest of the day, Charlotte's coolness towards Wincey was melted away by the happy preparations for the wedding. By the time the neighbours started to arrive, it was as if there had never been any bad feeling between them. Charlotte was not a person to harbour ill-feeling for long.

Mrs McGregor arrived with her three eldest girls, Lexie, Minnie and Jeannie. Each one of them brought a bottle.

'Oh here,' Teresa laughed. 'Do you want us all to get drunk?'

Then came Mrs Donaldson and her two girls, Mary and Joan. Then a couple of Charlotte's friends from the church, Sarah and Betty. By this time the kitchen was packed and so they all moved through to the front room. There Wincey started the gramophone going with a cheery record of 'Seventy-Six Trombones', which could hardly be heard above the excited chatter. They were all coming to the wedding and were eagerly looking forward to it.

By the time they'd had a few drinks, Mary and Joan Donaldson were well away. They got up to sing a duet—first of all 'Some Day My Prince will Come' and then, for an encore, 'I'm Wishing'. Both efforts sent everyone into a splutter of giggles because unfortunately neither Mary nor Joan had the slightest chance of a prince or any other man coming, no matter how much wishing they did. For one thing, they'd inherited their mother's ample girth, chubby faces and short-sightedness, which required very thick pebble glasses. Blissfully unaware of the cause of everyone's mirth, however, the girls continued to put heart and soul into their performance, even going on to their tiptoes and doing a little dance for good measure.

The party, including the supper that Teresa had prepared, was a huge success and everyone agreed that it was much better 'havin' a pairty in yer ain hoose—ye can let yer hair doon'. Even Granny agreed that it had been 'a rerr night'. She had also treated the company to a couple of songs, first of all 'The Bonny Wells o' Weary', then, after another few drinks, a rousing rendition of 'The Red Flag'.

The next day everyone had a long lie in bed. Teresa as usual was up first and making a pot of tea. Soon everyone was milling about trying to get ready.

'This is ridiculous, Mother,' Florence complained. She'd recently changed from addressing Teresa as Mammy to Mother. Copeland & Lye's was having a terrible influence on

Florence, Granny said. Who would have thought it, her of all folk.

'She's been totally corrupted by the bourgeoisie, She'll be callin' me Grandmother next!'

'What's ridiculous, dear?' Teresa asked.

'This awful dump of a house. I mean, that black hole of Calcutta of a toilet for a start. And out on the stairs, Mother! It's just not hygienic. And not being able to have a bath without traipsing about a mile up the road. It's high time we moved to a decent place with a room for each of us, and a bathroom.'

'Now, now, dear. It's just a wee bit of a crush today because of the wedding. Give yourself a wash at the sink.'

'That's another thing. It's not hygienic to sleep, eat, cook and wash in the one place. And Granny's chanty is absolutely disgusting. We'll have to move, Mother.'

'Ye'll be auld yersel' wan day,' Granny wailed.

'Now, now, Granny,' Teresa soothed. 'She didn't mean that you're disgusting, dear. Just your chamber pot.'

Charlotte said, 'We've offered to pay the rent of a bigger place with a bathroom, haven't we Wincey?'

'Yes. And it's an awful nuisance having to go out to the close for the toilet, right enough, Teresa. Especially in the winter. And the girls should have a room of their own, and not a room that has to double as a sitting room either. And now that Granny has her wheelchair, we could hurl her into the bathroom no bother.'

Teresa sighed. 'Right enough. A bathroom would be a great help.'

Florence, forgetting her poshness for a minute, shouted out, 'Oh Mammy, does that mean we can move to a better place?'

The twins joined in. 'Please Mammy. Please.'

'Och well, as long as it's still in Springburn.'

'Hurray!' Florence and the twins joined hands in a circle and danced around.

Charlotte said, 'I'm going through to the room to get ready.'

'All right, dear. I'll just see to Granny. I've just her hair to give a wee tidy.'

Granny's hair had once been long and jet black. Erchie always cut it for her, making it neat and short. She wore it sleeked down with a side parting and fixed on one side by a large brown kirby-grip. Teresa gave the dark grey head a gentle brushing and then replaced the kirby-grip.

'There you are, Granny. All smartened up.'

'Them shoes are killin' me. Ye know how bad ma feet are.'

'You can't wear your old slippers to a wedding, Granny. Try and suffer them till after the service. At the reception I'll slip them off under the table. Will that do?'

'Ah suppose it'll huv tae.'

Soon the packed kitchen was rustling with taffeta dresses in pale blue and lavender. Then the kitchen door opened and Charlotte came in looking like an angel in her white dress and veil. Tears came into Erchie's eyes.

'Oh hen, ah'm that proud o' you. Ye look that nice.'

Wincey embraced her. 'You look lovely, Charlotte. I'm so proud to be your bridesmaid. We all are, aren't we girls?'

There was an enthusiastic yell of agreement. Once more, Wincey made a secret prayer.

16

Virginia left the house and entered the Botanic Gardens by the side gate. With its famous Kibble Palace and pleasant grounds, it was a popular park for residents of the West End of the city. It was after lunchtime. She'd eaten the meal alone, as usual. Nicholas was shut away in his writing room with his flask of coffee and sandwiches to have if and when he remembered.

Walking in the park in the warm May sunshine was better than sitting at home doing nothing. May Day was past, with its exciting marches and colourful banners carried aloft. Then all the rousing speeches. Nicholas hadn't even taken a day off for that. She had gone with Mathieson and a crowd of other socialist activists. Afterwards they'd enjoyed a meal and lots of heated talk in Miss Cranston's famous Willow Tearoom in Sauchiehall Street. It was designed by Charles Rennie Mackintosh and much admired for its unusual furniture and decor. The talk as usual had been wide ranging and not solely about politics. It had been an exhilarating day altogether. In the days since then, quietness and loneliness had crept up on her once more.

Nicholas was not enthusiastic about having friends round very often while he was working on a book. Nor did they go out as much as they used to. At least not to the jazz evenings which had been so lively and such fun. They had got to know quite a few musicians. They had met them through Andy Daisley and his Balmoral Enterprises. Andy represented many of the best musicians and organised festivals and concerts in Glasgow. Through him, famous musicians from all over the world came to perform in the city. All she and Nicholas seemed to do together nowadays was visit his mother, even though, she suspected, this was more of a duty than a pleasure for Nicholas.

The park was quite busy with strollers like herself. Some wore nanny's uniforms and pushed prams. Virginia entered the heat of the Kibble Palace and wandered among the tropical plants, trees and statues. Virginia killed a half hour or so admiring the plants and passing the time of day with one of the workmen. He told her that they made up a yearly seed list which went out to all the botanic gardens in the world. Requests came back for seeds from countries as far away as Czechoslovakia and Australia.

The heat made her feel thirsty and so she left the Kibble Palace and walked towards the main gate, beside which Gizzi's Cafe was situated. Or the Silver Slipper Cafe, to give it its proper name. It was the usual thing after a stroll around the gardens for people to go and have an ice cream in the cafe.

Afterwards Virginia went down Byres Road to do a bit of shopping. She passed the subway with its special smell—a mix of archangel tar and water. Virginia had often seen women with children suffering with their chest standing at the side and letting the children breathe in the subway air. It was supposed to be good for them. She bought a paper on the way back and once home, made a cup of tea and sat down at the kitchen table to read the paper. There were pictures of the King's gilded carriage drawn by eight white horses passing through Trafalgar Square in London. It was on the way to the

Abbey for the coronation. There was a big picture of the newly crowned King on the balcony of Buckingham Palace. The King, Virginia thought, appeared a serious but sensitive man. His Queen looked pleasant and smiling, and the two children, Elizabeth and Margaret, were also smiling happily. They looked quite ordinary little girls. Behind the royal family, though, were other royal ladies and peeresses wearing elbow length gloves and coronets on their heads. Their supercilious stares and primped mouths were all too familiar to Virginia. They were the type of employers she and countless other poor girls had suffered under. Women who thought they were far superior to the 'servant class' and treated them like dirt. Women who lived in pampered luxury, enjoying one round of pleasure after another, while their servants slaved for a pittance from the crack of dawn until they dropped exhausted on to their attic beds. 'Useless, upper-class twits!' Virginia thought, as she turned the page.

Inside there was a picture of the wedding of Charlotte Gourlay, owner of the prosperous Gourlay factory which made clothing for the armed forces. Her bridegroom apparently had been one of her employees. 'Well, well,' Virginia thought, 'things were surely looking up and getting more democratic.' She looked a nice gentle girl, and no doubt she was a good and a kindly employer. It said that that four Gourlay sisters had all been bridesmaids. They weren't in the picture though, only the bride and the groom. It was obvious what the gentle looking factory owner saw in him. The paper described him as 'the handsome groom', although he wasn't the type that Virginia thought attractive, with his creamy fair hair, brows and lashes, and pale blue eyes. 'Oh well, good luck to her,' Virginia thought, turning another page.

★　　　★　　　★

Florence's boyfriend lived at the St George's Cross end of Great Western Road and he and Florence did quite a lot of their courting in the Botanic Gardens. During the summer at least. One day, not long after Charlotte's wedding, Florence invited Wincey to come on a picnic with them to the Botanic Gardens. Part of Wincey longed to see the place again—the beautiful gardens, the elegant Grosvenor Hotel and terraced houses opposite, and further along, Great Western Terrace. Then on the opposite side of the road from that, rearing up from the grassy bank, Kirklee Terrace and her original home. At times she longed to see her mother and father again, but sadly the longer time passed, the more certain she was of how impossible that was.

'No, Florence. It's very kind of you and Eddie but I'd rather not play gooseberry. You ought to know me by now. I prefer to be on my own. I'm just funny that way.'

'You certainly are,' Florence said. 'But are you sure?'

'Yes, honestly. I thought seeing it's such a nice day I'd either go up to Springburn Park or even to Glasgow Green. I'd like to visit the People's Palace again.' Glasgow Green was an important historic site and one of the great battlefields of Scotland. In many ways, the history of the Green was the history of Glasgow itself. A thousand battles had been fought there. Meetings and demonstrations had been held on the Green in the struggle for a living wage. The fight for political freedom—first one man, one vote, and then one woman, one vote—had taken place there. Different wars against all sorts of social injustices had been conducted on the Green. It was also the place where not only did women do their washing, but everyone enjoyed their leisure time. At school, Wincey had learned that it was here that the idea came to James Watt that changed the entire course of industrial and human history—the steam engine.

Wincey enjoyed her walk on the Green, watching all the people, and at the same time immersing herself in the colourful history of the place. She made straight for the People's Palace. It was different from other museums inasmuch as its collections all related to the history and the industry of the city and the life of the ordinary working people. It also housed a heated winter garden which was designed and arranged to serve as a hall where musical performances were given to large audiences. So it was a unique municipal enterprise, with the combination practically under one room of a museum, picture gallery, winter garden and music hall.

Wincey had barely stepped inside the entrance when she had an unexpected shock. She saw a familiar face. She had felt sure that neither her parents nor her grandmother would ever come here, unless there was some sort of political rally going on. Then her mother and some of her mother's political friends might turn up. Wincey had made sure before she'd ventured out that no such rally or meeting was taking place. She had not, however, considered the possibility of meeting one of her mother's or her grandmother's servants. But here, only a few feet from her, was Mrs Rogers and her two children.

Wincey quickly turned away and retraced her steps through the doorway and out onto the Green again. Her heart was thumping in her chest, making her feel as if she was in danger of fainting. She tried to calm herself with the thought that Mrs Rogers had not seen her. She was almost certain the older woman had not seen her. Nevertheless, as she hurried away, she wished she'd had a scarf with her to tie over her head. Her red hair was the thing that might draw attention to her. She couldn't get back to Springburn quick enough. Never had a tram car seemed so slow.

Only once she was in Springburn, hastening into the close and then safely into the house, did she feel secure. It had been as if she had relived the horror of her grandfather's death again and her dreadful part in it. Her panic had been exactly the same.

'What's wrong, dear?' Teresa asked. 'You look as white as a sheet.'

'I don't know. I just felt a bit faint.'

'Och, you've been working too hard, Wincey. Sit down, dear. Try to relax now and I'll make you a cup of tea.'

Granny wailed, 'Ah'm needin' ma medicine. If she had tae suffer aw the bloomin' agonies that ah huv tae, she'd know aw aboot it.'

'Now, now, Granny. You'll get your medicine with your cup of tea. The kettle doesn't take a minute on the gas. These gas rings are marvellous. They're so much quicker than the fire. Are you all right, Wincey?'

'Yes, I feel much better now that I'm home.' She must always remember that this was her home. There was no use allowing memories of her childhood home in Kirklee Terrace to creep into her mind. How could she explain to anyone why she'd run away and why for so long she'd stayed away? There could be only one explanation and that was guilt. Everyone would know that without her attempting to explain. She could offer no excuse for what she'd done. Even now, as an adult, she knew that by refusing to give her grandfather his medication, she had caused his death. She couldn't make the excuse that she hadn't known what to do to help him. Everyone was well aware that she knew perfectly well. How could she bring herself to say, 'He was a pervert. He was abusing me. That's why I let him die.' No-one would believe her. Her grandfather had appeared such a pleasant, loving, generous old man. Her grandfather, of all people! Anyway, such a thing had never been heard of. Everyone would revile her and despise her for even thinking of such disgusting behaviour. They would believe it was nothing more than an example of her dirty mind and they would be a hundred times more horrified at her callous treatment of her own grandfather. As far as everyone else was concerned, the old man had been nothing but good and kind to her from the moment she was born.

Wincey gratefully accepted the cup of tea from Teresa who said in surprise, 'Wincey, you're trembling. What on earth's the matter? Has something happened to upset you? Is that what it is?'

'I nearly got run over by a motor car. That's all.'

'That's all?' Teresa cried out. 'Oh my, you might have been killed. Oh Wincey, now I feel all shaky. You know you're as dear and as precious to me as my own flesh and blood.'

Wincey felt guilty about lying to Teresa and tears of shame welled up in her eyes. 'Thank you, Teresa.'

'Nothing to thank me for.'

'Where's ma medicine. It's well seen naebody cares about me. Ye'll be auld yersel' wan day, the pair o' ye.'

17

At last they made the move to a handsome red sandstone tenement near the top of the Balgrayhill. For Granny's sake they had waited until a bottom flat had become available. It was a spacious, high ceilinged four-room and kitchen and bathroom. It also had quite a large square hall. Granny said, 'Ye'll huv us aw votin' Tory next.'

The twins shared a room. Wincey had a room to herself, and so had Florence. The other room was to be the 'best room', used only for entertaining visitors. Granny had refused to move from the kitchen, nor would she countenance being left to sleep alone.

'Ah cannae get up on the bed in the kitchen or anywhere else. Ah'll aye huv tae use the hurly. So there's nae reason fur you an' Erchie no' tae stay in the kitchen bed. Anyway, what if ah needed tae "go" in the middle o' the night? Ye'll be auld yersel' wan day.'

They had to buy more furniture. For the sitting room, as Florence called it, they bought a three piece suite—a settee and two easy chairs, so cushioned that you sank deep into their comfort. But as Erchie said, 'We'll need a crane tae lift

Ma oot o' them chairs.' A walnut china cabinet was also purchased. It was filled with a coffee set with a cream coffee pot in a fashionable angular shape, with a geometric pattern of orange, yellow and black. A milk jug and sugar bowl and matching cups and saucers were proudly arranged alongside it. On the shelf underneath, there was a matching biscuit barrel. On the remaining shelves, there were crystal glasses. On a table beside the tiled fireplace sat a lamp in the form of a bronze lady holding a beach ball aloft. Another larger walnut table over against the opposite wall had a folding leaf to save space. On it were photographs of Charlotte's wedding.

Above the mantelpiece hung a large mirror and along the mantle shelf were two bronze figures of dancing ladies and a stylised black panther. On either side were low book shelves. The floor was of highly polished linoleum, covered with a large carpet. The carpet had a striking design of figures entitled 'The Workers'. It was a purchase insisted on by Erchie and Granny. They both said, 'Ye've aw had a say in everythin' else and we're no' that keen on any o' it. But we like this rug. That's the rug for us.'

'Carpet, Daddy,' Florence corrected.

Eventually everyone capitulated. Admittedly the carpet was a very modern design and it did fit in with the overall style of the room. But no sooner had they all settled into the new house when Florence announced that she was going to get married. She and Eddie had found a place in Clydebank, near Eddie's work. She refused a big wedding like the one Charlotte had. All she wanted was a quiet registry affair and then to a restaurant afterwards with the twins and their boyfriends. Granny loudly proclaimed, much to Florence's affront and embarrassment, 'Aye, it's well seen it's a shotgun affair.'

Teresa sighed. 'It'll be the twins next. I just hope they don't follow Florence and Eddie away to Clydebank. What's wrong with old Springburn?'

'Ah telt ye,' Granny said, 'they're aw gettin' above theirsels. Springburn's no' good enough for them noo. Even the Co-op. *The Co-op.*' Granny repeated the word with high pitched incredulity. The twins had followed Florence into Copeland & Lye's. Both were in 'Mantles'.

'You mean frocks,' Granny had said, but the twins just rolled their eyes.

'What worries me, Granny, is that they've always been so close. The girls, I mean. And even their boyfriends are brothers. It's good that they're close, of course,' Teresa added hastily. 'It's just I hope they won't follow Florence away to Clydebank. I'll miss them.'

'Aye,' Erchie said, 'the house'd be awfae quiet without the girls.'

'Quiet as a grave,' Granny wailed. 'We'll aw rummel aroon' this big, empty hoose like peas in a drum.'

'Now, now. It's not empty, Granny. The twins won't be getting married for ages yet.'

As it turned out, Teresa was wrong in this pronouncement. No sooner had Florence and Eddie tied the knot than the twins announced that they too planned to marry. Florence's wedding went smoothly. She was a June bride and looked very pretty and smart in a white embroidered linen dress with short puff sleeves and a wide brimmed navy hat trimmed with white flowers. The twins wore navy jackets and skirts and white satin blouses. Wincey looked unusual in a dark green dress, matching cape, and a brimmed hat pulled down over her eyes. But then, as Teresa said proudly, 'Our Wincey always looks that wee bit different and mysterious.' Wincey smiled wrily at the word mysterious. If only Teresa knew.

It had been a quiet afternoon affair, just as Florence wanted. Nevertheless, Teresa insisted on giving her, as she said, a decent send-off. 'Just a wee family party, dear.'

And so that is what they had in their new sitting room on the evening of Florence's wedding. Although Teresa cheated a little and had the neighbours in as well. Their old neighbours, as Teresa called them, from their last close. They hadn't got to know the new neighbours yet. They seemed to like to keep themselves more to themselves. A good time, including a few energetic reels and a hokey kokey, was had by one and all. Granny, in her best black dress and her hair slicked to one side with water, sang loud and long with the rest of them.

The twins had a winter wedding. Fifth of November to be exact. Granny said, 'They'll huv fireworks soon enough after they're married, an' no' just the kind they're buyin' in that fancy shop in the town.'

'Och, Granny, it'll be good fun. It'll be a laugh. I'll hurl you round to the park.' We're going to have quite a crowd. All our old neighbours are coming, and Mrs Chalmers from upstairs.' Mrs Chalmers was the only neighbour up the new close that Teresa had really got to know and become friends with. Although young Mrs Beresford, also on the top flat, usually smiled and said good morning or good evening. But she always seemed to be in such a hurry. The next-door neighbour on the bottom flat, Miss McClusky, was even worse. She was always rushing about like a ferret with a duster in her hand.

Granny said, 'A right house-proud horror, that one! She's aye beatin' carpets an' cleanin' windows an' even sweepin' oot the bins. An' ah'm sorry for the poor auld faither o' hers. Fancy her no' lettin' him huv his pipe in the house!' A chair was always placed in the draughty close and the old man had to sit there to have his pipe. And his daughter, a spinster who obviously wasn't used to men or pipes, always came out afterwards and wafted a tea towel about like mad to rid the close of any smell of smoke. 'Whit she's needin',' Granny said, 'is a big man an' a crowd o' weans.'

The neighbours one up the stairs were Davy, an old bachelor, and next door to him was Jock. Jock was a widower. Granny said, 'Here, Wincey, ye should set yer cap at him. Ye could walk right intae a ready made house.'

Wincey laughed. 'Are you wanting rid of me or something? He's far too old for me, Granny.'

'It's no' good for a woman tae be left on her own. Or a

fella for that matter. Jock cannae be more than forty. An' he's got a good job on the railway.'

'You *are* wanting rid of me.'

'No, ah'm no'. But the likes o' you cannae be too fussy, hen. Ye're nae oil paintin' wi' all them freckles. An' no' everybody goes for a ginger heid.'

'Now, now, Granny. Wincey's got very nice hair and it's not ginger. It's a lovely warm auburn shade. And he *is* too old. Wincey's not yet eighteen.'

'Och, she's near enough. An' anyroads, she's auld fur her age, an' looks it.'

Teresa rolled her eyes but Wincey just laughed again. She was well used to Granny by now and had grown to be very fond of her.

The twins' wedding was a great success and a great crowd of people, many of whom they didn't know, joined in the fireworks party in the park—until the 'parky' came and put them out because he was going to lock the gates. After they'd all said their goodbyes at the park gate, Wincey was still waving enthusiastically to the twins and their new husbands in their retreating car, and without realising, she stepped out into the road. There was an immediate screech of brakes, and screams from Teresa and Granny, who had already crossed to the other side. A man leapt from a car and glared furiously at Wincey.

'What do you think you're doing, you idiot?'

The car's front bumper had barely touched Wincey but she felt terribly shaken and angry.

'How dare you call me an idiot?'

'You ran right out in front of me. It's a bloody good job there's nothing wrong with my brakes.'

Erchie came hurrying over. 'Come on, hen. Say ye're sorry tae the man an' we'll be on our way.'

'I'll not do any such thing. I wasn't running anywhere. If anyone's the idiot, it's him.'

'A right little charmer,' the man remarked, turning away

and getting back into his car.

'Come on, hen,' Erchie repeated, putting an arm around her. 'Ye're jist upset.'

'I'm not upset,' Wincey said, shaking Erchie's arm off and glaring at the driver, who cast her a look of disgust before driving away.

'What an insufferable man,' Wincey said as she walked across the road with Erchie to join Teresa and Granny. Charlotte and Malcy had gone into their house but had rushed out again to see what the screaming was about.

Granny said, 'Dae ye no' think ah've enough wi' ma arthritis, without givin' me a heart attack as well?'

'It wasn't my fault. He must have been driving too fast.'

'If he'd been drivin' too fast, he'd huv splattered ye aw over the road. Ye wernae lookin' where ye were goin'.'

'Och well,' Teresa said. 'You're all right, dear. That's the main thing.'

'Oh look,' Charlotte said. 'He's stopped at that big house at the end of the road. He's turned into that garage.'

'Well, thank you, Wincey,' Malcy said. 'That's all we needed to help us get on with our neighbours.'

Wincey felt like bursting into tears. She was still shaken and now angry with herself. More than anything she regretted giving Malcy a chance to score a point over her.

'Come on, Wincey.' Teresa began pushing Granny's wheelchair. 'We're all dead beat. It's time we were home. Good night, Malcy. Good night, Charlotte.'

Wincey gratefully followed Teresa away along Broomfield Road, and then round onto the Balgrayhill, where Erchie took over the chair. Granny said, 'Ma tongue's hangin' oot fur the want o' a cup o' tea.'

'All right, Granny. I'll put the kettle on as soon as we get in.'

Teresa hurried on in front and up the close to unlock the door. Wincey took off her coat and hat and scarf and in the privacy of her room, breathed deeply a few times before she could get control of her emotions. A cup of tea was a comfort and she was able to say, 'I'm sorry for giving everybody a fright. It was my fault, right enough. I was so taken up with waving the twins off.'

'Och, just forget about it, dear. You're all right. That's all that matters.'

Wincey drank another cup of tea before going to bed. Then she lay for a long time feeling strangely uneasy and apprehensive.

18

'I don't know what the world's coming to,' Virginia said. 'You would have thought that some kind of lesson would have been learned from the last war. But no. Did you see that terrible picture in the papers of that Chinese baby sitting among the debris of Shanghai's railway station, screaming for its dead mother? Poor wee thing.'

'I know.' Mathieson shook his head. 'The Japanese air force were responsible for that. But what about when the Chinese were supposed to be bombing Japanese warships on the river, and the bombs fell on an amusement park. Over a thousand civilians were killed that time. They reckon over two thousand civilians have been killed so far. That's the insanity of war. Life's short enough as it is, but instead of making the best of it, and learning how to live in peace with each other, the whole human race is hell bent on exterminating each other.'

Nicholas sighed. 'Burns knew what he was talking about. "Man's inhumanity to man", and it's not just the Japanese and the Chinese, by the look of it. The Germans and the Italian Fascists are just as crazy.'

'Yes,' Mathieson said, 'I don't like the sound of what's going on over there. Have you heard about the new 'concentration camp' the Nazis have built? Buchenwald, I think it's called. For years they've been these camps to imprison Jews, communists and trade unionists. But what signals have our government and our leaders been sending out? The Duke and Duchess of Windsor said they were charmed with Hitler and delighted by the Nazis. And look at the reception they got when they visited Germany. They certainly didn't give a damn about shaking hands with murderers.' Mathieson's face contorted with disgust. 'The aristocracy and all the religious leaders, including the Pope, have been doing the same old pals act. Have any of them condemned fascism or supported the Jewish people? Or the communists? Or the trade unionists? Not on your life! I'm sick to my soul of their hypocrisy.'

'I'm with you on that, James,' Nicholas said. 'Remember what the priest Camara said. "When I gave food to the poor, they called me a saint. When I asked why the poor were hungry, they called me a communist." '

'Yes,' Mathieson agreed, 'and it could apply to quite a few good socialists I've known.'

'If only someone like Maxton could stir things up and open people's eyes to what's really going on,' Nicholas said, 'But then again, I don't think he's been the same since Wheatley died. Wheatley had the long term vision.'

'The sad thing is' Nicholas continued, 'I don't think even Maxton could do much to influence the way things are going. It's just like last time—war's on its way and there seems to be no way of avoiding it. . . .'

Virginia had been making a pot of coffee. Now she filled the cups that were set out on the coffee table. Mathieson shook his head, then after a few sips of coffee, he said, 'How's the book going, Nicholas?'

'I've hit a tricky bit. I'm not sure where it should go from here.'

'What they call a writer's block, is it?'

'Not exactly. I've several choices and I'm just not sure which ones to take.'

'Would it help to talk about it?'

'Huh!' Virginia gave a sarcastic laugh. 'That'll be the day. Nicholas guards his writing as if he's got state secrets locked away in that room.'

'I used to talk to you about my writing,' he reminded her.

'That was a long time ago.'

'Yes.' Nicholas looked away. 'A lifetime, it seems now.'

'Well, it's not my fault you've changed,' Virginia snapped.

'For goodness' sake,' Mathieson said, 'nobody's said anything was your fault, Virginia. What's up with you these days? You're so touchy. I don't know how Nicholas puts up with you. No wonder he shuts himself away so much.'

'That's right.' Nothing made Virginia more furious than when Mathieson defended Nicholas. 'Gang up against me as usual. I'm getting sick of this.'

Putting down her coffee cup, she left the room.

'She's never been the same,' Nicholas told Mathieson, 'since Wincey disappeared. I don't know what to do. At the moment I couldn't share my writing with her, even if I wanted to. I'm in too much difficulty with it. I need all my concentration, but I keep getting distracted . . . I'm worried about Virginia.'

'She used to help you sort out difficulties.'

'Yes. But that was mostly with my poetry. Novels are different, and she wouldn't understand this one. I got the idea from Wincey's disappearance, you see. It's not Wincey but it is about a young girl who suddenly disappears.'

'I see.'

'I keep wondering what Virginia will think. It's death to the writing of a book if you feel someone's breathing down your neck all the time.'

'But she isn't. Time enough to worry about what anyone thinks once the book's in print.'

'That's normally my attitude. But this feels different.'

'It's only fiction. You're a novelist. Everyone knows that.'

'Yes, but . . . the girl in my book is still alive. I worry in case this could awaken the hope in Virginia that Wincey might still be alive. She's liable to grasp at any straws and I don't believe for one moment that my daughter is alive, James. I only wish the story I've worked out *could* be true. But it's only a story. And I'm just a storyteller.'

'A very good one, and much more, Nicholas.'

'Can you understand my dilemma, James? With Virginia, I mean.'

After a moment's silence, Mathieson nodded. 'Poor Virginia. You're right, of course. She hasn't been the same. Over the years, she has changed. But then I suppose we all have. She should realise that you loved Wincey as much as she did and you've suffered too. But life has to go on. It's over five years now, she can't go on grieving for ever. No-one would expect either of you to forget Wincey but life has to go on and there's your son to think of.'

Nicholas smiled. 'It's fortunate I suppose that Richard is so self-sufficient. I'm sure he felt as devastated as any of us about what happened five years ago but he's been getting on with his life. Doing very well in the RAF, by all accounts. Virginia thinks he looks very handsome in his uniform. She's very proud of him. So is my mother—she dotes on the lad, always has done. He's coming home this weekend.'

'That should cheer Virginia up.'

'I'm hoping so.'

'Can I give you a word of advice?'

'Fire away.'

'For God's sake, Nicholas, take the weekend off work. It might even help you. Maybe then you'd go back to it with a fresh mind and a new perspective.'

Nicholas looked worried again. 'I'll see.'

'Nicholas, you're not helping anyone by shutting yourself away so much.'

'It's the nature of this job. You've often said so yourself, James.'

'I know. But there's surely a limit. Anyway, I suspect that it's more than that. It's your method of escape. You've not properly accepted or faced the loss of your daughter, any more than Virginia has. Only she has no escape. And not much support from you either, by the look of it.'

Nicholas flushed with annoyance. 'Now that's not fair, and you know it, James. I don't work twenty-four hours a day. I do spend time with Virginia. But you see what happens when I do. It's like walking on eggshells.'

'Nicholas, just take the weekend off and be with your wife and son.'

For a few seconds, Nicholas looked like a trapped animal, then he suddenly capitulated. But not with good grace. 'Oh, all right, if it'll stop the pair of you nagging at me.'

'Cheers.' Mathieson lifted his coffee cup and took a careful sip. His twisted mouth made drinking and eating difficult but with careful concentration, he usually managed. Only rarely did he have a spill and he liked to have a napkin handy just in case.

'Is Richard going to get home for Christmas as well?'

'We're hoping so, but we're spending Christmas at my mother's this year. She insisted. She's still very strong willed, my mother.'

'Yes, I have noticed,' Mathieson said wrily.

'I'm sorry she's never very pleasant to you, James.'

'Oh, it doesn't bother me. We don't meet very often, after all.'

'We'll have the usual party here at Hogmanay though. You'll come to that, I hope.'

'Yes, I'll look forward to it.'

'What'll you do for Christmas? I hope you're not going to be on your own.'

'No, one of the other teachers at the college has invited me to his place on Christmas Day.'

'Good.'

Just then Virginia re-entered the room. 'What's good?'

'James has been invited to spend Christmas with one of his colleagues.'

'Did Nicholas tell you of the jolly Christmas we've to look forward to? Or at least, I have to look forward to. It'll be all right for him.'

'Here we go again,' Nicholas groaned. 'I don't know how much longer I'm going to be able to stand this.'

'How much *you'll* be able to stand this?'

Virginia's voice rose and suddenly Mathieson snapped, 'Oh, shut it, the pair of you. I'm off.'

'Oh, you're all right,' Virginia said bitterly. 'You can just walk away.'

'Virginia,' Mathieson said, his voice quiet again, 'look at me. And you say I'm all right.' With the help of his stick, he managed—but not without a struggle—to get up out of his chair.

'James, I'm sorry. Half the time I hardly know what I'm saying these days.'

'That's only too obvious, Virginia. And if you don't pull yourself together, you're not going to be all right. And that's putting it mildly.'

19

Wincey had been doing some shopping in the Co-op in Springburn Road when she heard the commotion. On approaching to investigate she discovered what was a fairly common occurrence in the winter. The cobbles were icy, causing a horse to slip and clatter down. On this occasion it was the coalman's horse.

'Come on, Mac,' the coalman was encouraging the terrified animal. 'Up ye come. Come on now, son.'

A crowd had gathered around watching in anxious sympathy as the beast struggled, with rolling eyes, to rear up and try to get hooves on the ground. Neighing loudly and struggling valiantly, it fought to reach a standing position. Then failing and crashing down again, it lay, eyes bulging, in helpless terror. Eventually the coalman was forced to loosen it out of its shafts. This took a bit of time and effort. Every strap and buckle had to be loosened until the animal lay free and had only itself to raise, with no shackling cart to make its task more difficult. Sparks flew from its hooves as, with a tremendous effort, it heaved itself up and found its balance.

As soon as this happened, a cheer went up from the crowd.

Wincey shared their relief. She was fond of horses. She remembered holidaying in the Highlands and being taught to ride a pony. It was one of the few really happy memories of her childhood.

She crossed the road, a shopping basket slung over her arm, and quickened her pace along Springburn Road. She had come out to do the shopping in her dinner break from the factory. Granny was suffering one of her bad turns and Teresa didn't like leaving her to go out to the shops. Wincey was very conscientious about taking time off work and never took advantage of her senior position in the firm. She expected her employees to be conscientious workers and time keepers, and believed that bosses should show a good example. The employees knew, of course, that there were occasions when she had to be away from the factory on business, and that was different.

Unfortunately, Malcy was neither as conscientious nor as good a worker as he used to be. He often disappeared from the factory floor and on more than one such occasion, Wincey had seen him with the local bookie. She tried to keep her mouth shut and not say anything, either to Malcy or to Charlotte. She felt it was Charlotte's responsibility to speak to Malcy and had no doubt that if she did complain to either of them, she would only be met by indignation and anger. In the first place, Malcy would deny his gambling and Charlotte would be only too eager to believe him. She'd heard him tell Charlotte when he'd returned to the factory after over three hours' absence that he'd been helping someone who had been involved in an accident. He described how he had administered first aid and then gone with the man to the hospital. It has been one of the occasions when Wincey had been out negotiating a new order. Returning along Springburn Road, she'd seen Malcy so she knew that he was lying.

And what a liar he was. He had looked genuinely offended and hurt at Charlotte, when she had asked him in her usual gentle way where he'd been.

'It's too bad if the husband of the owner can't take a few hours off for whatever reason, and not be quizzed like a common criminal when he returns.'

Charlotte had been upset and effusive in her apologies. He had taken his time in grudgingly forgiving her. Wincey felt like killing him and it was only with great difficulty that she managed to control her feelings.

By the time she reached the close, she was quite out of breath with hurrying the Balgrayhill, carrying the heavy shopping basket. She had forgotten her key and had to pull the door bell. A harassed Teresa opened the door and immediately turned back along the hall and into the kitchen.

'Granny's not been at all well. I was just saying that I think we should send for the doctor.'

'Och,' Granny said, 'fur aw the good he is, we might as well save oor money.'

'Now, now, Granny. Surely he can do something for you.'

'The same as he aye does. Gives me more painkillers an' if ah get any stronger wans, they'll be knockin' me unconscious. Ah'm half asleep aw the time as it is.'

'Well, at least we could get a prescription for more, so that we have plenty in reserve for you, Granny. I wouldn't like you to go short, and maybe run out on a Sunday when all the chemists are shut.'

'Och, please yersel'. Ye'll dae that anyway.'

'I could go to the surgery for the prescription, Teresa,' Wincey said. 'I could run along for it now.'

'You've had nothing to eat yet, dear.'

'It doesn't matter.'

'Yes it does. You can go for it after work, on your way home maybe. There's enough to keep Granny going just now. Just you sit down and have some stovies. And there's apple and custard for pudding. Erchie's been and away.'

'The coalman's horse fell down the road,' Wincey said as she took off her coat and draped it across the back of the chair. She kept her hat on. 'The poor beast was terrified but the coalman loosened it from its shafts and it managed to get up. It was still trembling though.'

Teresa dished a steaming hot plate of the potato, onion and sausage mixture.

'Och, the poor beast,' Teresa sympathised.

Granny said, in between groans of pain, 'Ah once saw wan gettin' shot. It broke its legs goin' doon.'

'Oh dear. Could you manage a wee spoonful or two of stovies, Granny?'

'Well, starvin' me's no' goin' tae be likely tae cure ma pain, is it?

Teresa settled herself on a chair beside Granny and began feeding her with careful spoonfuls. Granny usually managed to feed herself but today her hands had swollen up.

'I hope Charlotte's taking her share of the work nowadays, Wincey,' Teresa said unexpectedly.

'Oh yes, I've no complaints about Charlotte.'

'It's just I get the feeling you're getting the heavy end of the stick these days, dear.'

It was true that Charlotte was taking time off but that was as a result of Malcy persuading her to have occasional days in Edinburgh. Actually, they'd had quite a few days in Edinburgh now. He'd also taken her—for a special treat, he said—to the races at Ayr and they planned to go there again. Perhaps Charlotte had mentioned this to Teresa, but Wincey would never be disloyal to Charlotte, even to her mother. Charlotte genuinely loved Malcy and he could twist her round his little finger. That was Charlotte's trouble.

Wincey wondered how much money Malcy had bet at the races. No doubt a great deal. Surely Charlotte must realise now that Malcy was a compulsive gambler. At least Wincey hoped Charlotte wasn't still fooling herself. For the sake of the business, Charlotte must see the danger that might lie ahead if she didn't do something about Malcy.

Wincey tried to reason with herself that Charlotte would continue to think of the interests of the business, as she'd always done in the past. But at the back of her mind, there was a feeling of apprehension and worry. All she said to Teresa, however, was 'Honestly, I'm fine. Everything's fine.' The last thing she wanted to do was to add to Teresa's worries. Teresa had enough to do caring for Granny.

'Do you think we'll be able to visit Florence next week, Granny,' she asked the old woman. 'She's looking forward to showing us all around her new house.'

Granny nodded. 'Ah hope so, hen. Ah cannae thole tae be as bad as this for much longer.' The only consolation Granny had was that when really bad attacks flared up, they usually only lasted for a few days before calming down again.

Florence and Eddie had managed to get a two-room and kitchen bottom flat in Second Avenue, Radnor Park, and they had been doing it up. No-one was allowed to visit until the house was looking the very best they could make it. They were terribly proud of it. The family had been invited for lunch the following Sunday. Up till now, it had always been 'dinner' in the middle of the day in working-class homes. But for some time now, Florence had—as Wincey could imagine Mrs Cartwright saying—'ideas above her station'. The twins had become much the same. They both lived in Dumbarton Road now. They hadn't managed to get houses up the same close, although they had tried hard enough, but their houses were only a few closes away from each other. Euphemia, now Mrs Grant, had a top flat. Bridget, now Mrs Ferguson, lived one up. Both had one-room and kitchen houses.

'It'll give you something to look forward to, Granny,' Teresa comforted.

Wincey finished her stovies and began tucking in to her pudding. Immediately afterwards, she struggled into her coat again. 'I'm away. See you later on.'

'All right, dear.'

Hurrying towards the factory, Wincey wondered if she could discuss the problem about Malcy with Erchie. She decided against it. Erchie was friendly with Malcy, always had been, and Erchie himself enjoyed what he called 'a wee flutter'. To criticise Malcy's gambling could risk Erchie becoming defensive and thinking that she was also casting aspersions at his gambling. In truth, she didn't mind in the least Erchie having his wee flutter, because that was all it was. He worked hard, earned his wages, and was entitled to spend them in whatever way he wished. They all contributed a share of their wages to the housekeeping, and what Erchie did with the rest of his own money was a matter for him and Teresa. Wincey had long ago insisted that she paid the biggest share because, after all, as a partner she had more money than him. She was too fond of Erchie now to risk offending him or making him feel guilty.

She was no sooner back at the factory office when a crisis erupted beside one of the machines. One of the women had tripped on something, and as she fell, her head banged against the corner of one of the tables. Her forehead was bleeding from a cut. It didn't look very deep and the girl said she would be all right, although she looked very shaken. Wincey said, 'It might need a few stitches. I'll take you to the doctor.'

The girl protested that she didn't want to go to the doctor's, or to bother anyone, but Wincey insisted. 'I've a prescription to pick up anyway.' She fetched a towel from the office and told the girl to hold it against her forehead. Then she led the white-faced girl out to Springburn Road. The doctor's surgery was only a few blocks away. Wincey had never had occasion to visit the surgery before but she had met the old doctor when he had visited Granny. Granny complained that all he ever did when anybody went to the surgery was asked them if their bowels had moved that day, then stuck a thermometer in their mouth. A receptionist led the girl into the doctor's room. Eventually she re-emerged to join Wincey.

'Gosh,' she whispered. 'You should see the handsome doctor. He gave me three stitches and I didn't feel a thing. I was so excited.'

'Handsome?' Wincey echoed in surprise, remembering the

white haired Doctor Houston.

Just then, the doctor emerged from the room, but it wasn't the Doctor Houston she'd seen before. Wincey immediately recognised him, however, as the driver of the car which had nearly run her down. He was looking across at her, and she suddenly made up her mind. She went over to him.

'I believe I owe you an apology. I was upset the other evening, and I behaved badly. I am sorry.'

He smiled with his eyes as well as his mouth. 'Apology accepted, Miss—?'

'Gourlay.'

'Not one of the Gourlays of Gourlays' factory?'

'Yes, one of the Gourlays of Gourlays' factory.'

'How interesting. My father has quite a few patients from there. He tells me it has a very good reputation.'

'Thank you. Are you Doctor Houston's son then?'

'Yes, I am.'

'Well, perhaps you could give me Mrs Gourlay senior's prescription for painkillers, please. I promised I'd collect it.'

'I'll go and look it up.'

In a minute or two he'd returned with the prescription, but he said, 'You can take this just now, but I think I ought to pay Mrs Gourlay a visit. She may need a change of medication.'

'Oh?' Wincey was taken aback. 'She didn't really ask for a visit.'

'Nevertheless, I'll call to see her this evening. I noticed by her record she lives quite near me. I'm round in Broomfield Road. I'll call on my way home.'

'All right,' Wincey said uncertainly. 'I'll tell her to expect you.'

He stood watching her as she led the girl away. She could feel his eyes burning into her back. Suddenly she felt nervous and upset, but she didn't know why.

20

'It wasn't the old doctor,' Wincey explained to Granny and Teresa. 'It was his son.'

'Ye knew fine ah didnae want a visit.'

'I told him, but he insisted. What could I do? He passes here on his way home, he said.'

'Ah dinnae like the sound o' him.'

'He's good looking, Granny. Strong chin and very dark eyes.'

'Oh yes?' Teresa laughed. 'Are you sure it's Granny he's coming to see?'

Wincey's heart began to thump but it wasn't with pleasure. She didn't want any man to be interested in her. She didn't want anything to do with men. She could cope with them in the line of business, but that was all.

'Here, Granny, would you look at her blushing,' Teresa said. 'Maybe she's found a sweetheart at last.'

'Teresa, don't be ridiculous,' Wincey snapped. 'I've only seen the man once and he's a doctor.'

'A doctor's still a man, dear, and you know you can call me a hopeless romantic if you like, but I do believe in love at first sight.'

'For goodness' sake,' Wincey groaned, and left the kitchen.

In the privacy of her room, she took deep, calming breaths. There was absolutely no need for her to feel threatened, she kept telling herself. She had just managed to calm herself, and was on her way back to the kitchen, when the doorbell jangled. As she was nearest to the door, she was forced to go and open it. Doctor Houston towered in the doorway.

'Good evening, Doctor,' Wincey said stiffly. 'Do come in.'

He followed her into the kitchen. 'Mrs Gourlay senior and Mrs Teresa Gourlay,' she introduced. 'Granny, this is the doctor I was telling you about.'

Doctor Houston nodded a greeting to Teresa, then he went over to crouch down beside Granny and gently took one of her swollen hands in his. Then he looked down at her feet.

'Your ankles and feet look awfully painful too, Mrs Gourlay.'

'Och, ah'm sore aw over, Doctor. Even ma jaws. Ah cannae even eat wi' ma teeth in nowadays. Ah cannae walk or do nothin'. An' tae think ah wis aye that active. If ye'd seen me a few years ago, ye wouldnae huv recognised me.'

'Yes,' Teresa agreed, 'Granny was out there marching behind Johnny Maclean. She was in the middle of the riot in George Square as well. You wouldn't be born then, Doctor, but maybe you'd have heard of it.'

The doctor smiled. 'Oh, I was born then, all right. And I remember it very well.'

Granny said, 'It wis the polis that started the riot. They charged at a crowd of unarmed men, women an' weans. But ah got a hold o' wan o' the polis an' me an' some other women stripped him naked. Mair than wan o' the polis, in fact, by the end o' it. By Jove, that done for them. They didnae know where tae put themselves.'

Doctor Houston laughed. 'Good for you, Mrs Gourlay. I like a woman of spirit. Now, I'll tell you what I'd like to do to help you.'

'Och, ah've got a big enough stock o' painkillers as it is.'

144

'No, I didn't mean that. There are other drugs. I'd like to try dealing with that inflammation in another way. There's quite a variety of new treatments. I believe some of them would help you, including diets and special baths. But for that you really need to be in hospital and have full time supervision and nursing.'

Granny looked startled and frightened. 'Ye're no' puttin' me away intae any hospital. Ah'm stayin' here in ma ain hame.'

Wincey said, 'It wouldn't be forever, Granny, and if it would really help you—'

'You shut yer mooth. Ye've nae right. Ye're no' even a Gourlay.'

The doctor flicked a curious look at Wincey before saying, 'Only for a few weeks. Think of the relief of pain. You'd be made so much more comfortable. I promise you, you'd be well looked after.'

'Ma Teresa looks aifter me well enough. Ye wouldnae want tae get rid o' me, would ye, hen?'

'No, of course not, Granny. Nobody wants to get rid of you, dear.' Teresa turned to the doctor. 'I'll do my best. She would be so unhappy away from the family.'

'Well,' Doctor Houston said reluctantly, 'I still think she would be better in hospital. But if that's how you both feel, I'll write a prescription for the new treatment and I'll pop in as often as I can to keep a check on her.'

'Thank you, Doctor,' Teresa said.

But Wincey detected a note of fatigue in Teresa's voice and couldn't help thinking that Granny was being selfish, expecting Teresa to cope with so much. It was bad enough with two of them—and often Erchie as well—struggling to lift and lay the old woman. Wincey made a decision.

'Doctor, would it be possible for a nurse to come in, say a couple of hours—perhaps twice every day—to help Teresa. I could afford to pay for a nurse so there wouldn't be a financial problem.'

Doctor Houston nodded. 'Yes, that would be better. Leave it to me. I'll arrange it as soon as possible.'

'Dinnae bother askin' me of course,' Granny said. 'Ah'm just a poor auld woman.'

'It's more for Teresa's sake,' Wincey said firmly. 'She'll be having to go to hospital soon if we go on much longer as we have been. She needs help.'

'Aye, well . . .' Granny said, slightly mollified. 'For aw the help she gets frae you!'

'Now, now, Granny. That's not fair. You know fine Wincey does her best to help whenever she's at home. She's working all day, don't forget.'

'Aye, well . . .' Granny muttered.

'Two nurses would really be needed,' the doctor said. 'I was thinking especially of getting you in and out of the bath.'

'Two nurses!' Granny echoed incredulously. 'Huv they nothin' better tae dae?'

The doctor laughed. Then to Wincey he said, 'Will that be all right with you?'

'Yes, of course.'

At the outside door, he turned to Wincey and asked, 'May I ask what relation you are to the Gourlays?'

'I'm sorry. I'd rather not answer that question.'

The doctor shrugged. 'Very well.' But his eyes betrayed his interest. Wincey closed the door after he'd gone and leaned against it for a minute. Curiosity about her real identity was the last thing she wanted. She wished she'd thought of some imaginary explanation that he could have accepted, and then forgotten about. He looked a man who would not rest until he got to the bottom of any mystery, medical or otherwise. She felt annoyed, as well as afraid.

As if she hadn't enough to worry her at the moment with Charlotte and Malcy. In the first place, Charlotte had taken a very large sum of money from the business in order to buy the villa in Broomfield Road. Renting a house wasn't good enough for Malcy. Wincey hadn't said anything at the time, for Charlotte's sake. Charlotte had been so happy in her lovely home with her loving husband, and still was. But expenses of one kind or another were piling up, just as Wincey had always feared. A time would come when she'd have to say something, for the sake of the business if nothing else.

'Well,' said Granny, when Wincey returned to the kitchen, 'ye've opened a right can o' worms.'

Wincey secretly agreed with her but she was thinking of a different can of worms from Granny.

'It's a miracle ah'm no' gettin' pit away. If it had been up tae you, ah wid. Bad enough strangers invadin' the house. God knows whit they'll dae tae me.'

'They'll make you feel better and more comfortable, Granny,' Wincey said. 'And you'll soon get to know them and look forward to their daily visits. Try to think of Teresa, Granny. If she loses any more weight, there'll be nothing left of her.'

'Aye, well . . .'

While Teresa was filling the kettle at the sink and Wincey was getting cups and saucers out of the press, Teresa whispered, 'Thank you, dear.'

Wincey felt a wave of gladness then. She had done something that would, she felt sure, be of real help to Teresa. To herself too, of course. They both missed the assistance of Florence and the twins. Now, to come home from a hard day's work every day to face the struggle of looking after all the old woman's needs was proving to be extremely exhausting. It was far worse for Teresa, who was tied to Granny the whole day.

'I see what you mean,' Teresa said, as she poured the tea. 'About him being good looking. If I was a bit younger I'd fall for him myself.'

'I haven't fallen for him,' Wincey protested. 'Will you get that idea out of your head. I'm perfectly satisfied and happy with my life as it is now. I like to be independent, and you've said yourself often enough in the past, I'm a loner. That's exactly what I'd like to remain, Teresa.'

'Yes, dear, you may believe that now. But one day you're bound to—'

'No, I'm not,' Wincey interrupted. 'Now, can we please change the subject.'

Teresa helplessly shook her head. 'You're a funny girl at times. Most girls would jump at the chance of a good looking doctor. He finds you attractive, dear. I could see.'

'Teresa!' Wincey groaned.

'All right, all right,' Teresa capitulated. 'Not another word.'

They sat in silence for a minute or two, sipping their tea and gathering strength for the back-breaking task of getting Granny undressed, wheeled to the bathroom, lifted in and out of the bath, then lowered at last on to her hurly bed.

21

There could be no hiding from the fact that the doctor was going above and beyond the call of duty. He was visiting the Gourlay house practically every day on his way home. Erchie had eventually remarked, 'Ah think he's adopted this place as his second home.' The doctor now regularly stayed to enjoy the cups of tea and home-baked scones that Teresa offered him. He now called everyone by their first names, except Granny, who was just Granny to everyone.

Teresa widened her eyes in mock innocence at Erchie's remark. 'I wonder why, Erchie. Is it my scones, do you think?'

'Aye, well,' Granny said, 'it's no' me. Ah hardly get a second glance noo. It's time that you'—she glanced across at Wincey—'woke up an' put the poor fella oot o' his misery.'

'His misery?' Wincey said. ' He looks happy enough to me. And I never asked him to keep coming here. It's ridiculous.'

'Now, now, Wincey. Do you not think it could be you being ridiculous, dear? What can you possibly have against that nice, kindly, good looking man?'

'Nothing. Nothing.' Wincey cried out in desperation. 'I just . . . I just can't be doing with it.'

Seeing Wincey's genuine distress, Teresa asked worriedly, 'With what, dear?'

'I can't talk about it. I'm going out before he comes.' She got up and went for her coat.

'Wincey,' Teresa called. 'It's blowing a blizzard. You can't go out.'

But the front door had banged shut and Wincey was away.

Granny said, 'There's something far wrong wi' that girl.'

'I think you might be right, Granny. I'm really worried about her.'

Erchie said, 'Aye, it's no' natural, the way she works aw the time an' never goes oot tae enjoy hersel' like other lassies. An' ah'll tell ye another thing—she cannae thole bein' touched.'

'How do you mean?' Teresa asked in surprise. 'I've never noticed anything different about her there. She's always been very demonstrative with me. More so often than Florence or the twins. You've surely seen her giving me a hug often enough.'

'Aye,' Erchie said, 'but no' me. Huv ye ever seen her gie *me* a hug? An' ah've long since learned no' tae touch her. Even if ah put ma hand on her shoulder, she shrinks away as if ah'm gonnae attack her or somethin'. Even after aw this time an' her knowin' fine ah widnae hurt a hair on her heid, any mair than ah wid ma ain flesh an' blood.'

'I wonder,' Teresa said thoughtfully, 'if you've maybe solved the mystery there, Erchie.'

'How dae ye mean, hen?'

'I wonder if poor Wincey was attacked before she came here. Remember how Florence found her crying in the street, poor wee soul. Maybe that's why she was crying.'

'Aye, right enough, hen. That'd explain a lot o' things about oor Wincey, right enough. It must have been some swine o' a man as well. She's fine wi' everybody else, but see if any man even looks at her in what she thinks is the wrong way, she either explodes wi' anger at him, or gets off her mark, just like she's done the night.'

'Oh dear, poor Wincey. I wonder what we should do, Erchie.'

Granny was quick to answer. 'Keep yer neb oot o' other folks' business.'

'How can you say that, Granny? Don't you care about Wincey?'

'Ah'm sayin' that because ah know the chances are ye'll just make things worse for Wincey. Ye're mair likely tae frighten the life oot o' her than be any help tae her.'

'You don't know that at all, Granny.'

'Ah know,' Erchie said. 'How about askin' the doctor for advice? That's his job, helping folk.'

'Huh,' Granny snorted. 'Wincey's gonnae love the pair o' ye fur that!'

'Now, now, Granny. She doesn't need to know. This would be a good chance tonight while she's not here. I'll have a quiet word with Doctor Houston. It can't do any harm.'

'Huh! Did ye come up the Clyde in a banana boat?'

'Come on, Ma. Teresa's just trying her best tae help Wincey.'

It was then the door bell rang.

'That'll be him.' Teresa rose in some agitation. 'Should I take him through to the room, do you think? Have a private word there?'

'Aye, you dae that, hen. Then Granny'll no' get the chance tae poke her nose in.'

'Me! Poke ma nose in?' Granny howled. 'Whit dae ye think she's doin'?'

Teresa hurried from the kitchen.

'Oh, come in, Doctor. Eh, would you mind coming through to the sitting room first? I'd like a wee word in private.'

He made a gesture with one hand to indicate that Teresa should lead the way. Once in the room, Teresa sat down and asked him to do the same. For a moment, there was silence and then Doctor Houston said gently, 'Would you like to tell me what's worrying you, Teresa?'

Teresa nodded. 'It's about Wincey.'

'Oh?' His expression, his whole body, tensed with interest. 'What about Wincey?'

'Well, it's difficult to explain, and of course we could be wrong . . .'

'About what, Teresa?' he prompted.

'Well, we've come to notice over the years that she keeps clear of men. Won't have anything to do with them. She even dislikes my son-in-law, and a nicer man and a better husband to my daughter you couldn't meet. The only man she gets on with is Erchie, but even he tells me he daren't touch her, take her arm or anything. It seems to make her frightened.' Teresa hesitated. 'We've been wondering . . . We've wondered if she had a bad experience at some time in her young life.'

Another silence followed. Then Doctor Houston said, 'First of all, Teresa, can I ask how you came to know Wincey? She's not a relation, is she?'

Teresa shook her head. 'Will you promise to keep this strictly between you and me, Doctor. She'd never forgive me otherwise, and maybe we'd lose her forever. I couldn't bear that—she's like a daughter to me.'

'What passes between doctor and patient is always strictly confidential, Teresa. You have my word on that.'

'Well,' Teresa began unhappily, 'years ago, Florence found her sitting in the street crying and brought her home with her. She said that Wincey's mother and father had been killed in an accident and she'd nobody. So the authorities were going to put her in an orphanage—or the workhouse, Florence said. But I have to confess, Doctor, that Florence used to be troubled with a terrible imagination. She's mostly grown out of it now but at the time—'

'What did Wincey say?' the doctor interrupted. 'Did she do along with this story?'

'The poor wee thing was in such a state, I think she would have agreed with anything as long as we didn't put her out in the street again.'

'And she's never spoken about her background since?'

'Not a word. She immediately clams up if we mention it, or ask her any questions. We've given up trying. We're just glad to accept her as one of the family. But now we're getting really worried about her.' Teresa avoided his eyes for a moment. 'If you'll forgive me, Doctor, she seems to have got worse since you've been calling so often. Tonight she ran out in all this weather, just so that she wouldn't be here when you arrived.'

The doctor stared at Teresa in silence for what seemed a very long time. Then he said, 'Leave this with me just now, Teresa. I'll have to give this matter some serious thought, and also make a few discreet enquiries.'

'Oh, Doctor, please don't let Wincey or anybody . . . *anybody*,' she repeated, 'know anything about this.'

'I assure you, you've no need to worry. I'll be very discreet, very discreet indeed. Rest assured, Teresa, this is strictly between you and me.'

Teresa sighed. 'Erchie and Granny know I was going to talk to you. Erchie won't say anything, but I'd better warn Granny.'

Doctor Houston smiled. 'Tell her I'll pack her off to the hospital if she says one word. That'll do the trick.'

Teresa rose. 'Thank you so much, Doctor. I feel a bit better now that I've confided in you.'

He rose too. 'I'd better say good evening to Granny. And I'd especially appreciate my usual cup of tea tonight.'

'Come on through, then, and I'll put the kettle on.'

Granny greeted him with, 'Aye, well, huv ye had a good gossip then? Are ye gonnae interfere in Wincey's life as well?'

'I don't gossip, Granny,' the doctor said with the patient good humour he always showed the old woman, 'and my concern is for the happiness and well-being of my patients, especially you.'

'Aye, well, you watch ye dinnae open a can o' worms that'll destroy oor Wincey.'

Doctor Houston gazed at her very seriously. 'Granny, listen to me now. I'll do nothing, nothing, do you hear, that would ever hurt Wincey in any way. Trust me. And I want to be able to trust you. I want you to promise me that you won't mention to Wincey anything that's been done or said in her absence this evening. It's especially important that Wincey does not know that Teresa has spoken to me about her. Do you promise me?'

'Aye, well, ah suppose so.'

'Right.' He smiled again. 'Now, where's my tea?'

22

Time passed and they heard nothing from Doctor Houston. Christmas came and went, then Hogmanay was nearly upon them and still he hadn't made an appearance. There were no more visits, either to see Granny or for any other reason. They all wondered about this. Wincey thought, with a mixture of sadness and relief, that he had given up on her at last. Teresa, Erchie and Granny wondered if he was busy finding out about Wincey's past.

Eventually Teresa asked the nurses when Doctor Houston was coming back to see Granny. The nurses said that they were to report regularly on Granny's condition and if the improvements she was now enjoying ceased, or if in their judgement she needed a visit, they were to contact the surgery.

'We haven't of course, because Granny is so much better. All she needs is her present treatment to continue. Anyway, involving him would be a last resort as far as we are concerned. Doctor Houston has enough on his plate.'

'How do you mean?' Teresa asked.

'He's had a very heavy workload because Doctor Houston senior became ill a while ago, and then started getting worse and worse. And well, I'm sorry to say he died yesterday morning.'

'Oh dear, I'm so sorry to hear that. We knew the old man was semi-retired but just thought it was his age. We've known him for years. Oh, I am sorry.'

'He wisnae a bad soul,' Granny conceded, 'but aw he ever asked wis . . .'

'Yes, all right, Granny. We know all about that,' Teresa hastily interrupted. 'It's a bad time of year to suffer a bereavement too. It won't be a happy New Year for Doctor Houston.'

As soon as Wincey came in from work, Teresa told her the news.

'Such a nice old man too,' she added.

'Aye,' Granny said, 'but aw he ever did was ask if yer bowels had moved an' stuck a—'

'Yes, all right, Granny, you've told us that before.'

Granny's memory was beginning to fail her and she often forgot she'd already said something. Or she couldn't remember what she wanted to say. But physically she was a good deal better. The swelling of her hands and feet had gone down and as a result she wasn't in nearly so much pain.

'Ah just wish ah'd got the son earlier. If ah had, ah might no' huv been stuck in this chair the day.'

One of the nurses said, 'I believe Doctor Houston junior worked in the Royal before. He came into the practice to help his father once the old man began to go downhill.'

'Actually,' Wincey said, 'I found out earlier on today. The obituary was in today's *Glasgow Herald*. I was going to tell you.'

The nurses were ready to leave. They had settled Granny in her hurly bed although it was, as usual, far too early for bed time. Granny had indignantly—and loudly—objected at first.

'Ah'm no' a wee wean that has tae be in bed the back o' six o'clock.'

'You can sit up in bed for as long as you like,' the nurse told her, ' but at least you're in bed. This way it'll save Teresa and Wincey struggling to undress you and get you down.'

Granny grumbled and muttered, but eventually accepted defeat. The nurses had become too valuable and important in Granny's life for her to want to cross them. Often she looked quite anxious if they were late in arriving. They came every morning to get her up and bathe her, and then every evening to settle her down. She even had once admitted to Teresa, 'You aye did yer best, hen. Ah know that. But by Jove, them nurses really help me. They make me feel that much better. Ah don't know what ah'd do without them now.'

Tonight, however, she had been—as she told the nurses—'black affronted'. 'It's Hogmanay. Ah cannae be sittin' here in bed an' aw ma clothes off when the first foots arrive.'

'All the more need that we get you settled,' the nurse said. 'Nobody would be able to do anything for you by the time they have a few drinks. You're wearing your nice shawl—you look fine.'

And so Granny accepted defeat again.

Teresa sighed. 'It'll kind of dampen any enjoyment of our Hogmanay thinking of the sad time it is for poor Doctor Houston.'

'Och, he'll huv his family around him for support,' Granny told her. 'An' ah'm sure he widnae want us tae be down in the dumps. Our time'll come soon enough.'

'I don't think he has any family. He was an only child, as far as I know. And his mother's long dead.'

'Och, there'll be aunties an' uncles an' cousins. They aw come oot the woodwork at funerals. It wis the only time ah used tae see aw ma relations.'

'I suppose you're right, Granny. I wonder if I should ask Mr McCluskey to come in for a wee while. I feel sorry for him in this freezing weather. He has to sit out in that draughty close to have his smoke. I've asked him more than once to come in here to enjoy his pipe but I think he was frightened he'd get a row from her.'

'Mind he did come in once,' Granny said.

'Yes, but she was away in town that day.'

'Here,' Granny suddenly chortled. 'Ah could solve his problem. Aw he needs tae dae is get merrit tae me. Ah'd soon sort that wan oot.'

Wincey laughed. 'I believe you'd do it if you were given half a chance, Granny.'

'Her trouble,' Granny said, 'is she cares more about her bloomin' hoose than her auld father. Aye scrubbin' an' polishin'.'

'I know,' Teresa agreed. 'I even saw her out the back sweeping the middens. And dusting the railings. Dusting the railings! Would you credit it?'

Granny rolled her eyes.

Teresa said, 'Mrs Chalmers is coming and Davy and Jock from up the stairs. I asked young Mrs Beresford but she said she was going to stay with her folks over New Year. They come from somewhere over in the West End.'

The mention of the West End startled Wincey but she managed to calm herself, Hundreds, if not thousands of people lived in the West End. Mrs Beresford's parents would no doubt live in the tenements, not in one of the big villas. Also, Mrs Beresford hardly ever saw anyone in the Gourlay house, far less spoke to them, so how could she know about anybody's background?

'I think she must be a young widow,' Teresa said, 'and she's had to go back out to work. She's always dashing away, isn't she? Never has time to talk.'

'Or disnae want tae,' Granny said. 'Stuck up, probably.'

'No, dear. I don't think so. She's got quite a nice smile. Just a bit harassed. I wonder what it is she does. Anyway, she'll not be here for Hogmanay.'

'Did ye warn Malcy nae tae first foot us, him wi' his fair heid?'

'Yes, don't worry, Granny. He knows it's bad luck. No, Davy from up the stairs is dark enough. I've told him to knock the door first.'

Wincey was thinking that Malcy could bring them enough bad luck without being their first foot.

'Well,' Teresa said to Wincey. 'We've had our tea, dear. Yours is in the oven. This is my day for acting house proud. That's why Erchie is away out the road. It's bad luck not to have everything spotless to greet the new year.'

Wincey used a tea towel to lift her plate of stew and dumplings from the oven. Then she settled at the table to enjoy the meal.

'Wait till I've finished this,' she told Teresa, 'and I'll give you a hand. Although the place looks spotless already.'

'Yes, well, I've cleaned and dusted the rooms and the lobby. But I've still this floor to scrub. I'll leave emptying the ash pan to the last minute. Maybe you could do the brasses, dear.'

'I could scrub the floor as well.'

'No, no, dear. I'll manage the floor. It won't take a minute. But I must change that bed first. Could you go through and change yours?'

'As soon as I finish my tea.'

By eleven o'clock the house was sparkling and Teresa and Wincey had spread a crisp white tablecloth over the table and were now setting it with plates of fruitcake, cherry cake, Madeira cake, black bun and shortbread. Erchie was laying out the bottles and glasses.

'Whisky for the men,' he said, 'an' plenty beer. Sherry an' gin for the women.'

'I hope you've got soft drinks as well, dear.'

'Soft drinks?' Erchie cried out in disbelief. 'Who's goin' tae want soft drinks?'

'I mean to put in the gin, Erchie, like tonic water.'

'Oh aye, ah've got some o' that.' He rubbed his hands in glee as he surveyed the table. 'A good spread, eh?' He turned to Granny. 'You look grand as well, hen.'

Granny's hair was well slicked down and held in place not by her usual brown kirby-grip, but a fancy one with a sprinkle of tiny diamante. The new grip had been one of her Christmas presents from Wincey, who had also given her the beautiful crocheted shawl that was now draped around her plump shoulders.

She looked pleased at Erchie's compliment but she said, 'But son, dae ah no' look daft sittin' here in ma bed? What'll folk think?'

'Och Ma, ye're an auld woman, an' ye're no' well. Everybody'll just admire ye for bein' sae spunky. Relax an' enjoy yersel'.'

'Aye, well, put another cushion at ma back, would ye?'

'Sure, Ma.'

The fire crackled brightly as they settled around it, all gazing up at the alarm clock on the mantelpiece as it ticked away the last few seconds of 1937. Then suddenly Erchie got up and rushed over to tug the kitchen window open. Everybody for miles around was doing the same thing, allowing the old year out and the new year in, and hopefully with it, good fortune. There were shouts of 'A Guid New Year' all around, both outside and inside the kitchen.

The new year greetings inside the kitchen, however, could hardly be heard for the riotous sounds from the river of the ships' hooters. Then there was a loud battering at the door. Teresa ran to open it wide and welcome in their first foot.

'Davy, Happy New Year.' She gave him a hug and a kiss. Davy grinned and blushed and handed over the lucky piece of coal, the packet of shortbread and his bottle of whisky.

'No dear, you keep a hold of your bottle so that you can offer Erchie and the other men a drink from it.'

'Oh, aye, right.' Davy was obviously not very used to socialising. Either that or he was a bit shy. Or both.

Behind him crowded Jock and Mrs Chalmers and, coming up noisily behind, Mrs McGregor from the old close, and Mrs Donaldson and her two plump bespectacled daughters, Mary and Joan, who were famous locally for their romantic but unintentionally hilarious duets. The merry crowd made for the kitchen where they knew the table would be loaded with the usual festive fare. Everyone made a great fuss of Granny and plied her with drink from each of their bottles. Soon Granny was insisting on treating the company to a song.

As Erchie said next day, she was giving it such big licks, she nearly fell out of the bed. Even Wincey had become a little tipsy but, although she laughed with the rest and joined in the community singing, she felt secretly weighed down by sadness. She wondered how her mother and father would be bringing in the New Year and her brother and her grandmother. Normally she never allowed herself to think about them. Now she realised that although she had adopted a new family and loved them dearly, her feelings for her original family were still there, buried deep in her heart. She could have wept, yet no-one noticed that anything was wrong.

Afterwards, Wincey blamed the drink and vowed to avoid alcohol in future. She had been reminded of what Granny had once said when talking of how she'd felt when she'd lost her other children with the fever. 'Ma hairt wis sair.' Wincey's heart had felt sore too.

1938

23

Wincey was about to enter the office when she heard something most unusual. It was Charlotte's voice raised in—perhaps not anger exactly—but certainly acute exasperation. She was saying, 'I couldn't give you a week's wages in advance, even if I wanted to. Wincey keeps the books and sees to the wages. Anyway, Malcy, what have you done with all your money? You get paid enough, and it's not as if you put any of it into the housekeeping. I'm paying for everything now. No, I'm not going to be soft-soaped any more, Malcy. We're already taking more money than we should out of the business. No, Malcy, please . . .'

Wincey felt self-conscious standing outside the office door. Everybody at the machines behind her could see her. It might look odd if she suddenly walked away. She turned the door handle and went in. Malcy had his arms around Charlotte and was trying to kiss her.

'Oh, sorry,' Wincey said and made to leave again, but Charlotte called out, 'No, it's all right, Wincey. Come in. Malcy was just leaving. I'll see you when I get home, Malcy.'

His pale eyes were cold with annoyance as they met Wincey's

for a brief second, but he smiled back at Charlotte before leaving.

'See you later then.'

'Trouble?' Wincey asked after he'd gone.

'You'd like that, wouldn't you?' Charlotte said with some bitterness. 'You've always had it in for Malcy.'

'No!' Wincey protested. 'I've never wanted trouble for you, Charlotte. I swear it. Or for Malcy. But it's his gambling, Charlotte. That's what's always worried me. And it's got worse, we both know it has.'

Charlotte avoided Wincey's eyes and her voice was barely audible. 'I'll speak to him.'

For all the good that'll do, Wincey thought, but decided it would be wiser to let the subject drop—for the moment, at least.

Later, Charlotte said she was going out to the shops for something for Malcy's dinner. Wincey always went home in the middle of the day for a bite to eat. She had been out in Springburn Road when she remembered the pair of shoes to be mended that she'd left in the office. She wanted to hand them in to the cobbler on the way to the Balgray. She hurried back into the factory.

The girls were all huddled at one corner of the machine hall—chatting, drinking tea and eating sandwiches. They didn't notice her reappearance. She went through to the office and, on opening the door, nearly bumped into Malcy who was coming out. Before she could say anything, he said, 'Just looking for Charlotte.' And he was off.

Wincey picked up the shopping bag that contained her shoes and then hesitated. A thought had struck her. At first she dismissed it with the unsaid words, 'Surely not.' But then she opened her desk drawer and saw right away that the petty cash box was empty. There had been quite a few pounds in it that morning. Wincey stood looking at the empty box, inwardly groaning and wondering what she should do now. It was one thing Malcy trying to wheedle extra money out of

Charlotte. But this was different. This was thieving. She thought of confronting Malcy—privately and discreetly perhaps. She suspected though that Malcy would immediately act the injured victim and go straight to Charlotte. He would complain that Wincey was always trying to get at him.

He was a master at appearing the hurt innocent. Wincey often thought he should have been in the acting profession— he even had the looks for it, with his curly blond hair and even features. She tried to imagine ways she could frighten him, warn him, but couldn't think of anything that would work. In the end she decided that, for now at least, she'd just have to depend on Charlotte's business sense. Surely Charlotte would call a halt if things began to get too serious. Hadn't she been trying to do that when she had been interrupted in the office? Wincey felt less anxious when she remembered what Charlotte had been saying to Malcy. She had used such an unusually strong tone of voice. Yes, Wincey assured herself, Charlotte was too good a business woman to allow anyone—even Malcy—to ruin what she'd worked so hard to build up.

So Wincey said nothing to Malcy about the stolen money. But she couldn't resist giving him some cold and knowing looks. Even when he and Charlotte came visiting, she never addressed a word to him if she could avoid it. When Charlotte invited the family to Sunday lunch in the villa, it was as much as Wincey could do to be civil to Malcy. She hated him for what he was doing to Charlotte, as well as what he might do to the business.

Charlotte's normally sweet, open face had developed a strained and worried look. Even Erchie had begun to notice it.

'Are ye aw right, hen?' he asked on one occasion. 'Ye're no' lookin' so well.'

'I'm fine, Daddy. I just get a headache now and again. Maybe I need my eyes tested.'

'Maybe ye should get Doctor Houston tae gie ye a wee check over, hen. Jist in case yer sair heid's caused by somethin' else.'

'Yes, all right, Daddy. Maybe I'll do that.'

Wincey kept quiet, but not without some difficulty. She was thinking—what use was a doctor? It was a good divorce lawyer that Charlotte needed.

Then for a time, all seemed well. Charlotte looked more relaxed and happy. On catching Wincey staring at her one day, she laughed and said, 'No need to look so perplexed, Wincey. I told you I'd speak to Malcy, and it worked, bless him. He's been as good as gold. I'm so happy, Wincey. I'm as much in love with him now as I've always been, and he with me. Aren't we lucky?'

Wincey smiled and nodded, and Charlotte went on, 'So many couples get into a bad patch in their marriage and instead of discussing the problem with each other and trying to sort it out, they just allow things to go from bad to worse. I always think it's so sad when that happens. Love's such a precious thing. I only hope one day you'll find the same happiness as I have, Wincey.'

God forbid, Wincey thought, but she tried to feel glad for Charlotte. She tried to believe that Malcy had changed. But somehow she couldn't convince herself of his sudden conversion.

Then one day, after Teresa had hurled Granny down to the Co-op to do some shopping, Granny burst out, 'Here, Wincey. Ye'll never guess whit we saw the day!'

'Now, now, Granny.' Teresa appeared very anxious to stop Granny in mid flow. 'We could have been mistaken. Drink up your tea, dear.'

Granny was not so easily put off her stroke, however. 'Malcy, comin' oot o' Mrs O'Donnell's place.'

'Who's Mrs O'Donnell?' Wincey asked.

'Och, it's well seen ye hide yersel' away in that factory too much. Everybody knows Mrs O'Donnell.'

'Granny, dear. I've got nice chocolate digestives. Would you like one to dip in your tea?'

Granny cocked her head in Teresa's direction. 'She's black

affronted, an' nae wonder. Naebody in oor family his ever gone tae a moneylender before. Never in oor lives! We'd rather starve first. Right capitalist rascals. Ah remember an auld neighbour o' mine was ruined by the wicked interest they charged her. She ended up committin' suicide ower the heid o' it.'

Wincey looked over at Teresa and Teresa said, 'It might have been somebody else.'

'It was Malcy!' Granny insisted. 'Ye know fine it was Malcy.'

'I mean, he could have been seeing somebody else. He could have been visiting a friend up that close.'

'Pull the other wan,' Granny said. 'Ah'm no' as daft as ah look!'

Teresa gazed worriedly over at Wincey. 'Is the business in any difficulty, dear?'

'No, the business is fine.'

'Well, I don't understand.'

'I do,' Wincey said. 'He's a gambler. He always has been.'

'Oh, but . . . Erchie likes a wee flutter as well, but I don't think he would ever . . . I mean, I don't understand.'

'There's a big difference, Teresa, between the odd wee flutter, or even a regular wee flutter, and a compulsive gambler.'

'Aye,' Granny said, 'Wincey's right. It's like an alkie. An' an alkie never can jist take wan wee drink. He's aye tae scoff the bottle.'

'Oh dear. Do you think Charlotte knows?'

'She knows he's that kind of gambler but she thinks he's cured. I don't think she knows about the moneylender.'

'Oh dear. And Malcy's such a nice man. And I'm sure he loves Charlotte. She certainly loves him. I hope this isn't going to cause any trouble between them.'

She turned to Granny. 'Now you listen to me, Granny. Don't you dare upset Charlotte by letting on about this. Do you hear me?'

'Oh aye,' Granny said. 'There'll be nae need for any o' us

tae put oor oar in. She'll find out soon enough for hersel'.'

'Maybe he'll have a big win soon,' Teresa said without much conviction, 'and be able to sort himself out.'

'Huh!' Granny gave Teresa a sarcastic look. 'Mair like some o' Mrs O'Donnell's hard men'll sort him out, if ye ask me.'

'We're not asking you, Granny,' Teresa said with unusual sharpness, 'so just keep quiet.'

Granny lapsed into a huff. 'Ye'll be auld yersel' some day.'

Again Wincey was in a quandary. She asked Teresa for advice.

'No, dear,' Teresa said firmly. 'I don't think any of us should interfere. It's between Malcy and Charlotte. They should be left to sort it out themselves and in their own way.'

All very well, thought Wincey, but it could involve the business. It was already doing so. However, she took Teresa's advice and just hoped that Malcy and Charlotte would be able to sort themselves out.

Anyway, just shortly after that, she had something more to worry her—even closer to home. Doctor Houston turned up again. Teresa and Erchie had gone to the Princes Cinema and she had been in the middle of reading to Granny from Granny's favourite paper, *The People's Friend*. Although Granny always insisted it was a lot of sentimental rubbish, and it was really Teresa who liked it.

After Doctor Houston's usual chat with Granny, Wincey saw him to the door. There he said, 'Could you come to the surgery tomorrow on your way home from work, Wincey?'

'Why?' Wincey said abruptly.

He smiled. 'There's no need to look so scared. I just want a little chat about Granny and the family. There's just one or two problems needing to be discussed.'

'Oh, all right,' Wincey said. She thought it might be about Charlotte and Malcy. Maybe Charlotte had been seeking the doctor's advice.

The next evening, when she arrived at the surgery, she was

the last patient to be seen. Even the receptionist had left by the time Doctor Houston ushered her into his consulting room. Wincey suddenly felt nervous. More than that. As she passed close to the doctor in the doorway, she felt sick with apprehension. Especially when he took her by the arm and led her across to a mirror hanging on one of the walls.

'Look into that, Wincey. What do you see?'

She saw, standing behind her, a tall, broad shouldered frame, a handsome face, straight black hair and very dark eyes.

'I don't need to look in a mirror to see you,' she said. 'What's the idea?'

'The idea wasn't to look at me, but at yourself.'

'Why?'

'To see for yourself your white, frightened face. And I can feel you trembling. As a doctor, I have to ask myself why.'

She shrugged. 'I didn't come here to talk about myself.'

'Don't you think it's time you did?'

'I don't know what you mean.'

'Wincey, part of my training was to observe people, and I've been observing *you*. I wanted to help you, and so I've been trying to think, first of all, of why you are like this. I have, as a result, been making a few discreet enquiries.'

Wincey felt faint. 'My God,' she thought, 'my God.' She had to sit down. The nearest chair was one in front of Doctor Houston's desk. He went round and sat behind the desk. She felt trapped, like a wild animal . . . too afraid to move. She looked over the desk at the man sitting there . . . he was wearing a white coat and he had a stethoscope hanging around his neck . . . she fixed her eyes on the stethoscope, trying desperately not to faint.

24

Virginia sat in silence, staring dully at Nicholas and Mathieson. They were talking about Sigmund Freud, the founder of psycho-analysis. The Nazis had been persecuting Freud for some time.

'It's a disgrace,' Mathieson said. 'A frail old man like that being hounded from pillar to post. A man of ideas. The Nazis couldn't put up with that, of course. Not in a Jew anyway.'

'But at least he's had permission to come to Britain to live,' Nicholas said. 'And his family and some of his students as well. He'll be all right here. Thank God for Roosevelt's intervention, he'd never have got an exit visa otherwise.'

'Yes, but what about all the other Jews who haven't been able to get special permission, Nicholas? America and Britain have known all about them for years, but what have we done about it? Even the Pope hasn't raised his voice in protest or tried to defend the Jews or anyone else in Nazi Germany. On the contrary, the only people who ever raise their voices against fascists are the ordinary working folk. Look how they saw Mosley off—and not only in London. They chased him off Glasgow Green.'

Nicholas grinned, remembering. 'Yes, good old Glaswegians. That was a sight worth seeing.'

Virginia thought, 'I might as well not be here.' They were two of a kind, Nicholas and Mathieson. Oh, they looked very different but they were both men of words, and both were equally obsessive. How ironic that she had chosen to marry each of them. Talk about out of the frying pan into the fire! At least Nicholas had been a better lover than Mathieson—much more romantic. Her eyes glazed, remembering how they'd danced naked in the woods and made passionate love on the mossy, fragrant ground. She remembered the beautiful love poetry he'd written and read to her. Tears began to well up in her eyes and she hastily blinked them away. They hardly ever made love now. The romance had gone. How often did they even speak to one another? Nicholas spoke far more to Mathieson. She and Nicholas had drifted far, far apart. Yet he seemed perfectly happy, sitting there relaxed and enjoying his glass of malt whisky and his conversation with Mathieson.

She was beginning to come round to Mrs Cartwright's way of thinking, or at least some way towards it. Mrs Cartwright claimed that it wasn't decent for her ex-husband to be so friendly with her husband. Certainly Virginia had begun to resent the friendship. Although she suspected that even if Mathieson never came near Kirklee Terrace again, it wouldn't make the slightest difference to her relationship with Nicholas. More than likely it would only make matters worse. Nicholas would sink into one of his silent moods, or he'd emerge from his writing room less and less.

She took a deep shuddering breath. Maybe it would be best if she just disappeared into thin air, like Wincey, never to be seen or heard of again. The thought settled like a stone in her mind, weighing her down, draining away her energy.

Nicholas was saying, 'I fancy a bite of supper, James. How about you?'

'I wouldn't mind.'

'Right. Virginia . . . Virginia,' he repeated.

'What?'

'Supper?'

She rose automatically and without saying anything, walked from the sitting room. While she did so, she had the distinct feeling that Nicholas was shaking his head. She had caught him doing it before, after she'd said or done something. He'd shake his head at Mathieson as if to say, 'See what I've to put up with?' Or 'See what I mean?' Or 'What can I do with her?'

She banged shut the sitting room door—anger and resentment had brought energy rushing back. Who did he think he was? What did they both think they bloody were? How dare they treat her like this? Let them make their own bloody supper. From the hall, she shouted back towards the sitting room, 'Make your own bloody supper.'

She went through to the spare bedroom and locked herself in. It seemed safest to be alone. Rage was building inside her, and she could not face the idea of sleeping in the same bed as Nicholas tonight. She punched the door, then leaned against it and wept. She didn't know what was happening to her life.

Next morning, Mathieson arrived on the doorstep. Nicholas was shut away in his room. Virginia turned away from the door and went through to the kitchen. Mathieson hirpled after her, his stick thumping on the hall floor. She put the kettle on and placed a couple of cups and saucers on the table.

'I hope you haven't come to give me one of your lectures, James. I'm not in the mood.'

'I have, as a matter of fact.'

'Well, you might as well leave right now. I'm sorry but—'

'You're not sorry at all,' Mathieson interrupted. 'You're wallowing in self pity. You've often used the word *obsession* about me and now Nicholas, but at least we're obsessed with something outside of ourselves. You're just self-obsessed. You can't see past yourself and your problem.'

'Is that it?'

'No, it's time you did something for others less fortunate than yourself. All right, you lost a daughter. But here you are in a comfortable—no, luxurious—home with a talented husband, a handsome son and a wealthy mother-in-law. Has it ever occurred to you that there are people out there who have lost children, but have no comfort and are struggling with a thousand other worries? Or drunken husbands who abuse them, and no money for food. Need I go on?'

'I'm sorry, but there's nothing I can do about other people.'

'Yes, you can. There are innumerable societies and charitable organisations who work to help the poor, the ill and the desolate. They're all desperate for volunteers. Seek them out. Offer your help. Do something really practical for a change. And do it now, Virginia. For your own sake, as much as anyone else's.'

'I've done my share of all that in the past. I've lived in the world of tenements and suffered poverty myself.'

'All the more reason to help now. You know what it's like. You more than most will understand. I appreciate the work you've done for me, Virginia, but by doing something like this, you'll be putting your politics into practice. You'll not only be arguing that the poor should have a better deal, you'll be at the grass roots helping them to have it. I'm sure you'd feel you were doing a worthwhile job. People like Maclean and Maxton always believed that the workers and the poor should be educated, so that they can help themselves in the fight for equality and a decent life. Both of them used their teaching skills at a practical level, and so have I. It's time now for you to do something practical, Virginia.'

She made the tea and sat down at the table. 'I'll think about it.'

'You're thinking too much, that's your trouble.'

'Oh, all right. Anything to get you off my back.'

He gave her one of his grotesque twisted smiles. 'That's my girl.'

'Shouldn't you be teaching this morning?'

'I haven't a class until eleven. I'd better be off as soon as I've finished my tea.'

After he'd gone, Mrs Rogers arrived after having packed her children off to school. She helped herself to a cup of tea and Virginia went through to the sitting room, out of her way. The sitting room was heavy with silence. Virginia went over and gazed from the window, down over Kirklee Terrace and the grassy bank onto Great Western Road.

Mathieson was right, she supposed. She was lucky in many ways. She remembered the tenement close in the Gorbals where she'd once lived with her mother and father and brothers, and her sister Rose. Poor Rose had died of tuberculosis. One brother had been killed while working in the munitions factory, the other killed in the war. When she thought of all that her poor mother had had to suffer, and yet she had kept going with such courage and unselfishness, she felt ashamed. Not only had her mother coped with all the family tragedies, but she had had to struggle with life in a terrible slum. She had to fight to rid the place of bed bugs and to slave endlessly for some level of cleanliness, not only in the room and kitchen house, but in the overflowing lavatory out on the landing.

Virginia leaned her forehead against the window. Oh, her poor mother! No doubt there had been many other working-class women like her. No doubt there still were—the unsung, unknown heroines, often with a wonderful sense of humour despite the tragedies in their lives.

Mathieson was right. For far too long, she had been blinded by self pity. She had been wallowing in it. But not any more. She was shaken by what he had said. Yes, Mathieson *was* right—she must do something.

She was suddenly impatient. Where to start though? Should she ask at the nearest church? She wasn't a churchgoer, however, and still had no inclination to become one. Nor was she a member of the Salvation Army, who did so much good work in the city. They had always been more practical and certainly more visible in the poorer districts, doing their best to help people, and *they* were courageous. Their female members with their bonnets tied under their chins did not shrink from going into the rough male bastions of pubs to collect money for good causes. Virginia, however, couldn't imagine herself either wearing the uniform, or going into the pubs. Again she felt ashamed. Where had all her courage gone? She used to have a reputation of being a really spirited young woman. Spunky was the word often used to describe her. She wasn't young any more, of course. She wasn't all that far off forty. 'Forty!' she thought incredulously. Where had all her life gone?

She forced her mind back to the problem at hand. There must be lots of charitable organisations that she could help, even if it simply meant dishing out hot soup at street corners to the unemployed and homeless. She'd seen them queuing up in the streets of poor districts and she'd heard about soup kitchens. She would phone around. She would speak to one of her Labour councillor friends. She would ask a doctor. Not her local West End doctor but a doctor from one of the poorer districts. She would talk to people at the next political meeting Mathieson organised. She had long since given up going to most of these meetings, but just this once, she would go to seek advice. There must be something worthwhile she could do, especially—as Mathieson said—with her life experience. She would not be just another middle-class do-gooder, she would know from first hand experience what it was all about.

For the first time in years, she felt drawn to go back to her roots, even just for a brief visit. On an impulse, she went for her coat and hat. It was a fur hat and the coat she put on was a rust coloured wool with a huge fur collar. She immediately took them both off again and found instead a Burberry tweed travel coat and a plain, soft brimmed hat. She decided she wouldn't take her motor car. Instead she went in search of a tram that would take her to the Gorbals.

25

He knew her real name. He'd consulted not only the police missing persons files, but those of the Salvation Army. She felt angry, as well as afraid. How dare he interfere in her life!

'You had no right!' she told him.

'I keep telling you, Wincey, I just want to help you.'

'I don't need your help.'

'I think you do.'

'I don't care what you think. I'm living a new life and I was perfectly happy until you started interfering. The last thing I want to do is go back to my old life. You say I look frightened. Nothing fills me with more fear than the thought of that.'

'Why? What happened, Wincey? It might help you to talk about it.'

'You've done enough harm as it is.'

'I've done nothing to harm you, and I've no intention of ever doing so. If you want to go on living as you are—as Wincey Gourlay—I'll respect that. And I'll also respect and keep confidential anything you tell me about yourself, or anything I already know about you.'

'What *do* you know about me, apart from my name?' She couldn't keep herself from asking the question. Nor could she control the anxiety in her voice.

'I know that your previous address was Kirklee Terrace in the West End. And your mother and father are Virginia and Nicholas Cartwright. Your grandmother and grandfather lived in Great Western Road and it was in their villa that you were last seen. It is believed that you found your grandfather dead—or the heart attack that killed him was witnessed by you—and you ran from the house in grief and panic.'

And so he knew everything—or nearly everything.

'Promise me, please, that you'll never tell anyone—*anyone*—that you know who I am, or where I am.'

'Wincey, I thought I'd already made that clear. You have my word. I swear to you that no-one, either in your past or your present life, will know one thing about you from me.'

She tried to relax. 'I need to believe you.'

'I know. And you can.'

She nodded, still wide eyed and anxious. She felt weak and trembling, as if she'd been through a terrible ordeal. Or as if she'd experienced a nightmare that she still wasn't quite able to shake off.

'I think,' the doctor said gently, 'we've talked enough for today. I'm going to drive you home now.'

'No, I'm all right.'

He smiled. 'I'm the doctor, remember, and you my dear girl are proving even more perverse and difficult than Granny.'

She couldn't help smiling herself then, despite her inward trembling. She allowed herself to be led from the room and the surgery, and helped into the doctor's car. He drove the short distance in silence. Then when they arrived at her close, he smiled at her as she was getting out of the car and said, 'Don't worry. You're perfectly safe, and you *are* going to be all right.' She nodded and hurried away into the close.

Granny had been sitting in her wheelchair at the front room window, gazing avidly at what was going on outside.

179

'Wis that the doctor's car ah saw you gettin' oot o'?' she bawled from the room.

Wincey called back, 'Yes, he kindly offered to drop me off on his way home.'

'Wid wan o' ye hurl me back tae the kitchen. Ah'll be losin' ma voice next. As if the power o' ma legs wisnae enough.'

Wincey answered her call and pushed the wheelchair through to the kitchen.

'You can't say you're frozen any more, Granny. That's a grand big fire in the room.'

'Aye, aboot time tae. Whit wis the doctor sayin' aboot me that he couldnae say tae ma face?'

'Nothing. He was just summing up your progress. He's really very pleased with you.'

'Seems funny he couldnae sum it up tae me.'

'He's a busy man, Granny. He can't keep coming in here to visit you now that he's running the practice single-handed.'

'His auld faither did that for years.'

'Yes, but you know what he was like.'

'Aye, well, whit's for ma tea?'

Teresa said, 'A nice wee bit of cod, Granny, and stewed apples and custard.'

Granny's eyes lit up and her jaws began chomping at the mere idea. She liked a nice bit of fish softened with one of the tasty sauces that Teresa made. Granny admitted that Teresa was 'a dab hand at comin' up wi' tasty sauces'. And stewed apples and custard slipped down without any bother.

'How did you get on at the doctor's?' Teresa asked. 'Granny said he'd asked you to go to the surgery tonight.'

'Yes, I was just saying—he's too busy to keep spending so much time in here. He was just explaining about Granny's progress and how we'd no need to worry. But if we do need him to make a visit, we've only to let him know.'

'Oh, isn't that kind of him. He's a nice man. Clever as well.'

'Yes, he is very clever,' Wincey agreed.

'Are you all right, dear?'

'We've been awfully busy. I'm exhausted but I'll be fine after I've had my tea.'

In the homes of Florence and the twins, the evening meal was now referred to as dinner. Lunch was in the middle of the day, dinner was in the evening and tea was only something one took mid-afternoon. In the Gourlay home, however, it was still dinner in the middle of the day and tea in the evening.

Erchie arrived then with the paper, after having enjoyed a couple of pints in Quinn's with his mates on the way home. Quinn's at the bottom of the Balgrayhill had one entrance on the Balgray and another on Springburn Road. The place was a landmark in Springburn with its tower on which there was a large clock. Erchie flung the paper down and rubbed his hands.

'By Jove, ah've a horse's appetite on me the night. How long's tea gonnae be, hen?' he asked.

'Just about fifteen minutes.'

Granny said, 'Tell me whit's in the paper while we're waiting'. I don't suppose there's anythin' cheery?'

'Naw. It gets worse every day. Noo there's whit they're callin' spring cleanin' of thae Austrian Jews.'

Teresa, busy over at the range, shook her head. 'Spring cleaning? Is that not awful? Poor souls!'

'Aye,' Granny said. 'Thank God we wernae born Jews, that's aw ah can say.'

Erchie lifted the paper. 'An' it's been carried oot at great speed, it says. Jews huv been dismissed from their professions, Jewish judges huv been dismissed, shops huv been forced tae put up placards saying "Jewish concern". It says as well that theatre an' music halls huv been already "spring cleaned" an' among the artists that Vienna will know no more are Richard Tauber an' Max Reinhardt.'

'Is that no' awfae?' Granny said. 'Whit's the world comin' tae, him such a good singer as well?'

181

'An' here's a bit about a church leader—Pastor Niemoeller. He's been detained in Sachsenhausen concentration camp where he's tae join three thousand inmates under the "Death's Head" Battalion o' the SS.'

'The poor soul,' Teresa said. 'A man of God. How wicked can anyone get?'

'Here,' Granny said. 'Ah mind in the war, the British an' the Germans were slaughterin' each other by the million. Half the time just for a few yards o' muddy ground, as well. An' good men like oor Johnny bein' tormented in jail because he stood up against it.'

Teresa sighed. 'Must you tell us all this before we eat our tea, Erchie? It's enough to put us off.'

'Sorry, hen, but Granny—'

'I know, I know, but as I've said before, you can read to Granny through in the room after we have our tea.'

Granny snorted. 'Hiding' yer heid in the sand never does anybody any good, or solves anythin'. That's the trouble wi' a lot o' folk.'

'You were hoping for something cheery yourself earlier on,' Teresa reminded her.

'Aw ah said wis, ah didnae suppose there was anythin' cheery in the paper. An' aw wis right!'

'I used to think Erchie's *Daily Worker* was awfully serious, but this paper's just as bad.'

'It's no' the *Record*'s fault, hen. It's what's goin' on in the world. The *Record* jist lets us know.'

'Yes, yes, but just do me a favour, Erchie, and keep it until after tea.'

'Anythin' you say, hen.'

'You're awful quiet, Wincey,' Teresa said.

'When's she ever been a blether,' Granny wanted to know.

Wincey tried to pull herself together and pay attention to her immediate surroundings. She had been far away in Kirklee Terrace, remembering her home there and the way her mother sang as she moved about. She remembered the loving looks that passed between her mother and father. How happy and so much in love they'd been. She'd never seen—before or since—such a happy, loving couple.

'I'm sorry, I was dreaming,' Wincey said.

'Nothing to be sorry about, dear. As long as you're feeling all right.'

Wincey smiled. 'I'm fine. Can I help you dish the tea?'

'No, no, sit where you are. Everything's under control. Granny, can you manage on your own?'

'Aye, now the swellin's down in ma hands, ah'm no' that bad at aw. Ah wish ah could say the same for ma hips an' ma knees.'

Teresa put a tray on Granny's knee. Then she tucked one of Erchie's big hankies into the top of the old woman's dress. 'I've mashed it up nice to make it easier for you.'

'Ah'm no' a wee wean. Ye didnae need tae dae that!'

Teresa rolled her eyes and served Erchie, Wincey and herself with plates of fish in a cheese sauce. Then she put a dish of boiled potatoes on the table. 'Wire in now.'

'Ah saw Malcy earlier the day,' Erchie said. 'Ah forgot tae tell ye at dinner time.'

'What do you mean, Erchie?' Teresa said in a puzzled voice. 'Surely you see him every day in the factory?'

'Aye, ah know, but this was dinner time. He wis comin' oot o' O'Donnell's close. Ah didnae think he knew anybody up there.'

Teresa and Wincey exchanged glances and Erchie caught their look. 'My God, dinnae tell me it was O'Donnell's he wis at!'

'Now, don't you say anything, Erchie,' Teresa warned. 'We're best not to interfere. Leave it to Charlotte. Any problem they have is between them. They've worked things out all right before. Charlotte can be quite firm when she wants. And she loves him that much. I'm sure he loves her as well, so they'll come through this.'

183

'Ye're probably right, hen. Ah like a wee flutter masel' as you know, but ah've been thinkin' for a while now that Malcy seems tae have been goin' over the score. Ah widnae like tae get on the wrong side o' Mrs O'Donnell though. She's got quite a few hard men at her biddin'. But och, if Malcy's got in too deep wi' Mrs O'Donnell, Charlotte'll bail him out an' save his bacon. He'll be OK.'

26

'I was thinking it might be a good idea,' Doctor Houston said, 'if we met for a quiet meal and a talk in a more relaxed atmosphere. Somewhere away from the surgery.'

His car had drawn up beside Wincey as she was walking home.

'I'm your patient.' Wincey felt a bit shocked, as well as frightened. 'You're not supposed to take your patients out.'

He laughed. 'If we're going into the ethical and legal niceties, you're not actually registered with me, are you, so you're not officially my patient.'

'Well no, but you said—'

'I'm a doctor, yes. And yes, I want to help you. And it's true that I respect anyone's confidence. Would it make you feel better if I said I just want to help you as a friend. Forget I'm a doctor if you like.'

'I'm on my way home. Teresa will be expecting me for my tea.'

'We'll make it tomorrow then. I'll pick you up at seven thirty.'

'Wait a minute—'

But he'd wound up the window and the car had slid away.

What a terrible cheek! He'd struck her as the kind of person who always had to get his own way. She felt harassed, as well as everything else. Her emotions were in turmoil. She couldn't eat her tea.

Teresa looked worried. 'Are you sickening for something, dear?'

'Ah'll eat hers,' Granny eagerly volunteered.

'Granny,' Teresa chided, 'you'll do no such thing.'

Wincey hesitated, then thought she may as well tell the truth. They would be sure to find out, or one of the neighbours would probably see her getting into the doctor's car.

'I'm a bit taken aback, that's all.'

'What about, dear?'

'Doctor Houston has asked me out for a meal. He says he's calling for me tomorrow at seven thirty.'

Teresa's face lit up with delight. 'I knew it! Didn't I tell you? I knew he liked you, Wincey. Oh, I'm so pleased for you, dear.'

'Aye,' Granny said, 'it's high time she had a man.'

'I don't want to go out with him, but he didn't give me a chance to say no.'

'Good for him,' Granny said. 'He's the fella for you. It's a strong fella you need tae sort ye out.'

'Now you must wear something really nice,' Teresa said excitedly. 'And take time off tomorrow to get your hair done, dear. Get a bit cut off that fringe. You always look as though you're trying to hide underneath it.'

'You're making me feel nervous with all this fuss. I told you, I don't want to go.'

'Oh, don't be silly, dear, of course you'll go. And you'll have a lovely time.'

'Ah'll gie ye a loan o' ma good kirby-grip wi' the diamonds on it,' Granny offered.

In a sudden impulse, Wincey rushed over and gave the old woman a hug and a kiss. 'Thanks, Granny, you're very kind.'

'Away ye go an' don't be daft.' Granny looked embarrassed but pleased at the same time. Teresa looked pleased as well, and Wincey thought there was nothing for it but to keep the appointment with Doctor Houston, if for no other reason than to avoid disappointing Teresa and Granny.

The next day, she couldn't concentrate on her work. Charlotte noticed, and even Malcy's eyes kept wandering curiously towards her. Charlotte said, 'Has something happened, Wincey? You look all flushed and sparkly-eyed.'

'Not really. I'm going out for a meal tonight, that's all.'

Charlotte clapped her hands in delight. 'Oh, at last, Wincey. I was getting worried about you. It's not natural never to go out and enjoy yourself. It's a boyfriend, isn't it? You wouldn't be all aglow like this if you were going out with a girl.'

Wincey fussed and tutted and protested she was nothing of the kind, but Charlotte just laughed at her. The truth was of course that she *was* excited. But it was an excitement tinged with apprehension. She tried to be sensible. Doctor Houston was a perfectly respectable, kindly man who just wanted to help her. Why on earth should she feel so nervous of him? She felt angry with herself. She told herself not to be so stupid—all to no avail. The more she thought about it, the more she began to convince herself that nothing she could ever do or say would cure what was wrong with her. It had nothing to do with Doctor Houston. It was an irrational fear that was always there, deep inside her. No doctor had any pills or potions or could give any advice that would ever help her.

'For goodness sake, dear,' Teresa said, as seven thirty was drawing near, 'try to look a bit cheerful. You'd think you were going to a funeral, not out for a meal with a handsome man.'

'Aye,' Granny said, 'she's never been wan tae talk much, but noo she's gone completely dumb. Ah sometimes think she's aff her heid, that yin.'

Still Wincey didn't say anything. Even when they heard the car hooter, she just left the house with only a wave and a faint smile to the two women.

'Quick,' Granny shouted at Teresa, 'hurl me through tae the room windae.'

Doctor Houston got out of the car and opened the door for Wincey. The faint nervous smile stuck to her face as Wincey climbed into the front seat. He slid in beside her and the car moved off. They didn't talk much until Doctor Houston said, 'You're looking very nice.'

'Doctor—' Wincey began.

But he immediately corrected her, 'Robert. Friends, remember?'

'Robert,' she said, although it felt very odd to be saying it, 'I'm nervous of sitting in a restaurant in town in case one of my family or their friends might see me.'

'Don't worry, I've thought of that. I'm taking you to a little hotel I know out near the Campsie Hills.'

'Oh.'

'So relax.'

She nodded, and they lapsed into silence again. The hotel was an old coaching house and the restaurant had once been the stables. It still had the original flagstones under foot, whitewashed stone walls and dark oak beams. A huge log fire crackled cheerily in the ancient hearth.

'This is lovely,' Wincey said.

'I thought you'd like it. I'll go over to the bar and fetch some drinks. What'll you have?'

'A gin and tonic, please.'

'Right.'

She watched him stride over to the bar and smile and chat to the barmaid. She noticed that above the bar there hung horse brasses and horse shoes. Her attention kept being drawn, however, to Houston's muscular back and his head of blue black hair. Even from this distance, she could sense the strong aura of masculinity and self-confidence emanating from him. He returned and sat down opposite her. He raised his tankard of beer.

'Health and happiness.'

'Health and happiness,' she echoed, raising her glass.

After a moment, he said, 'Wincey, your grandfather was an old man and there's no doubt he died of natural causes. You do know that, don't you?'

She stared down at her drink and said nothing.

'I just wondered if you felt guilty in some way about his death, and that's what made you run away—and stay away,' he added. 'But believe me, you had nothing to do with his death. I've looked into this and he died of a heart attack. He had a heart condition. There's absolutely no doubt about that.'

Just then a waitress came to take their order for the meal and Houston said, 'Let's concentrate on enjoying the meal. We can talk about that afterwards.' And he turned the conversation round to Granny, reminding Wincey of some of Granny's hilarious pronouncements. Soon Wincey was laughing and adding some anecdotes of her own that he had not heard. She enjoyed the meal and afterwards they took their glass of wine over to one of the more private areas that had wooden partitions on each side. Wincey guessed that perhaps they had been where the horses would have been stabled.

'So,' Houston said, 'was I right about the guilt?'

She hesitated, her heart thumping. 'In a way,' she managed at last.

'In what way?' he asked gently.

She shook her head. 'You won't understand. You'll just hate me. Everybody would if they knew.'

'Try me.'

Wincey didn't answer.

'Wincey, try to let it out. You've obviously been harbouring some secret that you believe is terrible. And for so many years. It's time you got rid of the burden of it and got on with your life. As a doctor, I've seen and heard some terrible things. I've long since stopped being shocked at anything. If

I ever was shocked at all. I've always been able to take things in my stride—you have to be like that working in the Royal in Glasgow. That's where I was before.'

Wincey took a deep breath. 'I killed him.'

Houston shook his head. 'No, no, Wincey. I've just told you—'

'I watched him.' In anguish Wincey closed her eyes. 'I can still see him gasping for breath. I'll never forget it. And how I let him die.'

'My dear girl, you were only a child. You couldn't have done anything.'

'Yes, I could have run upstairs as I'd done before, and fetched his tablets. But I didn't. I just stood there and watched him die.'

'Wincey, you were a child. You were in the house alone with him. You were in shock. It stands to reason, especially when it was someone you loved. Anyone would have understood that. My dear, believe me. You weren't able to do anything but just stand there like that.'

Wincey looked down at her hands. She was twisting them tightly together. 'Perhaps.'

'No perhaps about it. I've seen too many people in shock to have any doubt whatsoever. You were in shock,' he repeated firmly. 'You must rid yourself of all these guilty feelings.'

Wincey kept twisting at her hands. 'You don't understand. I wanted him to die. I hated him. He had . . . he had . . .' her hands now moved, instinctively, down between her legs, in an unconscious attempt to cover and protect, even from the memory . . . 'he had been touching me, doing things . . . for years. It was wrong, horrible . . . but what could I do? He was my grandfather . . .'

'Oh my dear!' Houston's big hand covered hers. 'My poor Wincey. Now I really do understand.'

Tears began gushing down Wincey's cheeks. He moved closer to her and put his other arm around her shoulders.

'It's all right. You're going to be all right, do you hear?'

She tried to nod and after a minute or two, he said,

'It's one of the terrible things about this kind of abuse. The victim gets the idea that it's their fault. This is totally wrong. It's always the fault of the abuser. But I've known this to happen over and over again. Whether the victim is a child or an adult, they feel dirty and they feel guilty. And these feelings can ruin their whole lives. I've known elderly women who were abused as children, and were still suffering deep inside as a result. They've never got over it. It's tragic. You mustn't go on suffering like that, Wincey. I won't let you.'

She raised a tear-stained, anxious face. 'You don't hate me?'

'Wincey!' He drew her head down against his chest. 'Of course I don't hate you. Quite the contrary. Now, in a minute or two, I'm going to go and fetch you a glass of brandy. That'll steady you up a bit. Then I'm going to drive you home. You'll have a good night's sleep and I'll see you again tomorrow. All right?'

'All right,' she murmured into the hard warmth of his body.

27

As Virginia walked about in the Gorbals, memories of her past life came flooding back. It was almost as if she was back in the teeming tenements of her youth, with their cavernous closes—man-made tunnels between the bottom of stairs and the streets. They were dark, cold and draughty places which the sunlight could never penetrate. She knew the worn stairs, and the flickering shadows of the gas light, and the stench of the overflowing lavatories. She heard the children crying, the racket of husbands and wives arguing, the drunk men, some aggressive and some maudlin. She returned to the close where she had been born. Seeing it, Virginia wondered how she'd ever survived in the place. Many others had not.

She heard again the deep melancholy booming of a foghorn from the river. The Gorbals had been the subject of a great many stories in newspapers and books in the past few years and had acquired a terrible reputation for violence. Reading these stories led outsiders to think that it was an area of constant violence and one pitched battle after another. But this had never been Virginia's experience. The main problem as far as violence was concerned was wife beating. And it took place on Friday or Saturday nights, after the husbands came home from the pub. She'd often seen women with black eyes and bruises at weekends. It was quite common to see or hear a child rushing along the street to the Southern Division police station shouting, 'Ma faither's killin' ma mither.'

There were two other types of violence Virginia had witnessed. One was caused by men coming out of a pub where they'd been talking and arguing, and continuing the argument in the vicinity of the public lavatories at Gorbals Cross. Another was at the intersection of Gorbals Street and Cumberland Street, near where she'd lived. Again it usually happened on a Friday or a Saturday night. An argument would become heated and lead to a street fight. This was always conducted with fists, and as a rule by no more than two men. A crowd of spectators would gather around though, and fair play was always insisted on. If the police saw the crowd and heard the disturbance, they would come along and order the fight to stop. It usually did. The policemen were often big Highlanders, well known and respected by most of the locals. If the police order was ignored, or if one of the fighters abused or attacked the police, there would be an arrest, with the policemen grabbing the offenders by the scruff of the neck and marching them off to the local police station.

The only other form of violence Virginia knew of was street fighting—but between youths of seventeen and under. They named themselves 'Cumbies' from Cumberland Street and 'Billy Boys' from Bridgeton. There was another gang of older men, she remembered, called the 'Beehives', after a shop at the corner of Cumberland Street and Thistle Street. They were unemployed men who used to hang about nearby and air their grievances. Sometimes their bitterness and resentment would boil over and once or twice a year, they'd gather together on a Saturday evening and march along a few streets, shouting and waving sticks. Sometimes groups of youths formed themselves into gangs and had tussles with the Beehives, but again only fists and sticks were used.

Virginia often wondered why this myth about the Gorbals as a hotbed of vice and violence had arisen. Mathieson said it was government-inspired—all part of an attempt to discredit men like Maclean and the other Red Clydesiders. In his view, this was why every minor incident that occurred in the Gorbals was blown up out of all proportion in the press and made to sound like a civil war was going on.

Virginia had a heavy heart as she wandered through the familiar streets. She remembered her mother and father and brothers, and many kindly neighbours and friends of long ago. She hardly knew anyone in Kirklee Terrace. It suddenly occurred to her that she missed the teeming life of the tenements, the closeness of neighbours and the involvement in each other's lives. Had she still lived in the Gorbals when Wincey disappeared, she would no doubt have had much sympathy, compassion, support and practical help from everyone around her.

Nevertheless, she could still imagine her mother and other working-class women, even without any help, soldiering on with courage and tenacity. It made Virginia feel ashamed of her own weakness and dependency. She made her way through the Gorbals streets with their crowds of ragged, barefoot children at play and women, some wrapped in plaid shawls, standing in groups at close-mouths or leaning on folded arms on windowsills, having what they called 'a hing'.

By the time she'd boarded a tram car and was on her way home, she had made a vow to be stronger from now on. To look forward with courage and optimism, not backward with sadness and regret. On the main street, she saw a placard outside a stationer's advertising the Empire Exhibition in Bellahouston Park and, feeling more cheerful already, she suddenly took the notion to sample the wonders of this new Glasgow venture.

As soon as she got home, she prepared a special evening

meal for herself and Nicholas and while they were eating it, she suggested that they should visit the Exhibition together.

'I don't think as a writer you should miss this experience, Nicholas.'

His eyes brightened with interest. 'Yes, you could be right.' And so it was arranged—their first outing together for longer than she cared to remember.

On the way to Bellahouston Park in the car with Nicholas at the wheel, she made a point of showing interest in his writing. She'd shown nothing but bitterness and resentment towards it for too long.

'How is your work progressing, Nicholas? I hope it's going well.'

He glanced round at her in surprise but he also looked pleased. 'I've been having a bit of a struggle for a while,' he admitted.

'I'm sorry,' she said, 'if I've been less than helpful or encouraging recently. I know I've been far too self-obsessed.'

'Darling, if anyone's been self-obsessed, it's been me. I should be the one apologising. Come to think of it, I haven't been of much help or support to you. I've withdrawn so much into myself as well as into my room. I'm sorry.'

'Never mind. Let's both try again, shall we? Let's make a go of our marriage, I mean. It's been drifting dangerously near the rocks, don't you think?'

He nodded, his eyes still on the road ahead. 'Yes, we've been needing to talk for a while.'

'And we will,' Virginia said, 'but let's relax and enjoy our visit to the Exhibition. Let's pretend we're a young courting couple again and we're out on an exciting date.'

He grinned. 'Well, if we're going to act as we used to, you're not going to have much chance to talk, Virginia.'

'We can't behave exactly as we used to. There are no woods around here for a start.'

'There's the trees in the park, and lots of nice springy grass.'

195

She laughed and playfully smacked his hand. 'Do you want to get us arrested?'

'It would be worth it. I'm game if you are.'

She tutted and shook her head, but she was light-hearted with happiness.

After Nicholas parked the car and they entered the park, Virginia linked arms with him. He looked down at her with surprise and pleasure lighting his eyes again. Soon their whole attention was riveted by the fantastic sights all around them. There was the Highland clachan built beside a loch among a grove of trees. It consisted of thatched roofed cottages. clustered around an old castle. At one of the cottages, wool was being spun. In the castle, ceilidhs were being held, songs were sung, and stories told that had been handed down from father to son for centuries in the Highlands.

There were the noisy thrills and spills and looping the loop of the amusement park, including a scenic railway, and the Rocket ride. Virginia and Nicholas stood for a time admiring the lake with its beautiful fountains and cascades. Everywhere there were magnificent pavilions, each representing a different part of the Empire—Australia, Canada, and Africa—all illustrating the Exhibition's theme of modernity.

Eventually Virginia said, 'We'll never be able to see it all in one afternoon. I'm exhausted already, aren't you?'

'Yes, let's have a leisurely meal and then make for home. We can come back again another day. In fact, I think we'll have to come back several times, Virginia, if we're to see everything. Next time, let's come in the evening, so that we can see the illuminations. I've heard they're really special.'

'Right.' Virginia was studying her map. 'Let's go to this treetop restaurant. It's on the first storey of the great Tower of Empire. It says the tower is a three-hundred-foot-high triumph of engineering. It certainly looks impressive, doesn't it?'

They strolled towards the tower and were soon settled at a table in the unusual restaurant where trees were growing up through the floor and enormously high windows sparkled all around. They had champagne with the meal and Virginia became quite giggly.

'If I don't get you home right now,' Nicholas told her with mock seriousness, 'you're going to give me a showing up. Come on.'

Arms encircling each other's waists, they made their way back to the car. On the way home, Virginia leaned her head against Nicholas's shoulder.

'Oh, Nicholas, I'm so thankful we've still got each other.'

'Don't go all maudlin on me now.'

'No, I'm not. I mean it.'

'I know, darling. I feel the same. I love you. I've never stopped loving you.'

As they drove along, she said, 'I want you to make love to me.'

He glanced round at her with laughing eyes. 'I know I'm a genius but my talents don't include making love and driving at the same time.'

She punched his arm. 'You know what I mean.'

'Yes, as soon as I get you into the park . . .'

'Don't you dare.'

They were the young couple again that they once had been, laughing and teasing, loving and passionate. Back at home, he carried her to the bedroom and they undressed one another and caressed one another, as if for the first time. They made deep, passionate love, and afterwards she lay in his arms and he said, 'I thought I'd lost you, Virginia, and it was my own fault.'

'No, it wasn't, Nicholas,' she told him firmly. 'It wasn't anybody's fault. We were both just struggling to cope with the loss of our child. And we were both feeling guilty. But I've come to see that people always feel guilty to some degree after a loved one's death. I remember my mother saying things like "If only I'd said this", "If only I'd done that" after my brothers died. And my father was the same after my mother's death.'

It was the first time Virginia had accepted, and openly admitted, that Wincey was dead. She knew Nicholas had never truly accepted the truth either.

'Oh, Virginia.'

'Shh . . . Shh . . . '

She put her arm around his neck and pulled his head down and nursed it against her breast.

28

The next time they had a drive out to the Campsies, Wincey took a picnic basket. They spread a travelling rug on the grass and Wincey poured homemade soup from a flask into cups. There was a plate of salmon sandwiches and a crisp apple tart baked by Teresa. A flask of coffee finished the meal.

Houston said, 'That was a feast. I really enjoyed it. And look at that view. That's a feast for the eyes.'

Wincey gazed into the distance, where Glasgow was out in the valley below. She remembered a short poem called 'Glasgow'. It must have been the same view, only in the evening, that had inspired the poet,

> *A huge town*
> *Lying in a plain*
> *With a valley*
> *Atwinkle with lights*
> *Defies time*
> *And radiates warmth from a million hearts*
> *Back to the skies.*

'I wouldn't want to live anywhere else, would you?'

Houston shook his head. 'And I've been around and seen a few places. The thing that annoys me, though, is what a bad reputation Glasgow seems to have, especially down in London.'

'I know. I could hardly credit it recently when I invited one of our English customers to visit us in Glasgow. He seemed quite shocked. "Oh no," he said, "I'd be too frightened to go up there." ' Wincey laughed, remembering. Houston laughed too.

'A Glasgow accent stands you in good stead in an English pub, though. As soon as any thug looking for a fight hears it, they give you a wide berth.'

After they finished their coffee and Wincey had packed everything back in the basket, Houston said, 'Wincey, have you given any thought to what I said the other day?'

'About contacting my family?'

'Yes.'

'It hasn't made any difference, Robert. They would be liable to die of shock if I suddenly appeared. You told me I'd been given up for dead.'

'I wasn't suggesting you suddenly turn up on their doorstep. You could write them a letter.'

'But what would I say? After all this time. It would seem wicked of me to have let them suffer for so long. It *was* wicked.'

'No, it was not,' Houston said firmly. 'How often have I to spell it out to you? Your grandfather had been abusing you for years, and you'd only begun to realise what he'd been doing to you. You felt confused and betrayed. But you also thought it was somehow your fault. You didn't know what to do. When he had his heart attack, you were still confused, Wincey, and you were in shock. Then you felt horrified and guilty, and afraid, and you ran away. The longer you stayed away, the more afraid you became, especially to go back and face your family. Now that's the truth, Wincey, and that is exactly what you must write and tell your mother and father.'

'What if they don't believe me about what he did to me? What if they think I'm just making up lies to try to excuse my behaviour?'

'What behaviour?'

Her expression strained with anxiety. 'He was such a successful and respectable business man, Robert. I suppose you could call him a pillar of the church, and the community. He was an elder in the church, and he donated a lot of money to the restoration of the building. Oh Robert, who would believe me? It makes me sick to my soul just to think of how people would revile me.'

'Darling!' He gathered her into his arms. 'Did I revile you when you told me?'

'You're a doctor. That makes you different. And . . .' She flushed and gazed up at his face, her expression still uncertain. 'You love me.'

'Yes, I love you. I love you very much. And I'm sure your parents love you as well, in a different way, of course. I want to make love to you, and don't look so anxious, darling. I've every intention of waiting until you want it too. Although . . .' His tone became teasing. 'You're really testing my curative skills as a doctor, as well as my will-power, to the limits. I hope you realise that.'

'I do love you, Robert, and I do want to make love to you, but it's just . . . it's just . . . this awful feeling comes over me. It's disgust as well as fear. Not disgust at you,' she hastily added. 'Oh, I know I'm being stupid.'

'No, you're not, Wincey. You just need time, darling. And you need to get all this out in the open. You must get all aspects of your life, and your guilty feelings, sorted out. I know you think you love me but—'

'Oh, I do, Robert, I do,' she cried out in distress.

'Wincey,' he continued firmly, 'you've got to learn to love yourself before you can really love someone else.'

'Love myself?'

'Yes, and accept yourself. Now, to get back to what I was

saying—are you going to write that letter?'

Worriedly, she hesitated. 'It's the terrible shock it would give them. I've left it too long, Robert.'

'It might have given them a shock if you suddenly appeared before them without any warning, but if you wrote them a letter, Wincey . . . You're just making excuses. It's far more likely they'd be absolutely overjoyed.'

'I'll . . . I'll think about it.'

'What good will it do to allow more time to pass?'

'I need more time to adjust to the idea, and to pluck up enough courage, I suppose.'

'You've got me now, remember.'

She smiled at him. 'Yes, you're my rock.'

'Well, I've been called many a thing, but never a rock. Is that meant to be a compliment?'

'Of course.' She thought he was going to kiss her but it was as if he suddenly changed his mind. He turned away and got to his feet.

'Do you fancy a walk, or are you ready to go back home?'

She rose too. 'It's getting a bit late, and we've both early starts in the morning.'

'Right.' He lifted up the picnic basket. 'Let's walk back to the car. Then we'll be on our way.'

The closeness that had existed between them earlier was now gone. On the way home they still spoke pleasantly to each other, but there was an edge of politeness that made Wincey feel sad. She suspected that if she didn't pull herself together soon, she was going to lose him. She couldn't expect him to be patient for ever. He would have no difficulty in getting any woman—for sex, or whatever he wanted. He didn't need to put up with a guilt-ridden neurotic.

He didn't come into the house with her but just carried the picnic basket into the close and deposited it on the Gourlays' doormat.

'See you again soon.' A brief wave and he was gone.

Wincey stood listening to the car start up and then the

sound of it fade away. Then she put her key in the door.

'Ah'm tellin' ye,' Granny was bawling at Teresa, 'there's gonnae be another war. Ah huvnae lived aw this time no' tae know aw the signs.'

Teresa didn't seem in the least perturbed. 'Och, you're always such a pessimist, Granny.'

'Whit dae ye think they're conscriptin' fellas o' twenty for? Tae send them tae Rothesay for their holidays?'

'Oh, there you are, Wincey.' Teresa greeted Wincey with some relief. 'Did you have a lovely time, dear?'

'Yes. That's the rain coming on now, but we got it dry for the picnic. Robert thought your soup was delicious, by the way. And your apple tart. He sends his compliments.'

Teresa flushed with pleasure. 'Such a nice man. And he'll make you a wonderful husband.'

Wincey forced a laugh. 'He hasn't even asked me yet.'

'He will, dear. He will.'

Wincey wished she could feel half as confident as Teresa sounded. Suddenly Erchie said, 'Ma's right, ye know, hen.' He had been sitting reading his *Daily Record*. 'First there's the conscription plans. An' now they're even havin' wee weans practice wearin' gas masks.'

'There was gas in the last war, wasn't there, Erchie?' Granny said. 'It did terrible things tae poor fellas in the trenches. See if they gas us over here, we're aw done for, gas masks or no. Anyway, where's oor gas masks?'

'Will you be quiet, the pair of you!' Teresa said.

'Aye,' said Erchie, ignoring Teresa's command, 'an' it'll no' stop in this war. There's aye another generation comin' up, aye ready tae be fooled an' indoctrinated an' encouraged tae hate their fellow men. Now German weans have been recruited by thae Nazis. Could ye beat it? Wee fellas o' thirteen, an' even younger, are marchin' intae a Jewish neighbourhood wi' brushes an' buckets o' white paint. They're daubin' the star o' David on Jewish premises pointed out tae them by the grown-ups.'

203

'Is that no' wicked? Wee weans,' Granny said.

'Aye,' Erchie agreed, 'an' it's forbidden tae play wi' or even speak tae Jewish weans.'

Teresa sighed and shook her head. 'I don't know what it's all coming to.'

'Ah telt ye,' Granny raised her voice again, 'it's comin' tae another war, that's what it's comin' tae.'

Wincey had been emptying the picnic basket and washing the cups and plates and she spoke up in an effort to change the subject. 'Does anyone fancy going to the Empire Exhibition. Some of the machinists have been and they were raving about it. Some of them have been two or three times.'

'Yes.' Teresa brightened. 'I was talking to Mrs McDougall just this morning, and she was telling me she had gone with her man and the family and she thought it was marvellous. And it was packed, she said. She'd never seen so many folk packed together before.'

'Whit? An' her wi' such a mob packed intae her room an' kitchen. She must have aboot a hunner by noo.'

'Now, now, Granny, don't exaggerate. Yes, I'd love to go, Wincey. How about you, Erchie? And do you think we could manage Granny's wheelchair if there's such a crowd?'

'Whit?' Granny said. 'Ah'll soon clear a path wi' ma brolly. Don't you worry.'

Wincey laughed. 'We'll probably all need umbrellas. I don't remember such a wet summer before, do you?'

'Maybe Robert will want to take you on his own. I think you should go with him, dear. We'll be fine with Erchie.'

'Yes, I am going with him, but I could go with you as well. We could go in the morning. That way Granny wouldn't get too tired. It's easier for Robert to get off at night after his surgery, and he was saying that in the evenings, everything's illuminated and looks extra beautiful.'

'Ah widnae get too tired. Ah'd just be sittin' in ma chair.'

'Now, now, dear. You know fine you fall asleep in your chair if we don't get you to bed before nine. And you need

204

your wee nap in the afternoon as well.'

'Dae you want tae deafen everybody in the exhibition wi' yer snores, Ma?' Erchie said.

Granny drew down her brows and sucked in her gums. 'Ye'll be auld yerself wan day.'

'Right,' Wincey said. 'I'll organise it, shall I? And we'll have a nice meal in one of the restaurants. My treat.'

'That's very kind of you, dear. I'll really look forward to that.'

Wincey looked forward to it as well, especially the evening when she was going with Robert. For one thing, she felt safer in the darkness. And for another, maybe that would be the moment that Robert would propose. As his wife, surely she would feel more secure, more safe, less frigid and neurotic. She would gladly give up the factory to concentrate on being a good wife to him, assisting him in his work, making him happy. Although in fact Robert wasn't in favour of women just staying at home. He said, 'Outpatient Departments are full of what you might call suburban neurosis—lonely women who are left at home all day with not enough to do and too much time on their hands, which they spend worrying about their troubles.' There had been several suicides and attempted suicides brought in when he had worked in the Royal.

'Even in this area,' he said, 'I have my share. It's become a grave social problem.'

Was she what he regarded as a suburban neurotic? Even though she had plenty to do. And she'd plenty to worry about. Charlotte was looking thin and pale and anxious. She had confessed to Wincey that Malcy was getting in deeper and deeper with the moneylender. Charlotte had paid Mrs O'Donnell off more than once and pleaded with Malcy to stop gambling. Often he did for a few days or weeks, and then he'd start again, worse than ever. He always believed that the next bet would be his lucky one and he'd be able to pay off everything he owed. Although it never worked out that way, he never lost his optimism and hope.

It made Wincey so angry. 'For goodness' sake, why don't you leave him, Charlotte?'

'I don't leave him, Wincey, and I'll never leave him, because I love him. He's not a bad man. He's been nothing but kind and gentle and loving to me. He can't help the gambling. It's an illness. We'd be perfectly happy together if only he could be cured of that.'

Wincey didn't believe he'd ever be any different. Even Erchie had become disenchanted with Malcy and had stopped helping him out with money. Everybody had now stopped giving Malcy any cash, except Mrs O'Donnell, and Wincey feared a time of reckoning was likely to come with the moneylender. Charlotte had recently, in desperation, told Malcy that she was no longer going to bail him out with what he owed Mrs O'Donnell.

'I had to tell him that I just couldn't afford it any more, and it's the truth,' she admitted to Wincey. 'I'm hoping that if he knows I'm definitely not paying off Mrs O'Donnell any more, he'll realise he'll just have to stop going to her. It just can't go on, Wincey. I feel I'm only encouraging him. The interest that that woman charges is wicked, really criminal.'

Wincey agreed and hoped and prayed that Charlotte's new strategy would succeed. But when Erchie heard, he groaned. 'If Malcy disnae pay up soon, O'Donnell's men will put the frighteners on him. Ah hate tae say this, but maybe a right doin' is the only thing that'll bring Malcy tae his senses.'

'Oh dear,' Teresa said. 'I hate violence.'

'It's Charlotte I'm worried about,' Wincey said. 'I don't care what happens to him.' And the flame of hatred she had felt for her grandfather now encompassed Malcy and burned stronger than ever.

29

Virginia spent the morning doing some shopping. Time hung heavy on her hands until Nicholas stopped work half way through the afternoon. After making a few purchases, she wandered along Sauchiehall Street, and then down West Nile Street. Trace horses were plodding up the cobbled road on their way to Buchanan Street Station and the factories in the north of the city. The carts' wheels trundled along the two broad stone lines, especially formed to make the journey smoother for the carts. In each case, the huge Clydesdale horse in front was yoked to the horse at the back, helping one another to haul the heavy load up the steep hill. A carter sat on the cart, a clay pipe stuck in his mouth, his sleeves rolled up. Walking along side the front horse was a trace boy, leading and urging the beast on with a rope attached to it. Then once the destination at the north of the city was reached, and the load delivered, the horses would be unyoked and the trace boy would mount astride the lead horse's back. With a whoop and a clatter, he'd joyously make a headlong dash down the hill towards the River Clyde again, sparks spraying in all directions from the horse's hooves. That is, if he was lucky and a policeman didn't catch him.

Virginia couldn't help wondering if the police, for the most part, turned a blind eye, because she'd so often seen the wild descent of trace boys with their horses, manes and tails flying. It was one of the most familiar sights in Glasgow. So too was the sight of young lads with home-made barrows and shovels, with which to scoop up all the horses' dung to sell to people with gardens or allotments.

She glanced at her watch. Hours to go yet. She thought of visiting Mathieson and then remembered that he'd be at the college. Anyway, she had made up her mind not to see so much of Mathieson, at least not without Nicholas. It was one thing Nicholas being such close friends with Mathieson, but it had begun to occur to her that it wasn't just Mrs Cartwright who thought her close association with Mathieson odd, to say the least. She had been helping Mathieson not long ago at one of his political meetings, and at one point another woman helper had said, 'Your husband is such a courageous man. What a wonderful spirit he has. Despite his disabilities he teaches others and works tirelessly for the cause in so many ways.'

'Oh, you mean James?' Virginia said. 'He's my ex-husband. I'm married now to Nicholas Cartwright, the novelist.'

The woman had given her such a strange look and later that day, she'd seen her in a huddle with some other women, talking together in lowered voices. They'd immediately stopped when she appeared. Virginia had no doubt they'd been gossiping about her. At first she'd thought, To hell with them. Why should she care what anyone thought? It wasn't as if she was being unfaithful to Nicholas. She wondered what the women would say if they knew it had been Mathieson she had been unfaithful to. But that was so long ago.

However, the more she thought about it, the more she realised that perhaps she had been visiting Mathieson too much on her own. Perhaps it wasn't fair to Mathieson, or to Nicholas. She should try to be more self-reliant. Her efforts to find charity work had so far not been very successful. It would have been easier if she'd been a member of one of the local churches, or the Salvation Army. Recently, however, she'd remembered from her youth the Model lodging house, a kind of poor man's hotel known simply as the Model. Why the word 'model' was applied to such a place, Virginia never knew—the dilapidated building had always looked ready to collapse. It housed weary-looking, unshaven, unemployed men, eyes deadened with hopelessness. They shuffled about in tattered clothing and boots with soles flapping off. She wondered if the place needed a voluntary worker, perhaps to dish out food. One morning she'd gone along to the Drygate, plucked up courage and walked straight into the Model. The first thing that hit her was the stench of frying fat and sweaty feet. A doddery man in a long army greatcoat flopping at his bare ankles shuffled past her. She called to him, 'Where can I see the manager?'

The man jerked his head towards a door. 'The kitchen maybe.'

Virginia opened the door and found herself in a large kitchen and dining area which had a broad, flat hotplate stretching the full length of the place. The fumes from greasy frying pans mixed with the stench of dozens of unwashed bodies. It all but overcame Virginia—she felt sick. One man who looked comparatively clean and was dressed in a blue shirt and grey flannels came hurrying towards her.

'Good morning, madam,' he said. 'What can I do for you?'

He indicated that she precede him back out of the door. Then he hastily led her across to another room which was obviously his office. 'I'm Mr Scott, the manager.'

'How do you do.' Virginia suddenly felt foolish. There wasn't another woman in sight. It looked as if no woman had ever stayed here, or worked here. 'I think I've possibly made a mistake. I was wanting to do some voluntary work and just wondered, in passing, if there was anything I could do here.'

Mr Scott looked shocked. 'Oh, I couldn't allow a lady like

yourself to have anything to do with a place like this. What would your husband say?'

What indeed? In fact when she got home Nicholas thought it hilarious. 'Darling, it's an old doss house. It'll be moving with fleas for a start. I bet you had to have a bath the moment you came home.' She had, in fact—after being horrified to see several fleas jumping about her person. She'd also had to wash her underwear and stockings and stuff her outside clothing into a bag ready to take to the cleaner's.

'I suppose it was a bit daft to try a place like that,' she conceded, 'but I was getting desperate. Surely there's some kind of voluntary work I could do.'

'Have you thought of the Red Cross?'

'Nicholas,' she cried out in delight, 'you're a genius.'

He grinned. 'I know.'

'I'll go to their office first thing tomorrow.'

'Good idea.'

'The Red Cross does a lot of good work.'

'Yes, all over the world. But,' he came over and gathered her into his arms, 'don't you dare go stravaiging all over the world, doing your good works. I want you here with me. I'm totally selfish, like all true geniuses.'

She flung her arms around his neck, a great wave of love for him engulfing her. She kissed him with all the passion that was in her. In a matter of seconds they were on the floor, tearing at one another's clothing, rubbing, licking, biting each other, making love over and over again. At last, exhausted, they rolled apart.

Virginia managed, 'Mrs Rogers'll want to know about dinner in a minute. I'd better go through to the kitchen.'

'Now that you've had your wicked way with me.'

Virginia gave him a quick kiss and scrambled up to fix her clothing back in place and tidy her hair.

'You'd better get up and make yourself respectable as well. Mrs Rogers could suddenly come in here.'

He propped himself up on one elbow. 'So what? It would

liven up her day. She needs a bit of spice in her life, by the look of her.'

Virginia shook her head. 'You're incorrigible. By the way,' she asked at the doorway, 'do you fancy going to the Exhibition later on? You promised we'd go and see the illuminations one night.'

'Yes, fine.'

Happily she went through to the kitchen for her usual talk with Mrs Rogers about menus and also to make out the weekly shopping list. Mrs Rogers had cooked a delicious roast of prime beef, surrounded by roast potatoes. In a separate dish were golden brown, light as a feather Yorkshire puddings. For sweet there was a fruit salad and cream. Because Mrs Rogers always left early, Virginia dished the meal, and afterwards Nicholas helped her to clear the table. In the kitchen, Virginia washed the dishes and Nicholas dried them. Eventually, arm in arm, they left the house, and soon were on their way to the Empire Exhibition in Bellahouston Park.

★   ★   ★

Granny's gums were chomping with excitement as she related to Mr McCluskey what a great show good old Glasgow had put on. Mr McCluskey was sitting in the close having his smoke, his thick straggly moustache wet at the ends with sucking on his pipe. Erchie and Teresa had brought Granny home just after lunch time. Then Erchie had gone off to the factory. Wincey was already at work. Granny had insisted on her chair being parked beside Mr McCluskey's so that she could tell him all about her adventures. She quite often parked in the close beside Mr McCluskey now.

'Ah'm the only wan the poor auld soul can enjoy a good blether wi',' Granny insisted.

Before she got started, Teresa had run into the house and fetched Granny's shawl and also a blanket to tuck around her waist and legs.

'Now, will I get you a scarf to tie round your head?' she asked the old woman.

'Stop yer fussin',' Granny said. 'Can ye no' see ah've got ma hat on. Away ye go an' make Mr McCluskey an' me a wee cup o' tea.'

'Can I fetch you a blanket, Mr McCluskey?' Teresa said.

'No thanks, hen. Ma long johns keep the cauld aff ma legs.'

He was also wearing a tweed bonnet with the skip pulled well down over his brow, and a big woolly scarf knotted high under his chin, and hanging down over his chest.

'A wee cup o' tea would be very welcome though, hen,' he said, and settled back in his chair to enjoy another few puffs at his pipe. 'And,' as he'd said many times before, 'a guid crack wi' Granny.'

Granny described in glowing detail everything from the hurly burly of the amusement park to the British Government pavilion with its steel and glass globe of the world, apparently unsupported in space. She took Mr McCluskey through the Scottish Pavilion South, with its hall of youth, and the Scottish Pavilion North, with its striking twenty-five-foot statue called The Spirit of Modern Scotland. Each Scottish Pavilion was coloured blue and each had a tower.

'Ma favourite though wis the Peace Pavilion. It wis tellin' ye about aw the things folk dae tae try to live in peace thegither. Well, no everythin', mind ye. Ah could huv telt them a thing or two tae put in there if they'd asked me. Still, it wis better than nothin'. Somebody or somethin's got tae speak up for peace at a time like this. Dae ye no' think so, Mr McCluskey?'

Mr McCluskey removed the pipe from his mouth. 'Aye, ye're quite right, Granny. Aw the generals an' high heid yins telt us the last war wis tae be the war tae end aw wars, an' we wis comin' home tae a land fit for heroes. Bloody lies, if ye'll excuse the French. Ye'll no' get me rushin' aff like an idiot tae jine up this time.'

Teresa, returning with a tray of tea and digestive biscuits, couldn't help smiling at the idea of poor Mr McCluskey rushing off anywhere.

'Here, Mr McCluskey, can you hold the tray on your knees?' Teresa said.

'Aye, fine, hen.'

Teresa took one of the cups and placed it between Granny's hands. 'Will I dip a biscuit for you, Granny?'

'Ma hands are fine. Gie me ower a digestive an' away ye go an' leave us in peace.'

After a while, Mr McCluskey's daughter came bustling into the close and started tutting the moment she saw her father's pipe.

'That woman jist hates that poor fella's pipe,' Granny had said. 'He's tae hang on tae it like grim death—even sleeps wi' it under his pillow, he telt me, in case she takes it aff him an' throws it in the midden. She's tried aw sorts o' tricks tae get her hands on it. He's that feart he loses it, the poor auld soul. Ah telt him no' tae worry—if the worst came tae the worst, ah'd get him anither yin.'

'Come on now, Father,' Miss McCluskey said, 'it's time you came in and washed your hands, ready for your dinner.'

Obediently the old man got up, still clutching at his pipe.

'Put that disgusting thing out,' Miss McCluskey yelped as if the pipe was going to leap up at her and bite her. 'I will not have its dirty fumes contaminating my house. It's bad enough out here in the close.'

'*Your* house?' Granny said in wide eyed innocence. 'An' here wis me thinkin' that the hoose wis in Mr McCluskey's name.'

Miss McCluskey flushed and pushed past them to unlock the front door.

'Ye're an awfae woman, Granny,' Mr McCluskey said, but gave her a wink.

After Granny had settled back in the kitchen, Wincey arrived and Granny said, 'That wis awfae good o' ye, hen, tae

213

take us tae the Exhibition an' pay for everythin' like ye did. Ah really enjoyed masel'. Glasgow's put on a rare show, eh? Good old Glasgow.'

Wincey gave Granny a kiss. 'Yes, but there's nothing old looking about the exhibition, is there? Everything's ultra modern.'

'You're not rushing out again, are you, dear? You must be exhausted.'

'No, I'm fine, Teresa. I'm just going to get changed.'

'Sit down and have a bite to eat first.'

'No thanks. Robert and I are going to have a meal at the Atlantic Restaurant at the exhibition. Remember that one that's been built exactly like the bow of a ship? And all the waitresses are dressed as stewards. I'm really looking forward to it. So is Robert.'

'A cup of tea then?'

'No, honestly, Teresa. I'll away through to put on my new dress.'

'The long black velvet one? Oh, wait until Robert sees you in that. You could pass for a film star.'

Wincey laughed, and once she was through in her room, they could hear her singing.

Teresa smiled and shook her head. 'What a girl! What would we do without her?'

30

It was raining yet again when they left the Atlantic restaurant. Wincey had just tied her headsquare over her hair when suddenly Robert grabbed her, pushed her against the hull, or wall outside, and started passionately kissing her. Wincey was too astonished to struggle. Robert was not a man who believed in indulging in uninhibited public displays of emotion. On the contrary, as a doctor, he always showed a quiet self-confidence and calm authority.

Eventually he let her go and she gasped breathlessly, 'What on earth was that all about?'

'Your mother passed within yards of us.'

Wincey paled. She was glad now of the wall at her back to steady her. At last she managed, 'How did you know? I mean, you've never seen her before, have you?'

'No, but I've seen plenty of photographs of Nicholas Cartwright, and she was hanging onto his arm.'

Wincey looked fearfully, wistfully, around. 'Where are they now?'

'They were going in the direction of the exit, I think. Anyway, the opposite direction from us, so don't worry. But you know, Wincey, it's bound to happen sooner or later. Glasgow's not all that big a place. One day you're going to give her a terrible shock. You've got to write that letter.'

Wincey nodded. She was still shaken. 'Yes, you're right. I'll do it this weekend.' Her heart was pounding at the thought, but as they moved away, she couldn't help being diverted and uplifted by the breathtakingly beautiful scenes all around them. Earlier she'd read Robert's copy of *The Times* and could now agree with what its arts critic had said.

'The best effect of the exhibition is at night, when to the straight lines and delicate colours of the pavilions is added floodlighting and the changing effects of illuminated water in movement. The lake, lit by submarine floodlights of changing colours, presents a magnificent spectacle. High up over all shines the fixed red, yellow and green of the Tower of Empire observation balconies. From the foot of the tower cascades descend, lit from below with changing colours, the water being made semi-opaque by aeration to give value to the colours.'

'This is like a dream world,' Wincey said. 'It's all so beautiful, isn't it.'

Robert agreed and, arm in arm, they wandered around speechless now with admiration. Although Wincey couldn't relax completely. Every now and again she'd gaze uneasily at people in the crowd. Eventually, Robert said, 'Relax, will you.'

'I am.'

'I can feel your tension. I told you, they went away in the opposite direction.'

She clung tightly to his arm, glad of the strong, hard feel of it. 'It's just been a bit of a shock, but I'm fine really. I'm glad we came. I am enjoying it. It's wonderful. Thank you for bringing me, Robert.'

He smiled down at her. 'Maybe I've been going about this in the wrong way.'

'Going about what?'

'Courting you. Do you realise that's the first time you haven't trembled or shrunk away from me when I've kissed you?'

'Oh Robert, I don't shrink away from you. I never—'

'Imperceptibly perhaps, but I'm not a doctor for nothing. You can't fool me.'

'Oh Robert, I'm sorry. It's not you . . .'

'Don't get all agitated. I know what it is. I also know that you'll never be free of the past, Wincey, and all the negative emotions that are still twisted up inside you, if you go on like this.'

'Like what? I've been trying to free myself of the past for years, Robert. I thought I had.'

Robert stopped walking and turned her towards him. 'Have you forgiven your grandfather?'

'What?' All the hatred she'd felt for the old man came careering back, making her tremble violently. 'Never!'

Robert said, 'You see. You haven't even begun to free yourself, Wincey. And this hatred only harms you, it doesn't do anything to your grandfather. He's long gone.'

'Change the subject, for goodness' sake,' she suddenly snapped at him. 'You're spoiling the evening.'

He shrugged and they began walking again, but this time not arm in arm. Eventually Wincey couldn't bear it any more and she said, 'Robert, I'm sorry. I'm over-tired, that's all. It's been a long day. Do you mind if we go home now?'

Later, alone in the silence of her room, she wept. A horrible certainty was creeping over her. She was going to lose him. That night she dreamt she was sinking deep into a quagmire and couldn't get a foothold, couldn't struggle up. She woke sweating and exhausted.

It wasn't a good start to what turned out to be a dreadful day—one of the worst days of her life. A day that banished everything else from her mind.

217

She could see right away that Charlotte was tense and upset and eventually she asked her, 'Charlotte, what's wrong? Please tell me. Maybe I can help.'

She knew of course it would be something to do with Malcy. Only he could make Charlotte look so desperately worried and unhappy. Charlotte shook her head. 'I'm trying hard to stick it out and not give Malcy any more money, Wincey, but it's been terrible these last few days. He's begged and pleaded and says Mrs O'Donnell's men have threatened to kill him if he doesn't pay up by today. Today's his last chance, he says. But he's lied to me so often before, Wincey. I don't believe him now. And I do so much want him cured of his gambling. I feel I really must hold out this time and not give him any more money. He always just goes and gambles it away, you see. But at the same time, I'm so afraid. I mean, what if he *is* telling the truth this time? I'll never forgive myself if anything happens to Malcy. It'll be my fault if anything does.'

'Of course it won't be your fault,' Wincey said. 'This is all Malcy's doing, not yours.' Wincey took Charlotte's arm and held her and Charlotte wept broken-heartedly on Wincey's shoulder.

After a minute or two, Wincey said, 'The only thing I can think of is if I go and speak to Mrs O'Donnell. Find out exactly what the true situation is.'

'Oh, could you, Wincey? Maybe if we went together. I probably should have confronted Mrs O'Donnell before, but to be honest with you, I never thought of it. I've just kept trying to talk to Malcy and sort things out between ourselves.'

'I don't mind going on my own,' Wincey said. 'You're upset enough.'

'But could you do it discreetly, Wincey? Without Malcy knowing. He'd never forgive me if he thought I'd allowed you to interfere. I'm sorry, Wincey, but you're not his favourite person at the best of times.'

'I know, but don't worry. I'll say nothing to Malcy about this. And I'll slip away just now while he's with Erchie through in the back workshop. I won't be long and I'll be able to tell you exactly what he owes Mrs O'Donnell, or if he owes anything at all. If necessary, I'll warn Mrs O'Donnell that her men had better not lay a finger on Malcy or I'll go to the police.'

'Oh, thank you, Wincey, and tell her if he does owe her something, I'll pay it. Oh hurry, Wincey, in case he comes back to the machine room and sees you.'

'It's all right even if he does see me, Charlotte. He knows I often go out on business.'

'But the sooner we know about what's going on, the better.' Charlotte was getting more and more agitated. 'I mean, what if we're too late and something happens to Malcy. Oh please hurry, Wincey.'

Wincey struggled into her coat, eyes averted from Charlotte in case Charlotte might detect the dark hatred she was nursing. It would be the best thing if, on this occasion, Malcy was telling the truth and he did get set upon by Mrs O'Donnell's hard men. However, for Charlotte's sake, she vowed to do her best to get things safely sorted out.

The moneylender's close was only minutes away from the factory and Wincey ran inside the close and up the stairs. At the door with the brass name plate which said 'Mrs Frances O'Donnell' she both pulled the bell and rattled the letterbox. There was no reply. Wincey tried again, this time battering at the door with her fists. Still nothing happened. She peered through the letterbox, she shouted through it. 'Mrs O'Donnell.' She knocked on the other door on the landing and after a few minutes, she heard the shuffling of slippers along the lobby. The door opened to reveal a frowsy looking woman with uncombed hair and a sallow, unhealthy looking face. She seemed to be having difficulty in breathing.

'Whit dae ye want?'

'I've been trying to get hold of Mrs O'Donnell. It's urgent. Have you any idea when she'll be back?'

'There's aye folk comin' an' goin' there. Her as well. Ah couldnae keep track o' them aw, even if ah wanted tae.'

'You've no idea where she could be?'

'Naw.' And she shut the door.

Wincey decided to try the other neighbours, just on the off chance Mrs O'Donnell might be visiting any of them. Again she drew a blank. Eventually she stood at the close-mouth wondering if she should look in at the local shops. Mrs O'Donnell might be out for her messages. But then she happened to glance at her watch. 'Oh God,' she thought, suddenly agitated and apprehensive. Soon it would be closing time at the factory. She could well believe on this occasion that Malcy might be telling the truth. He might well be in immediate danger. Not that she cared what happened to him but she cared terribly, urgently, about Charlotte. She began to run back along the road.

31

Nicholas circled Virginia in admiration. 'Yes, very smart. Sexy as well.'

She rolled her eyes at him. 'Don't be daft. How can a Red Cross uniform be sexy? But it is smart, right enough.' She went over to the full length wardrobe mirror and, hands on hips, surveyed herself this way and that. She liked the well-cut navy-blue costume and crisp white shirt, dark tie and navy cap with white bands and Red Cross badge and stiff peak. The cap had also a thin leather chinstrap. Navy stockings and shoes completed the outfit.

'The first aid course was interesting,' Virginia said. 'I quite enjoyed it. They had actors and actresses made up to look like injured people—blood and everything. It was very realistic. We learned how to do dressings and how to put on splints and all sorts of things.'

'Come away from that mirror. You'll be getting so big-headed your cap won't fit you.'

'I volunteered to do some nursing training in one of the hospitals. You don't mind, do you, darling?'

'Mind? Why should I mind? I have a job that I enjoy and

find fulfilling. Why shouldn't you, Virginia?'

Virginia smiled lovingly at him. 'Not every Scotsman is as liberal as you, Nicholas. I remember so many husbands where I lived who regarded their wives as part of their goods and chattels. All the poor women did was bear children and slave in houses that weren't fit places for animals. They struggled endlessly to keep their homes clean and respectable and to feed and clothe their families. The husbands—even the best of them—would never dream of washing a dish or doing anything to help in the house. It would have been considered unmanly. Maybe that's still the attitude, for all I know.'

'I wonder why that's so much the case in Scotland,' Nicholas said thoughtfully. 'I don't think it's like that in England. I must remember and do some research on that.'

Virginia laughed. 'You never stop being a writer, do you? Always curious about what makes people tick.'

'I know what makes you tick.' He made a lunge at her and, squealing with laughter and protesting, she struggled out of the room.

'Get your hands off my good uniform, you sex maniac. I've a Red Cross meeting to go to.'

In the hall, they bumped into Mrs Rogers and nearly upset a tray of dishes she was carrying.

'Sorry, Mrs Rogers,' Nicholas said. 'I didn't see you. I was too busy trying to ravish this woman.'

Mrs Rogers flushed, hurried past and disappeared into the dining room, dishes loudly clinking.

'Get back to your book,' Virginia said, 'and behave yourself.'

'I've done my stint for today.'

'Well, go to the Mitchell and do some research or something. Visit your mother. Or go and have a drink with James. I won't be more than a couple of hours at most.'

She blew him a kiss before leaving. Outside she got into her car and drove away down the terrace and onto Great Western Road. Her thoughts now took a serious turn. Despite their happy banter, both she and Nicholas had been concerned for some time about the way things were going in the country and in the world. So was Mathieson. They all agreed that it looked as if there was going to be another war. Above all, she was worried about what might happen to Richard. Losing one child was bad enough. To lose both children would be far, far too much to bear. She had told Nicholas, 'If anything happened to Richard, I'd die. I mean it, Nicholas. I know I just wouldn't be able to bear it.'

He'd tried to soothe away her fears. 'Nothing's going to happen to Richard, darling. If there was a war, it wouldn't be like the last one. There wouldn't be fighting in the trenches. There wouldn't be hand to hand fighting or anything like that. And Richard is a pilot, remember.'

She didn't see how that could make him any safer, and she was sure Nicholas didn't either. They tried not to talk about it but the subject of war was inescapable. Germany and Italy had made their pact of steel. Germany and the Soviet Union had signed a non-aggression pact. Two thousand Nazi guards had arrived in Danzig. Attacks on Poles had become a regular occurrence. Virginia felt as if she was living on the edge of a nightmare that was gathering in horror as each day passed. There could be no ignoring it, even at Red Cross meetings where they discussed every eventuality and what their role might be if the worst came to the worst. These days Virginia was often reminded of the well-known verse Robert Burns had written after witnessing a thanksgiving service after a victory in battle:

> *Ye hypocrites, are these your pranks?*
> *Tae murder men an' gie God thanks.*
> *For shame, gie ower, proceed nae further,*
> *God won't accept your thanks for murder.*

> *Then let us pray that come it may,*
> *As come it will for a' that,*
> *That Sense and Worth, o'er a' the earth*

Shall bear the gree, and a' that.
For a' that, and a' that,
It's comin' yet for a' that,
That Man to Man, the warld o'er,
Shall brothers be for a' that.'

★   ★   ★

At the Red Cross meeting, Virginia was given a list of things she would need for her nursing duties. It consisted of a light blue dress, a white bibbed apron (to be kept crisply starched at all times), a white 'butterfly' cap (also to be kept starched) and a broad navy belt and white cotton elasticated cuffs. The cuffs were to be worn over sleeves if and when the sleeves were rolled up.

After the meeting, she went straight into town and bought the lot. She had to report for duty in a couple of days' time at the Royal Infirmary, so instead of going home with her parcels, Virginia decided to go and have a look at the Infirmary. She'd seen it many times before, but just in passing, and had never paid it much attention. When the huge new building had been opened in July 1914 by King George V, it was the largest public building in the United Kingdom. It probably still was, Virginia thought, as she viewed its enormous bulk, blackened by the smoke that had belched out over the years from Glasgow's tenement chimneys.

Virginia parked the car, and in a few minutes found herself in the emergency outpatient department, where a disturbing number of real-life patients—no actors these—sat around or milled about in various degrees of bloody injury and obvious suffering. Virginia beat a hasty retreat, somewhat less confident in her ability to cope with the duties that awaited her. She had enjoyed the make-believe of the Red Cross classes where she'd ministered with such ease and success to the actor patients. Now she could see that enjoyment would definitely not come into it. However, she was undeterred. She had never shirked hard work, even dangerous hard work, and she remembered only too well her time working in the munitions factory in her youth. If she could survive that, she could certainly survive Glasgow's Royal Infirmary.

Thinking of the munitions factory reminded her of her poor brother. Ian had been killed in one of the many explosions in that death-trap of a place. Losing him, and then her other brother Duncan, had broken her mother's heart. And to think that munitions factory had been owned by George Cartwright, Nicholas's father. Who would have thought that the charming, smiling old gentleman of his later years was that same ruthless capitalist? Indeed, he'd always appeared to be the more kindly and reasonable half in his marriage. Mrs Cartwright was the one feared and hated in the Cartwright household, by all the staff at least.

As Virginia drove back to Kirklee Terrace, her mind kept slipping into the past. Her mother, her father, her brothers returned to her like ghosts. And Wincey. Poor shy Wincey, with her straight red hair and fringe, and her dear freckled little face. Had she lived, she would have been a young lady now, married probably. Virginia sighed and tried to banish all such gloomy thoughts from her mind. She drew up in front of her house, then gathered her parcels together.

Once inside, she greeted Nicholas cheerfully. 'That's me all organised. I'm starting at the Royal on Saturday.'

'In at the deep end, then,' Nicholas said.

'How do you mean?'

Nicholas shook his head. 'Darling, you are so innocent sometimes, despite your tough upbringing. Saturday night in Glasgow?'

'Oh, you mean the drunks. I know, but don't worry, I can cope with all that. Drunks don't worry me. It's the poor women who'll come in after being battered by their drunken husbands. That'll upset me, but I suppose I'll just have to get hardened to it all.'

He gathered her into his arms. 'I can't imagine you ever

being hard, darling. You're the sweetest, softest, most sensitive and caring person I've ever known.'

'Ah,' she smiled up at him, 'but you're prejudiced. You love me.'

'Yes, I do. More than anybody or anything in the world.' He held her close. 'God knows what's going to happen to the world. It seems to have gone crazy. Again,' he added.

'You really do believe there's going to a war, then?'

'Oh, there's going to be a war, all right, Virginia. The whole of Europe's mobilised. Children are already being evacuated from the cities.'

'Oh God!'

'By the way,' Nicholas said, 'James was on the phone. I've invited him to join us for dinner. Is that all right?'

'Yes, of course. He'll be upset about all this.'

'Yes, he's worried about what's going to happen to all the young men he's been teaching. War's such a waste.'

'I hate violence,' Virginia shuddered. 'I always have.'

32

'She wasn't in,' Wincey told Charlotte breathlessly. 'Where's Malcy?'

'Did you not see him? He left a few minutes ago. I wanted to lock up early and walk back with him but he said he didn't want to put me at risk. And anyway, he thought if he left early, he'd be all right. He said he'd be able to run home in a matter of minutes. He said no-one could catch up with him, even if they came early and saw him.' She took a bundle of keys from the desk drawer. 'But I'm still going to lock up early. I've already told the girls and the other men to go.'

'I saw them leaving right enough. I wondered what was going on.'

'I told Malcy I'd pay what he owed but that I'd go and see Mrs O'Donnell personally tomorrow. I was hoping you'd be able to tell me if he did owe her anything. But when he left early just now, I saw him racing away down the street. I knew then he must have been telling me the truth. She really must have threatened him. Quick, Wincey, I must go after him and make sure he's all right. I'm in such a state now.'

Wincey followed Charlotte out of the building and they'd

barely turned the corner onto Springburn Road, when they heard the commotion. Women were screaming. Someone shouted, 'Ye never see the polis when they're needed. There's a man bein' murdered along there.'

'Oh dear Jesus,' Charlotte cried out and began to run.

Wincey ran too, heart pounding. They could see ahead on the other side of the road three men kicking the figure of Malcy who was curled up on the ground in the fetal position, arms trying to protect his head.

'Malcy!'

Before Wincey could stop her, Charlotte had suddenly shot out into the road. It happened so quickly. One minute Charlotte was by her side, the next she had darted away. A car was coming along, and didn't have time to stop, or even swerve to miss her. Rigid with horror, Wincey saw Charlotte's body hit the car, fly into the air and land with a sickening thud on the cobbles. Wincey couldn't move. People were milling about . . . somebody had run to the doctor's surgery, the driver of the car was being sick, then the police arrived. The next thing she remembered was Robert kneeling down beside Charlotte. He was gently closing her eyes.

Wincey remembered no more until she came to in Houston's surgery. 'Oh Robert,' she wept, 'tell me it was only a dream. It was only one of my nightmares.'

'No Wincey,' he said, 'it wasn't a dream. Charlotte was killed instantly. Malcy's in the hospital but he'll survive.'

'Do Teresa and Erchie and Granny know yet?'

Houston shook his head. 'There hasn't been time. I'll drive you home now. I'll probably have to give them a sedative. You too. It'll at least help you all to get some sleep tonight.'

'Oh Robert, I can't bear it. It's not fair. It would have been far better if it had been me, not Charlotte. She's never hurt a fly, or said an unkind word to anybody in her life. Could *you* tell the family?'

'No, this is something you must face, Wincey. They regard

you as part of the family. It would be better coming from you.'

Normally Wincey would have walked the short distance home but now she was glad of being able to sit in Houston's car. On the way up the Balgrayhill, she dried her tears and struggled to find the strength to face the ordeal that awaited her.

With a trembling hand she opened the front door with her key and, followed by Houston, she went through to the kitchen. Erchie was sitting at the table reading his *Daily Record*. Granny was in her usual place beside the fire and Teresa was stirring a pot on the gas ring over at the range. She looked round, smiling.

'Oh hello, dear. You're early. And Robert . . .'

Her smile faded at the sight of the tragic expression in Wincey's eyes and the doctor's sad, sympathetic look.

'What's wrong? What's happened?'

'You'd better sit down, Teresa,' Houston said.

Teresa did as she was told, her face as pale as Wincey's now.

'It's Charlotte,' Wincey said. 'She's been killed in an accident.'

'Naw!' Erchie shouted. 'Ah said cheerio tae the lassie jist a wee while back. She let us away early the night. She wis fine.'

'She saw men beating up Malcy and she ran across the road to try and help him. She didn't see the car and the driver didn't have time to do anything.'

Wincey went over to Teresa and put her arms around her shoulders.

'She didn't suffer,' Houston said quietly. 'She died instantly.'

Suddenly, they became aware of a whimpering noise that turned into a terrible wailing. 'Oh Granny.' Both Teresa and Wincey ran over to try to comfort the old woman.

'She wis such a good wee lassie,' Granny sobbed, 'an' aye that nice tae me.'

'I know.' Wincey hugged and kissed her, while Teresa held and patted the gnarled, misshapen hands. 'And she wouldn't have wanted you to get all upset, Granny.'

'How can ah no'? She had aw her life before her, an' you say there's a God.' She turned a tragic gaze at Teresa. 'What kind o' a God's that.'

'God works in mysterious ways, dear.'

'Don't ye gie me any o' that claptrap. There's nae mystery aboot a lassie bein' run doon by a car.'

Erchie blew his nose. 'Teresa's only tryin' tae comfort ye, Ma.'

'Well, she's no' daein' a very good job o' it.'

Houston had opened his black medical bag. 'I'm going to give you all something that'll calm you and help you to sleep tonight.'

'Aye,' Granny said, 'they'll maybe knock me oot the night but ah'll still have tae face the morrow.' She wiped away her tears with the back of her sleeve. 'But ah'll face it, don't you worry. An' better than any o' them. Ah've had tae face the loss o' weans before.'

It was much later, after Houston had gone, that Teresa suddenly said, 'What about Malcy? Is he all right?'

'Oh yes,' Wincey said bitterly. 'He's all right. They're keeping him in hospital for a couple of days but he'll survive all right. His kind always do.'

'Wincey,' Teresa said gently, 'Charlotte loved him so much and he loved her. He'll be broken-hearted. We'll have to go and see him, give him a bit of support.'

'What? Oh no, Teresa, you can count me out of that.'

'Now, now, it's what Charlotte would have wanted.'

'I'm sorry, Teresa, I couldn't. It'll be as much as I can manage to be civil to him at the funeral.'

Erchie sighed. 'We know he had his weaknesses, hen, but he's no' a bad man. He was good tae Charlotte in his own way. He made her happy.'

'Oh really?' Wincey queried sarcastically. 'You think so?'

'Ye're an awful bitter wee lassie.' Erchie shook his head. 'Ye've aye felt the same about Malcy, an' he never did ye wan bit o' harm.' He hesitated. 'Have ye no' been mixin' him up wi' somebody else, hen? Are ye still daein' that? Maybe that's yer problem.'

'I have no idea what you're talking about, Erchie.' Wincey rose. 'All right, I'm off to bed. I feel the tablets beginning to work, don't you?'

'Thank goodness they've worked for Granny anyway.' Teresa gazed over at the hurly bed where Granny was lying, toothless mouth hanging helplessly open. 'Goodnight, Wincey,' Teresa added, 'although it's been anything but a good night, hasn't it?'

Wincey kissed Teresa, said goodnight to Erchie in passing and went through to her own room. There she quietly wept.

Next morning she got up very early and went to the factory to pin a notice on the door saying what had happened and that the factory would be closed for the rest of the week as a mark of respect. All the employees would be shocked, she knew. Charlotte was very well thought of by everyone. Then Wincey saw the undertaker about a date for the funeral before putting a notice in the local paper, as well as in the *Glasgow Herald*. Teresa had sent telegrams to Florence and the twins, and was now awaiting their arrival.

Wincey booked the Co-op for the funeral tea. They had all agreed that it was best to keep busy, and they were soon dealing with a steady stream of friends and neighbours coming to the house to express sympathy and to grieve with them. Teresa kept making pots of tea and putting plates of sandwiches and cakes and biscuits on the table. The blinds were kept pulled down, and during the day the kitchen and all the rooms were in a ghostly twilight.

'It doesn't seem right that Charlotte's lying in the Co-op undertaker's parlour,' Teresa said. 'She should have been here in our front room.'

'Naw, naw, hen,' Erchie said, 'her place wis in her own

231

front room, up in Broomfield Street. But ye can understand Malcy jist lettin' her go to the Co-op. He's no' gettin' oot till the funeral day, so he couldnae be wi' her in their hoose.'

'I suppose so,' Teresa said, 'but it doesn't seem right, not having a wake for Charlotte.'

'A wake?' Granny bawled. 'There'll be nae Popish carry-on while ah'm here. An' when ah go, don't ye dare hae one for me, Teresa Gourlay, or ah'll come back an' haunt ye. Ah'd birl in ma grave if ye did that.'

'Oh, all right, Granny. I won't have a wake for you. But it's not just folk of my persuasion who have wakes, you know. It used to be—'

'Never mind what it used tae be. It's no' gonnae be. Can you no' take a bloody tellin'?'

'Now, now, Granny. It's not like you to swear.'

'It's no' like me tae have a wake either.'

Teresa rolled her eyes and gave up.

Wincey sat quietly for much of the time. She was dreading the day of the funeral, not only because of her grief at Charlotte's untimely death, but also at the prospect of facing Malcy. As far as Wincey was concerned, Malcy—and Malcy alone—had been the cause of Charlotte's death. Never before had she hated him so much.

★   ★   ★

At the funeral, he looked a pathetic figure, with his bruised and swollen face, his head in bandages and his arm in a sling. He sobbed through the service. Everyone felt acutely sorry for him and Wincey hated him all the more.

'Look at the two-faced hypocrite,' she said to Houston at the funeral tea.

Houston stared at her in silence for a moment. 'He's genuinely upset, Wincey. I've spoken to him more than once in the hospital. He's more than upset. He's broken-hearted and he blames himself.'

'And so he should. He was to blame. I'll never forgive him. Never.'

'Just as you'll never forgive your grandfather? Do you think you'll ever change, Wincey? Do you think you'll ever forgive yourself? I'm beginning to wonder.'

She had begun to recognise the warning signals in his expression, in his voice. She was going to lose him all right.

After the funeral tea, he said he had to go. He had a patient to visit and so Wincey returned to the Balgrayhill with Erchie and Teresa. Erchie pushed Granny's wheelchair. Florence and the twins returned to Clydebank.

★   ★   ★

Eventually the time came to reopen the factory. Life had to go on. Wincey was sitting at her desk in the office when Malcy knocked at the door and came in.

'What do you want?' Wincey asked him coldly.

'I feel terrible about this, but I don't know what to do.'

'Do about what?'

He hesitated. 'They're still after me for the money. Charlotte said she was going to pay Mrs O'Donnell.'

'I'm not Charlotte.'

'Look, Wincey, I'll never gamble again. I swear. This has finished me.'

'I'm glad to hear it.'

'But if you don't come up with the money in the next few days . . . They've given me a week's grace because of what happened to Charlotte. But they're going to kill me. They've told me, Wincey. They said they'd finish the job this time. And I believe them.'

'All right. I've got a week to let you know. Now, if you don't mind, Malcy, I'm busy.'

'Wincey, don't do this to me, please. I feel bad enough as it is. I loved Charlotte. Maybe I didn't as much as I should have at the beginning, but who couldn't grow to love her once they knew her? She was such a sweet and loving person, Wincey.'

'She was indeed, Malcy. Now I really am very busy.'

After he'd gone she thought she'd feel some sort of satisfaction. But she didn't. She knew he was a weak man and she didn't believe his vow about never gambling again. She did believe, however, that Mrs O'Donnell's men meant what they said.

'Here,' Wincey thought, 'is revenge being handed to me on a plate.'

Yet it didn't feel sweet. She kept remembering Charlotte saying, 'I love him, Wincey. He's not a bad man. He's been nothing but kind and gentle and loving to me. He can't help the gambling. It's an illness. We'd be perfectly happy together if only he could get cured of that.'

'Oh Charlotte,' Wincey thought, 'if only I could be like you.'

She still felt Charlotte was near to her. There were two desks in the office, her own desk, and Charlotte's directly opposite. How often had they sat like this working quietly across from one another, every now and again glancing up and smiling at each other. If Charlotte had been here and heard how she'd just spoken to Malcy, how would she have felt?

'Oh Charlotte,' Wincey said to the empty desk, 'I'm so sorry.'

She sat for a long time struggling with herself. Then she went out to the machine room and said to one of the girls, 'Tell Malcy to come to the office.'

In a few moments, he had returned to stand in front of her desk like an errant schoolboy. She suddenly felt tired of hating him, tired of hating.

'This is what Charlotte wanted, Malcy.' She handed him the cheque. 'She also wanted to go to Mrs O'Donnell to talk to her and make it perfectly plain that there would be no point in lending you any more money. I'll do that now, shall I?'

'Thank you, Wincey.' He accepted the cheque. 'You can talk to her if you want, but there's no need. I won't be here to borrow money from her again. I'm joining the Army. There's nothing to keep me here now.'

'I see.'

Again she struggled with herself. 'Take care then, Malcy.'

He nodded and turned to go. Just before he left, Wincey said, 'I'm sorry we haven't always seen eye to eye, but rest assured, for all your faults and no matter what you did, Charlotte always loved you.'

He nodded and quickly closed the door.

A few minutes later Erchie came in, and without his usual knock at the door.

'What huv ye been sayin' tae Malcy?'

'Why?'

'The poor fella came oot o' this office an' across the machine room like a bat oot o' hell wi' tears streamin' doon his face.'

'Poor Malcy,' Wincey said. 'I just told him that, for all his faults, Charlotte always loved him.'

'Oh?' Erchie looked taken aback. 'That wis nice o' ye, hen. He did love her, ye know.'

'Yes,' Wincey said. 'I know.'

'Well,' Erchie said, 'ah'll see ye later, hen. Ah can see ye're busy the now.'

She managed to smile. 'Yes, I've an important letter to write.'

Then after she was alone again, she took up her pen and began.

'My dear mother and father . . .'